C000018095

Alice's Dérives in Devonshire

Phil Smith

With a Foreword by
Bradley L. Garrett

Published in this second edition in 2014 by:
Triarchy Press
Station Offices
Axminster
Devon
EX13 5PF
England

+44 (0)1297 631456
info@triarchypress.net
www.triarchypress.net

A catalogue record for this book is available from the British Library.

Paperback ISBN: 978-1-909470-39-2

Cover illustration: Rachel Sved

Foreword

Bradley L. Garrett

When we think about the spaces around us, the spaces that we inhabit, the spaces we care about, the spaces that matter, we begin to think of them as *places* rather than *spaces*. It's a slimy, smudged, shattered line between space and place, one that can be affected by our own thoughts, experiences and attachments and one that can be equally affected by the actions of others. Over time, often we find that unless we really work at it, spaces we call places begin to dwindle in number. For many people, home, work and the local pub or cafe are perhaps the only places left in adulthood – the rest of the world slips into an ethereal blur of places that could have been. We are, in the end, just too busy to keep trying to explore the world for new places or even to tend to places we know in a way that gives them the required thickness.

What would a world look like where our actions were driven primarily by desire rather than utility? What if exploring and imagining took priority over working, paying the bills and mundane everyday tasks? One vision of this world is perhaps rather dystopic. Here, hedonistic throngs eschew responsibility, wholly depend on the labour of others, eating and drinking, dancing and drifting their way through the world, leaving behind little beyond memories of good times and a few broken objects hastily swept under the rug. This rudderless lot have radically misinterpreted Buddhist philosophy, living not in the present as a state of concern, but allowing the past and future to fall away simply because too little attention was paid to either. In this rather decadent imagination, the credo of all might be "I want" rather than "I must".

Anyone who has children will be familiar with this behaviour; it's the natural state of youth. Why is it then that in our stable, reasonable adult years that we strived so hard to reach, we so

3

often look upon our childhoods with fond nostalgia and a vague impression of a paradise lost? Could it be that for many of us, we sense that the pendulum has swung too far the other way? What is it that still compels us to yearn for irresponsibility and reckless adventure? Perhaps it's more important than we realise to remember every so often what it is we want to do as well as what it is we need to do.

I grew up in Riverside, California, amongst the neglected remains of what was once the citrus capital of the Golden State. The condominium where I lived with my mother backed onto a few dozen acres of orange groves. My friends and I used to traverse the groves with a pellet gun shooting produce and lizards, spray-painting the bounding breezeblock walls and building forts in trees complete with central hearths, toilets and watchtowers. Every so often we would run away from home and live off oranges and irrigation water for a few days in a fort, pre-supplied for just such an abscondion. At other times, we would come back to the forts to find they had been raided by some unknown force, smashed up and robbed, branches sagging languidly, weighed down by wet toilet paper stolen from our ersatz loo. We would then stomp through the groves for hours, vowing revenge, but never actually encountering the culprits ("lucky for them!" we would shout).

My first kiss was on a windmill in these orange groves, atop a decrepit old hulking machine covered in graffiti that peeked just over the trees and only started up on the rare occasion that the temperature dropped below freezing in the Californian Inland Empire. In our teenage years, we had "orange fights" every weekend, where kids were split up into equal teams and try to nail each other with oranges from the opposing road. It was a messy business.

Throughout all of these citrus adventures, we were of course trespassing – and destroying other people's property to boot. But we never thought about any of that, not for a second. When I was in my late twenties and had long moved away from Riverside, I was told that our grove had been summarily bulldozed to build a school. Better than a shopping mall I thought.

I feel some sense of melancholy about the loss of the place. But I also know that as children we would have made the most out of whatever environment we lived in. Perhaps if the school had been built twenty years earlier, I would have fond memories of wandering around in the corridors after hours hunting zombies with that same pellet gun or geocaching secret stashes of stuff for others to find. We also would have made the shopping mall our place, somehow. What I can be sure of, in any case, is that those years were ruled by a desire to explore and a desire to explore together. At times, this led to conflict, heartbreak and loss but it also made our lives richer, more plentiful, more prone to encounter and surprise. As I grew older, I refused again and again to give over that desire to utility.

In *Alice's Dérives*, Phil Smith captures the wonder of childhood imaginations and reminds us of the importance of continuing to embrace desire, letting it play out through our imaginations. Phil reminds us of the continuing importance of transforming spaces into places. Alice and her friends encounter a world that seems at the same time completely familiar and bizarrely bleary-eyed; they are adept explorers of the everyday, finding the impossible all around them. In transporting us to this world from the perspective of a curious nine-year-old girl, Phil also reminds us that those experiences carry with them a hidden danger, the reason why we fear that rudderless lot: the wonders of the everyday waiting to be found are so tantalizing, so satisfying, that we may never emerge from them. This of course is what many of us are embarrassed to admit in adulthood – the compulsion to run away, to escape, never wholly vanished, we just suppressed it out of supposed necessity.

Even if we step over that line at times to escape into the wonders of the everyday we are so prone to ignore, to speak of the world as somewhere we simply go "out there" to encounter is of course too simplistic a formulation. Each of us builds very particular relationships to the people and places we encounter. Each of us will respond in different ways to the worlds constructed around and within us. And yes, this gets more difficult as we grow older and lose control of time. Yet as the philosopher Jean-Paul Sartre once wrote, freedom is what we do with what's been done to us. Sartre suggests that even a prisoner confined to a cell can make choices within that cell; the prisoner retains power of consciousness and is therefore free. The prisoner may find that the most alluring freedom then is in the mind, in the imagination, in the thoughts that cannot be imprisoned (yet) – there is always an open door in the mind, ready to run through.

In many ways, we all live in prisons now, though the walls may be difficult to render or even invisible. To be in the world today is to be chased constantly by an unknown spectre, the watchers, the guards of a panopticon. As the world becomes increasingly constricted, our behaviours surveilled, monitored and circumscribed, our ability to explore physically is challenged in new ways and we may find that our minds wander more; the mind will reach for the freedoms the body can't find. There is beauty and danger in this, as Alice, her friends and family, find. What we are left with at the end of these wonderful adventures is perhaps a sense that it is not the escape we necessarily covet, but rather the capacity to escape, if we so choose. Having that choice pulls the pendulum back toward the centre. And if Sartre is right, it is up to us to decide for ourselves how far we're willing to go to keep that door open. Some of us will inevitably get sucked through, never to return. Perhaps the rest of us can learn to live with that or to, at the least, be more sympathetic to the choices others make in (re)staking claim to their spatial sovereignty.

The Situationist International, that beloved group of Parisian urban explorers, once spray-painted a wall with the words "*sous les pavés la plage*" (under the cobblestones, the beach). It is a powerful phrase that has resonated for decades, far from the wall where it was initially penned. Its persistence as an idea is twofold. On the one hand, there is an obvious implication here of a city in the city, a hidden city, a city we perhaps can't see or don't know about and there is an imperative placed on finding that city at all costs, even if it means tearing up the city we know. More importantly however, the beach is a place of play, a place where childhood daydreams and mischievous adventures can stretch out, where beautiful castles can be built out of sand, though we all know the tide will eventually come in and wash them away. And that of course is the point.

As Alice and her compatriots learn on their drift, on the path of a vanished father in search of what is beneath everything, the most important things in life are perhaps those things you can't hold onto – but in trying we make them matter. Watching the sand castles dissolve into the tide, we realise that the paving stones will also, in time, disappear, and that the world around us is, in the end, a vast crumbing fiction. It is that fiction Alice must come to terms with in her drift. In that light, perhaps the greedy sensibilities of the perpetual present make more sense, because if the world is going to be created and recreated in every instant, it may as well be created by us, in our image, in the way children do, without shame or concern, out of love and starry-eyed marvel. The challenge to us then perhaps is to retain those vivid imaginations and desires that lead us to be active citizens in the creation of places rather than simply passive spectators in our own lives, passing through spaces created by others. And yet in that process, we must hold on tight to the people and places we care about because the ride will be a painful one, once you decide to start carving your own path again, now with a fuller awareness of the possible consequences of those decisions. Get our drift?

> Dr Bradley Garrett is a geographer at the University of Southampton with an interest in hidden spaces, secret geographies and places that do not appear on maps.
>
> He is the author of *Explore Everything: Place-Hacking the City*, an ethnographic account of the activities of the London Consolidation Crew (LCC), a group of urban explorers who exposed parts of London that had been lost to time. The explorations of the LCC, via Garrett, have been featured by news outlets across the world.
>
> His most recent book is *Subterranean London: Cracking the Capital*, an unsolicited photographic dissection of underground London from a range of (mostly anonymous) contributors.
>
> Find him at www.bradleygarrett.com

I beheld then that they all went on till they came to the foot of the Hill Difficulty, at the bottom of which was a spring.

(*The Pilgrim's Progress*, John Bunyan)

Beginning

Can a city fall to bits one day and put itself back together the next?

I think so, but I am crazy. So why should you believe me? Dad says it's OK to be mad. Bad is the problem.

And the city is bad. I saw its badness. For one day its glass was everywhere like broken teeth after a fight between lions and sharks. Big buildings leaning on each other like drunk dinosaurs. The new shopping centre was a cave full of smoke. And everyone was frightened of each other.

But I wasn't frightened. I could see that between the pieces of glass were shining gaps. And in the biggest building were passageways and tunnels and I could see that *that* was the good city. The city of holes and caves. Between the bad was the good, but only if you knew that before you looked.

A little while later – I'm not sure how long because that was when I was ill again – the bigger cities burned for real; life had a really bad dream. By then, though, I knew that the cities were always ruins, no matter what they looked like. And that you had to know how to see fire to find warmth.

Chapter One ~ Dad

Time: Midnight
Place: The hospital
Action: Stand holding your breath for as long as possible.
Then exhale loudly, catch your breath and run away.
(*Open City*, Andrew Brown, Katie Doubleday & Emma
Cocker)

Dad was a fireman. But one day, during the pretend riots, he breathed in a cloud. He wasn't allowed to be a fireman after that.

Dad had been trapped in a big fire at a factory where they made things they weren't supposed to, with things they shouldn't have. When the gangs burned it down Dad breathed in their mischief. He wasn't the same Dad after that.

"What am I going to do?" he asked Mum one day after the fires. Mum said: "You always wanted to save the world – now you've got time."

"I couldn't save a cat," he said.

After the fires they always spoke like they were joking, but they didn't laugh much.

Every week or so after that, our front room would fill up with huge men. I told Mum that they were too loud, but she said that firemen had to have big lungs. And, anyway, Dad was always the loudest.

After they'd gone Dad would cough for a while.

Dad had to be still a lot when he first came back from the hospital. Then it became a habit. Even my little brother wasn't allowed to bother him. Dad might have started to laugh again, but he would never go back to the fire station, Mum said. The people there wouldn't let him go back on the engines and Dad said he wasn't going to fly a desk. How could he have? At the time he said about the desk he was taking down his certificates and making weird gulping noises. Dad didn't ever cry, but he did a mixture of laughing and coughing bits of cloud. After that, when the big men came they still arrived loud, but went out quiet. Then they stopped coming altogether. It didn't matter. Because Mum's friends started coming instead and Dad would make them laugh. Mum put up some pictures she'd bought in town.

For a whole school term, from summer to nearly Christmas, Dad sat in the corner by the bookcase. He never seemed to move from there. Never took us on walks like he used to, no more setting off with no idea where we would end up. Now, when his visitors laughed it was as if Dad had crept up on them from out of a lair.

My little brother says that our Mum is a 'cynical cyclist'. She does go to work on a bike, but actually she looks after people who are ill in their minds.

My Dad's mind is fine, but he has the remains of a riot in his lungs. "Why don't you help me?" he sometimes says to her. "You won't let me," she says; then they go quiet when they see me. The one time I asked "won't let you what?" Mum went and made frankfurters (to teach me I suppose).

When Dad wasn't laughing he would read. He said he didn't mean to, but he couldn't see the telly properly from his chair. At first he just looked at the words, then he started to write notes on the edges of the pages. Soon our bookcase was full of new books that Mum fetched for him from town or got from her computer, so he started to build little piles around his chair. Mum told him off about writing in the books so he kept notebooks for when she was there. On one side of his chair was a shrinking pile of empty notebooks, and on the other was a growing pile of full ones.

"What are you making notes about, Dad?"

"Connections."

When Dad was in his chair he was like a giant king in a city of paper towers.

Dad never wanted to come out with us any more. He wanted to sit in his chair, all his body concentrated on breathing. He'd say to Mum: "I think I'd better give it a miss this time." One teatime Mum had called me into the kitchen, but I stayed hidden so I could read another page of 'The Coral Island'. (I'm hoping that if I read all 'the classics' one day a letter will come, with a key and membership.) Dad must have forgotten I was there. Mum came in to speak to him. In front of my eyes I saw him do his change. He'd been tapping on his chair arm, reading the latest weird present from his 'theory godmother' (Mum). Now he bent over and coughed. Mum said: "Naya's free to babysit if you want to come tonight."

"I think I'd better give it a miss this time," he said and coughed again.

Mum shrugged and went off shouting for me. Dad punched the air and rubbed his hands together like a clown. I stood up. He saw me. I wanted to shout: "Dad's a..." but he silently and furiously cut the air with his flattened hand. Backwards and forwards. His eyes were a difficult kind of funny. A kid doesn't know what to say when grown ups act like this. So I cut the air with my flattened hand and made his face back to him. He laughed. Or else I would have told Mum.

"I won't tell."

He made a thumbs up.

"But you have to tell me why you don't want to go out."

"I need to get on with things inside."

After that, if I ever thought Dad was putting on his poorliness to get to watch his old videos on his own I would make the sawing with my flattened hand. Mum caught me once. It was a good secret sign. She didn't have any idea.

Then Mum made Dad take all his books and notes and videos up to the loft. She said: "you'll have more room. Isn't that what we converted it for?" But she didn't use a question mark. So Dad disappeared up the ladder. Now he has to come down specially to see us. Mum says: "I wish I'd never said you could go up there, we never see you." But Dad won't move back down now. And when he does come down he always has a book.

"What's that one about, Dad?"

"Space."

"Rockets!"

"No, different kinds of space in the world, Ben, how people feel about those different spaces, how they see them."

That was the biggest sentence Dad had said to us since he swallowed the cloud. I knew it was important.

"I didn't know you were a geographer," Mum said.

I could tell Dad didn't like that because he started to do the washing up. So he could turn his back on us.

Because of my little brother the ladder to the loft always had to be pulled up. When he was tiny Mum had left it down and he had climbed all the way up to the top and terrified her, a little naked baby so high above the landing. Sometimes, before Dad lowered the trapdoor or Mum pushed it shut, I could see the bright blue ceiling of the loft.

Dad has a different sky to ours.

"They're here!" Mum would shout, pulling down the ladder and Dad would climb down backwards, already laughing. Dad would sit in his chair again, as if the buildings of paper were all around him, a king in his city of words. And he would tell stories and listen with a big smile on his face, and when he laughed I could see his teeth, jumbled like an animal's. But I never heard him talk to Mum's friends about the things he read in his loft, under his painted sky, never about connections and space.

And then, one day, when Mum brought us home from school in the car, Dad wasn't in his sky. Nor in his chair. He wasn't in the house anywhere. Mum was excited. The ladder had been down and she put it back up. She checked the coat cupboard under the stairs.

"Your father's gone for a walk, for the first time since the fire. You've got to tell him how well he's done when he gets back."

But he didn't get back.

Chapter Two ~ Just Us Now

Be wary of playing games of hide and seek, for there is always the risk that your cover will not get blown, that you will be forever left in hiding. Too effective a camouflage makes for a sad and solitary life.

('Making Room for Manoeuvre; or Ways of Operating along the Margins' in *Manual For Marginal Places,* Emma Cocker)

Mum knew exactly the right things to do. The police lady told us so. Dad hadn't come back yet, but it was nice to see people in uniforms in the front room again.

After Dad disappeared we carried on the same as before, but everything was twice as big and twice as fast. Mum did everything Dad used to do: read us stories at bedtime, watch scary programmes with us, help us paint without thinking too much, and cook meals that were bad for us. She got twice as angry, twice as worried, twice as forgetful.

I heard her tell her friends it was "for them". She had to be "strong for them". Was she secretly doing exercises? I wasn't sure if 'them' was us, me and my little brother, or if there was another 'them' – if Dad had been taken away by 'them', or tricked by 'them', or had gone off to be with 'them' instead of 'us'. And whether if 'we' could find 'them' then 'we' could get Dad back. But where are 'them'?

I told my little brother about 'them' and that if he ever told anyone else that I had, then 'them' would come and get him in his bed and Dad would never come back. I meant to make him cry a bit, but he just went quiet and his eyes got bigger. It was a game, like 'rockets', for him. He wanted to know what happened next in the story. So I told him. "I think Dad must have known about 'them' and that's what he was reading about and that's why he went to the loft. But 'them' still got him. 'Them' must have found out he was writing notes about 'them'. We need to get in his loft for clues."

We looked up. The trapdoor was still open, but the ladder was up. A policeman had been up there. He'd said there was nothing "immediately obvious" which I think was code.

We could see the blue ceiling.

"'Them' are something to do with space," I said.

"Rockets?" hoped Ben again.

"The other space. That people feel. That's where Dad is."

"How do you get there?"

"That's why we have to get up the ladder. Because I think Dad found out and wrote it down."

"What did Dad do before he was a fireman, Mum?"

"Goodness me, what made you think of that?"

I couldn't tell her the truth.

"Well, your Dad was ... *is* very clever, and he was always reading and he made these things, like machines..."

"Rockets?"

"No. He didn't like that sort of... science fiction thing. He liked strange, witty things..."

"Like machines?"

"Well, they were more art than machines – dancing things, made from pumps, hydraulics... er..."

"What's that?"

"I didn't really understand it, to tell you the truth. I suppose they were driven by some kind of liquid. Some of them you plugged in and they walked."

"What were they?"

"O, a funny mixture of things. Some of them were like mechanical people. Just their legs. They were for galleries and exhibitions. Silly, ridiculous, wonderful things. Chorus lines. Your Dad wanted to change this world, but all the things he knew how to do, do really well, didn't change anything... He could make people laugh, he could make them amazed, he could even make beautiful things when he wasn't thinking too much, but he couldn't save anything. Least of all his money."

"What was he, Mum?"

She laughed.

"Before he was a firefighter? He was a sculptor."

"What's that?"

"You know what a sculptor is. The things in the High Street – that family in stone that you touch, the thing you climb on about the war. Those were made by sculptors."

"Dad made those?"

"No. He worked with different materials... but Dad stopped making his sculptures a long time ago. Shortly after we got together. It wasn't his kind of world, really. You know what Nanna and Gramps are like, they're not arty people, are they? They like the telly and the bowls club – well, that's how your Dad grew up, with telly and football and looking at steam trains and aeroplanes and things... that's what he's like. So even though your father was very good at making the strange machines, and he did love it, he always felt it had led him into a world that wasn't for him, it was really for 'them' rather than people like him, and he'd never properly be part of 'their world'." (When she said 'them' and 'their world' she put on Dad's rumbly voice.) "Dad liked football and thrillers on the telly and going off on his own. He wasn't very good at mixing with the other artists. He didn't like the gallery system. So, he put all his art into a big pile and burned it."

"Were you there?"

"O, yes. We all nearly died of the fumes!" She laughed. "That's how your Dad became a fireman. We burned the sculptures on Gramps's allotment and Gramps got into terrible trouble. All the black smoke blew onto someone's washing and then the fire brigade arrived and we all had to run for it! Except for your Dad. He said: 'I'm going to be a fireman'. We all laughed at him, because it was like a little boy saying he wanted to be a train driver. But he did, didn't he? He was so happy. He could save the world."

"Was Dad a hero, Mum?"

"He loved trying to be one."

"Has he gone away because he can't be a fireman anymore?"

Mum didn't answer that for ages. Then she nodded and the nod made her cry. It tipped out the tears. They weren't pretend. I think she really, really believed it. But I knew she was wrong and that the real, real, *real* reason was up in Dad's loft and it was something about 'them' and 'their world' and 'space' and 'connections' and the 'something system'.

First we tried with teddy bears.

Dad had once got out of his cot when he was a baby by piling up his teddy bears. Great Nanna was looking after him in the shop. She'd heard a big thump and then the bell in the front go, but when she looked there was no customer so she went back to her dinner. Dad was crawling along in his rompers next to the big road when the lady from the sweet shop saw him.

We piled the bears up under the loft, but even with two fairies, a shark and a dinosaur we didn't have enough.

If only we could get the metal ladder past Mum. No chance. What game could we say we needed it for? Picnic, Battle, House, Den? Our plan had to fit with one. Den Mountain, then...

We put all my little brother's clothes drawers in a pile on the landing and leaned our mattresses against them. When Mum came up to dust we said they were the roof of our cabin.

"Big roof," she said. But she didn't stop us.

Inside the den, we planned until Mum went downstairs to warm up the dinner. Then we started. My little brother sat against the bottom of the mattresses to keep them from sliding and I began the climb. I could get my toes into the bits of the mattress where the buttons were and if I held my arms out wide I could hold on to the edges where there was a stringy ridge. Once I'd got my toes in the first button dip I pulled with my fingers, so I could bring my other foot up to the second button dip. Then I searched around for a grip inside it with my toes. I couldn't see them, but they felt like desperate little fishes panicking in a jar. Not like they were mine. At last the toes settled down, gathered round the button. I pulled myself up with my fingers again and all of me slid up the mattress. I could feel the springs pinging from my heart beats, even though I don't think real mattresses have springs anymore. I was scared Mum would hear the 'boing, boing, boing'. When I got my toes into the next button dip, I couldn't push off from the carpet any more. I wanted Mum's arms. I weighed like a schoolbag full of books and water bottles.

My little brother was trying to reach the arm of a plastic pirate that he'd noticed in the fluffy bit between the carpet and the wall.

I pulled as hard as I could and my toes nibbled madly round the next button dip. The loft ladder hung a little down from the trapdoor and I would get on to it with one more pull and toehold. I felt my toes grip on properly and I pulled again. The top mattress suddenly bent in the middle, pinging my brother in a somersault down the landing carpet. He veered off and rattled against the banisters. Under me everything went soft and I was dropping, not sliding, but coming down fast, then bump, I hit the point where the first mattress was still bent over the drawers and all my breath came out in one go. But it is a thick mattress and the bump was soft as well as sudden. I bounced a bit more and then sat down, hard on the carpet.

My brother was laughing, and I was gasping.

"Are you all right, you two?"

I couldn't speak, but my little brother wheezed that we were "only playing".

"Well, be careful up there."

I had to lie still for a while and try not to breathe too hard. I lay on my back and looked through the hole above into the sky that I couldn't get to.

Of course Ben had, famously, been up the ladder before. It was one of our Family Stories and in the car we'd get Mum to tell it to us again and again.

"I had to stay very calm," she would say: "Hello, little lad!" Because she didn't want to scare my brother by her being scared. "Come on in, little chappie in the nappy!" Which was strange, because in the story he wasn't wearing anything, he was just a little chappie in the nuddy climbing a huge ladder to the sky.

My little brother pretended he remembered what the loft was like, but I knew he made it up: "it's bigger on the inside than the outside" – he stole that from Doctor Who – "with controls and a fridge and lots of beer and all our Christmas presents." The last two bits were probably true, but the rest he was guessing.

Mum was always telling Dad off about drinking too much wine and beer and Dad was always telling Mum off for using his loft as "a rubbish dump".

We put the two mattresses up against the drawers again. My

little brother took off his socks and I sat against the bottom of the mattresses. He climbed on my leg, which hurt, and then on my shoulders, which tickled. And he was suddenly on the ladder and into the loft, his little blond head shining against the paint sky.

He whispered: "what do you want me to do?"

"What are you two doing?" Mum shouted up.

"Dens!"

I heard the clink and scrape of plates.

I whispered: "What can you see? What's it like? Be quick!"

Ben disappeared and then his frizzy head was back in the picture.

"There's some windows. And there is millions of books and things."

"What things?"

"There is things from outside – rocks and dirty things..."

"What kind of dirty?"

"Dirty soil and earth. Things from the street that dogs have weed on. And people... there are people..."

"Up there?"

"Little people, plastic people and metal people from other countries. And a write-tighter."

Probably the keyboard of Dad's computer. My little brother disappeared and when his head next appeared he was holding a thing next to it – it was made of a dirty gold and it was a small fat person with an elephant's head. I could see a piece of white paper on the bottom with a price on it.

"Like that."

He and the elephant headed person disappeared. I knew what it was. When Ben appeared again he had a piece of road. It was almost too big for him to hold. I could tell it was from a road because it had a part of a yellow line on it.

"It's got sea things on it."

I could just see by bending my neck, because I was looking at everything upside down, that they were barnacles.

"I think Dad's been out before, secretly – see if there are any messages or maps", I bossed my brother.

"What are you two whispering about up there?"

Very quietly: "Anything that might say where Dad is..."

Out of the hole in the blue sky one of Dad's notebooks dropped down.

"What are you two doing!!!!"

Mum's face was right next to mine! It was angry and staring at me through the banisters! Now we would never find Dad!

"Where's Benjamin?"

Ben appeared in the sky and Mum screamed. She started to run up the stairs.

I only had enough time to slide Dad's notebook under the mattresses because Mum slipped on the carpet by the bathroom. She made my little brother jump off the ladder into her arms and told us we were NEVER to do such a dangerous and stupid thing again and made us look over the edge of the banisters so we could see how far it was from the blue sky in the loft all the way down to the bottom of the stairs in the hall. I'd only noticed the different bits of those distances before then. I hadn't ever connected them up. And even though I wasn't on the mattress any more, trying to get my toes to stop slipping round the buttons, I was as scared as if I was, because I suddenly saw the empty space for the first time and that its different bits were all parts of some massive thing and I was tiny on it and wriggling to hold on.

"It doesn't mind," said Ben.

"It doesn't *matter*," Mum corrected. "And yes it does."

Mum took away one of the mattresses so that we couldn't get to the ladder.

"Stick to dens, please, you two – little monkeys! Come on, Alice, usually so sensible."

Ben didn't want to play dens. He went downstairs to watch an old 'Doctor Who' video of Dad's.

I always thought Mum and Dad would split up. She had brand new dvds with cellophane on and he had old videos.

I pushed the mattress a little higher on the drawers to make more room in the den. That let more light in from the blue above. Then I crawled in, slowly pulled Dad's notebook from beneath the corner of the remaining mattress, carefully so it did not rip. And I started to read.

Chapter Three ~ Long Ago

In the jungle is a city that moves. When its inhabitants
build new districts it is always to the west. Each time they
cut the ribbon opening a new quarter, an old one in the
east is abandoned... the ruins left behind in the east would
be perfect terrain for the dérive.

(*The Beach Beneath The Street*, McKenzie Wark)

"1987.

January 4th.

Still not feeling well. That's the last New Year's Party for me – ever.
Fell down the stairs, sick in the garden. Apologies to the roses.
What an idiot! Why should anyone fancy me in that state? Should I
be suspicious of this Nancy? She's a psychology student – aaaah!
Maybe she wants to analyse me? She's rung every day since, but
I've been too ill to see her. Got to get myself sorted out. Will get
dressed in a minute. See what happens.

January 6th

Went outside today. Things are weird. There's snow on the ground,
but no one seems to notice. I met Mister Binns in the pub again.
Everyone knows he has a secret, but countless pints will not get it
out of him. Why should I pour my money into him? He's deep and
scary – he looks small, but his eyes are wide like the moon, that
dirty coat of his is like a mountainside!

This morning, from the window, I saw people on the bowling green
again. They must have raked the snow off. Couldn't make out any
faces – there was mist rising from the main road. Didn't know they
let you bowl in January.

January 8th

Nancy called and talked all day and all night. She is the most
beautiful talker ever. How can someone be pretty and interesting
and right? She must have some terrible part of her locked in a
suitcase in her flat, scratching on the lining. Or not, hopefully.
The bowlers were back today – just one rink this time, but there are
too many players. What sort of game are they playing?

January 15th

What a week. A wonderful week! Rather keep it to myself. Are you jealous, diary? Are you curious?

This wasn't one of Dad's *new* notebooks. My stupid brother had thrown down some old diary of Dad's. So unless 'they' had been chasing him since 1987 – I don't even know how many years ago that is! – there wasn't going to be anything to help me find him in this.

I only kept reading because Mum's name is Nancy.

January 16th

Bowlers again. I counted them. Twice as many as there should be. I'll go over tomorrow and find out what's going on.

January 17th

No show from the bowlers. Snow again. The green square has disappeared. Everything white. Nancy calling in a minute.

January 25th

O! No, no, no, no, that cannot have happened!!! What a weird few days! Got to write this all down.

"Darling, come and get some tea!"

Mum said it didn't matter if I wasn't hungry, I still had to eat. Why does she have to make such huge meals now? It's like we're having to eat for Dad as well. That what we eat will feed him. Which is probably why we also have to do twice as many things as we did before. Mum said the best thing we could do was to carry on as we did before; but now we do twice as much. I have to read twice as many pages at bedtime, I have to go to twice as many clubs, we see twice as many films, and we eat twice as many sweets – infinity times more really, because Mum never used to buy us any.

Am I the only kid in the universe who hides sweets under their bed so they DON'T have to eat them?

And Ben watches videos Mum used to say he couldn't. And he's had to learn how to put his shoes on by himself.

After tea Mum let me play dens again. Ben was allowed to watch the end of the video.

Things started to get strange six days ago. No bowlers on the hill that day, but someone had cleared the snow. I'd had to go to Wally Eager's. He'd left a note the night before – pushed under the door. He thinks we're on to something. I think he's off his head! For the last few weeks, every night in the bar has been about the city, places in the city, empty buildings, tunnels, drains. About there being some sort of pattern to them. Great conversations! I couldn't wait to get to the bar each night, slipping into the warm bath of speculation. But lately, Wally seems to think we're all taking this stuff as seriously as he does.

At Wally's there was a fox on his front path. I shooed it away and rang the bell. After a couple of rings, a little kid from one of the other flats answered. She let me in. Her Mum was sick in bed, mumps – very nasty – she moaned more than talked, she said Wally had just gone out, should be back soon, said it would be OK to wait in his room. He didn't come back though, so I had a nose about. Lots of books – not the kind I'd expected – there were engineering books, stuff on electronics, design, war gaming and a whole shelf of 'The Pan Book of Horror Stories selected by Herbert Van Thal'. I thought Wally was more of a poet. When he didn't come back I left a note and told the sick woman on the mattress that I was going. Not sure if she heard me. Her little girl was making mountains from sugar cubes on a table. I took the chance to go up The Hill.

I wished this were a proper book where it says who all the characters are and what they're trying to do.

Something is going on up there. As I get closer I see cream figures on one slice of the green square. The sun's shining now, low and blinding from the white, but nothing's melting. I crouch behind the bushes that surround the bowling club. It's the noisiest game of bowls I have ever heard in my life. Everything they do they describe to each other – it's like they're teaching bowls to aliens. I climb through the bushes and half a ton of snow falls down the neck of my coat – thank you very much! But now I can see through the knotholes in the wooden fence and I work it out. Half of the bowlers are blind, the sighted ones are describing the play to them.

I made myself known, told them that my old man was club secretary. They invited me to have a roll-up with them, but I explained that there was someone I had to see. I think they could hear me blushing. "One wood at least!" Well, I could hardly not bowl one wood, so I stepped in for the blind number three's second wood. Our side lay pretty well: it was a long end and most of the woods were short, but we had a couple of chalked 'touchers' on the edge of the dyke, a yard beyond the jack. They had the 'shot' wood though, a foot in front of the jack. I'd have to make a perfect draw, or, even better, keep it just a little tight, put on a shade extra weight and slice the jack into the dyke, follow through and with the two other 'touchers' at the back we would lie three shots to the good.

I stepped onto the mat and bounced the number three's wood in my hand, checked the bias and admired the silkiness of the black lignum. Like polished coal, shining from somewhere deep beneath, and completely artificial. An *idea* of nature. At the other end of the rink, up around the jack, a member of our team, one who could see, was over-describing the shot to me. When he'd eventually shut up, I went into my usual 'thing', trying to feel the space, trying to simply 'place' the wood into its journey, just letting it happen. I stepped off the mat and swung into the delivery. I hadn't bowled since the summer, but it was all the better for that. Like touching a girl's cheek for the first time. Impossible to do wrong.

This is the most boring story I have ever read, Dad! What is this kind of bowling, anyway? Only old men like Gramps play it! So this has to be a code. Usual 'thing'? I think maybe it's about Mum and Dad doing things that Dad didn't want Nanna to read about.

The wood swung way out to the edge of the rink, but that was fine, it's a swinging green. I'd put a little wobble on the wood to keep the bias from working as much as it should. The sighted players up at the jack could see the way it was coming. "That's a perfect line, lovely weight, looking good…" They were clapping already, both sighted and blind. When my wood, rather than turning majestically to sweep the jack to the dyke for three shots, turned away and faded, alone, into the emptiness of the next rink.

"Drinks on you, young man!"

"He put the wrong bias on," someone explained to the blind bowlers.
They were all laughing, good-humouredly, jigging up and down, the ritual laughter necessary after this particular mistake. But it wasn't a mistake. I'd checked the bias. I ABSOLUTELY KNEW THAT IT WAS

NOT THE WRONG WAY ROUND. Somehow the wood had moved against the bias. It had defied nature and the laws of physics. Either that or something else had caused them to be briefly suspended.

There is something weird about The Hill.

I knew it would get more interesting!

I got home and had a bath, but I couldn't get it out of my head. There'd been no point complaining on the rink, no one was going to take me seriously. They had the evidence of their own eyes. I went out to see a film to forget about the whole thing.

Mum called me to get my pyjamas on ready for bed. When she came up with my hot chocolate I asked her about bowling and bias.

"How do you know about that?"

"Dad told me."

"Your Dad was a big bowler when he was young. He started when your Gramps was poorly after he retired. I think your Dad pretty much saved Gramps's life, spending time with him playing bowls. After that Dad carried on for a while on his own."

"What's a 'bias'?"

"You'll have to ask your..."

I pretended not to know what she was going to say.

"No, actually, I think I do know – it's something in the wood itself, isn't it?... that's what they call the balls they use – 'woods' – in the 'wood' I think there's some metal that makes it slightly heavier on one side so that when you throw it – or roll it, rather – on the grass, it makes the ball go in a curve, towards the side that the metal is heaviest."

"What if it went the way that the metal is lightest?"

"Well, it wouldn't..."

"But what if it did?"

"It can't."

"But just say that it did?"

"It wouldn't – it would always be pulled to the side that was heaviest. That's just how things are."

"Even so – if it did?"

"Even so? OK. Well, I suppose that would mean that things aren't 'just how they are' after all."

Chapter Four ~ Everything Is Wrong

"Even the Moon who now tiptoes
into the rectangle of my window
is no longer the same.

The moment when a human foot
first stepped on her
she was already dead."
(*The Selected Poetry of Jaroslav Seifert,* Jaroslav Seifert)

I hid Dad's diary under my pillow. After my bedtime story, which I couldn't seem to listen to at all, I counted a minute and slid out of bed. I could see the writing in a strip of light from the gap between the door and the wall. If I kept moving the notebook back and forward I could read the words. I knew now that Dad had known that everything that had happened so far would happen as it had and that he had left a message for me that could only be read in this way. Dad had discovered that things are not just how things are.

Like Mum said, Dad had tried to save things bit by bit – a cat here, things in a burning factory there – but it didn't work because those things aren't just how things are. You have to save things as if they are some other way. Save things from 'them'. Or maybe with 'them'. Dad always liked teams. I knew he wouldn't be alone. If I could work out who he was with I might be able to find him.

There wasn't much new on at the movies in town. I'd seen all the Christmas hits, I didn't fancy Zombie High or Meatballs III so just on account of the poster I bought a ticket for The Bedroom Window.

In the toilet some maniac had engraved into the tiles something about rays from outer space entering our brains. The film was better than I'd expected. It was a thriller. All about having to look at things from someone else's point of view, in order to get them out of trouble, and then how that got you into even worse trouble than them. I thought it wasn't very good at first, because none of the characters were attractive, but the story got you asking: whose eyes are you looking through? On behalf of exactly who are you witnessing these things?

Not the first time Dad's lost it, then.

At the end of the movie I did a really stupid thing. I tried to hide in my seat until the next showing. I didn't want to see the whole movie again, the end was ridiculous. Why should I pay for a whole new ticket just to see the first half? But I did want to get that feeling again, when the main character realises that pretending to see what someone else saw is an impossible task. Of course, after a few minutes the ushers started coming through the seats, clearing up the sweet packets and cartons. I slid down onto my knees – getting myself into an increasingly embarrassing position (at least if I'd stayed in my seat I could have pretended I'd fallen asleep) – now they were going to catch me. It was hardly a big deal, but I could feel my heart beating in stereo. If I'd thought at the time, I would have pretended that I'd lost something and was still scrabbling around looking for it. I didn't think. I jumped up and ran to the emergency exit by the side of the screen. Opening the door, I collided with a young man running *into* the cinema. I pushed past him and he pushed his way past me and as the door shut between us I saw him turn – what the hell was Wally Eager doing there?

The door clunked shut and I was in a dimly lit yellow corridor. Along one side were doors to the other screens. I knew exactly what I should do: go back, apologise to the staff, and find out if Wally was OK. It wasn't a good sign: that hunted look on his face. The only predator on Wally's tail was his own mind. But instead, I kept going, too embarrassed to turn back. At the end of the corridor was the door to the outside world, and I was heading towards it as fast as I could, when a few yards from the return of self-respect, one of the studio doors up ahead began to open. They were going to catch me.

'They'! Dad was being chased by them!!

I stopped in a dead panic. I could hear voices behind me, too. There was a door just to my right. I took the handle, turned and pulled. It opened, I stepped into the darkness and quietly closed the door behind me. It was open just long enough for me to see the mops, tins of cleaning fluid, a bucket and some brown overalls. I felt my way carefully around the tins and hid myself behind the work clothes. I felt for the wall, but found only another layer of clothing. So I pushed myself behind them too. Still no wall. Another layer, another and another – just overalls – a forest of them. Finally the texture changed, it felt cooler, suddenly chilly, and I touched the cold of brick. I squeezed myself against it, face between the shoulders of rough coats. I waited. Voices outside, shadows moving in the crack of light under the door. They came and went, shouted and laughed. They checked the storeroom four times, but not behind the coats. Only when there'd been no sound for a good twenty minutes did I inch around to look for another way out. Nothing doing.

After what seemed a very long time, I sat down against the wall. I didn't want to go out there. What if I opened the door and there was a posse of ushers and usherettes waiting in silence? Waiting to laugh at me? And I was warm amongst the overalls, anyway, I was fine there. I closed my eyes, and re-ran the movie behind my eyelids. Somehow I fell asleep.

When I woke up the light under the door had gone. I listened for a minute or so, then pressed my way forward, neatened up the work clothes and eased open the storeroom door. It was dark and quiet in the corridor. I reckoned on the cinema being shut by now. At the far end of the corridor the outside door had one of those PUSH fire exit levers that always seem to stick – I leant down on it and it clanged smoothly open. But I wasn't in the street. I was in a concrete nothing, no use for anything, no reason for being kind of place, brown-grey in the moonlight. Above was clear, with a few stars. And I could see my breath coming in nervous clouds.

Cut to the chase, Dad!

I found my way down the concrete alley, and out beside the front of the cinema. I checked the street. Opposite, in the shadows, a single orange light sedately throbbed. Some sort of security device. There had been talk of putting up TV cameras in cities to watch people. Suddenly the light dropped to the ground where it burst into a splash of yellow sparks and was snuffed by a large foot that reached down out of the darkness... snuffed by a large foot ... from the ... from the... snuffed by... the... snuffed by...

28

... there was a strange yellow-white light all around me, and I was staring over the soft edge of something, at this square of light... the same colour as my curtains... I couldn't think what this kind of feeling was... I heard voices... I was wrapped in something... faces stared at me... odd, frozen, stuck faces... my posters. I fell out of bed and into the light. I could hear Mum, muffled, shouting for me to get up and that it was almost eight and that I had school and we had to be early because there was a trip. I hadn't finished the story... no, it wasn't a story. Dad wasn't here. It was all real.

'They' had been after him for years. Even at the movies. O my god, 'they' mustn't find the... I reached around the covers for the notebook. Under the pillow. Under the bed. I shook out the bottom sheet. Nothing. Behind the toy box, then? Nothing. Under yesterday's clothes?

I knew by now it wasn't going to be there. 'They' had come. 'They' had been in my room. Even so I checked everything. NOTHING had been disturbed. Everything had been replaced exactly as it was, except for Dad's story... Dad's real story... that was gone.

I pretended everything was OK. I knew that was what you had to do. When 'they' have been. You don't tell. You don't talk. You keep it to yourself and you plan.

Downstairs Mum had made me two cheesy crumpets with butter and tea. I stirred in some sugar with my knife. Butter from the crumpets made oily patterns on top of the tea. Whole countries on the move, continents breaking up.

"Mum, where did Dad live when he was young – like as a young man?"

"Where are all these questions coming from, darling?"

I knew I was taking a chance.

"What did Dad do in 1987?"

"1987... 1987 specifically?"

"We're... doing it in history."

"1987 is history? Dear me..."

On the top of the fridge, next to the candlesticks and the

Spiderman present that Ben had already got and that we were saving to give to someone else, was the notebook. I saw the corner of its blue cover resting on the black and red web. Just where Mum would see it. 'They' were pretty smart.

"Mum, can I have some more orange, I'll get it thanks." I was dragging my chair to the fridge, using the open door to hide most of what I meant to do. I poked one hand above the door and pulled down the notebook. The spiderman toy smacked onto the shiny wooden floor. "Trap!" it seemed to say.

"What are you doing? We're saving that for one of Ben's friends?"

But by then Dad's notebook was in my school bookbag. Maybe 'they' weren't that clever after all. Maybe 'they' made mistakes too. Maybe we could still get Dad back?

"Mum found the book," Ben said in the car, whispering between the two booster seats. I knew then that we had to escape and find Dad on our own.

Mum was with 'them'.

Chapter Five ~ Underground

For every man worthy of the name is an initiate; but each
one into different Mysteries.

(*Lud-In-The-Mist*, Hope Mirrlees)

**"Wally stepped out from the shadows and waved me over. Even in
the ugly orange street light I recognised his short ginger hair,
squashed, meaningless face, and odd glasses. What was he doing -
still here? Wally told me the story. I have to write it down now
before I dismiss it as the nonsense it almost certainly is.**

Wally! What a let down! I thought Dad might have at least come
face to face with 'them'.

I'd had to pretend I needed to go to the toilet urgently. The
lights were sharp and nasty in the school toilets. I'd checked the
cracked tiles on the floor to see if there were any messages there.
Nothing about brain rays. Just patterns.

**Wally said he'd followed me to the bowling green. (Although he
wouldn't properly explain why.) He said he saw me bowl the wood
that defied nature. The blind bowlers must have told him. Anyway,
he said he'd spoken with them – they'd wanted him to join in the
game (same as me) and one of the blind players had taken him
inside the clubhouse to get him some flat-soled shoes. Wally said
that when the blind guy opened the locker of old kit, Wally could
see there was no back to this locker – instead it fell away into a
corridor. I said: "You sure it wasn't a mirror?" That didn't go down
well. Anyway, Wally had played a couple of ends, then excused
himself to use the lavatory and climbed into the locker. Four hours
later – he reckons – he found himself in a cupboard full of mops and
overalls at the back of the cinema, stumbled out, and that was
when I collided with him – he'd been in the same cupboard as me,
but I could only find a brick wall.**

"What were you running away from?"

He said: "I don't know. I don't remember what it was like inside."

And then he went home.

I couldn't sleep. I keep wondering if there is something under everything. I know there isn't, but the more you talk about it...

That was five days ago.

Yesterday, we took Wally to the hospital. He says he's fine, but he's not. He's been wandering around the streets on his own.

"The city is a dream, my friend" he says, repeatedly.

I don't think he's in control anymore. Anyway, the good thing is that he's not unhappy. And he's done nothing dangerous to himself or anyone else. It's just that everywhere is haunted for him; wherever he is, that place is haunted by everywhere else.

What's the point of the story if he doesn't tell us what Wally *saw* under the hill?

Then there were a couple of pages of stuff I didn't understand, I think it was psychology stuff that Dad was maybe getting from Mum. Anyway, it didn't make much sense. It certainly wasn't interesting and it probably wasn't right. So I skipped until I got to the bit that I was looking for. In the hospital Wally told Dad what he'd remembered about what was under the hill:

Inside The Hill is a world of upside down and inside out statues, monuments, places that have been planned but never built, ugly buildings, motors that are disconnected, lost things, thousands of single gloves all hanging down from the roof. As if all the secret things of the city are dropped down under it – all its loose connections and unwanted parts are in fact the levers and brakes and control sticks of the city, the control room for everything above the surface. As it is below, so it is above.

And that was it. Just as it was getting good the writing stopped. Only blank pages after that.

After school I put the notebook back on the fridge.

Mandy came round to play and I told her about the notebook, swearing her to keep it a secret. Mandy said: how did I know it was true because my Dad hadn't actually been there, he was just repeating what his friend told me and you should never believe what other people tell you unless you have 'evidence'. Her Dad is a solicitor. She thinks she knows everything.

"Then we better find this Wally?" I said.

She didn't like that because she couldn't argue with it. It was her who said to find evidence.

"But what if he's a mad axeman?"

I knew that didn't happen very often.

We looked up 'Eager' in the phonebook. There were none.

"Are you sure that's how it's spelt."

"It's in the notebook. E-A-G-E-R."

"Wally is short for Walter, which is like "alter", and Eager sounds like ego..."

"So?"

"Your 'alter ego' is like another version of yourself. It's Latin."

"Like clones?"

"No. A version that can do things you can't. It's like you, but it's got everything you haven't got... it fills in the gaps... I suppose if you could put you and it together you would be perfect. Or everything."

"Which is why someone might try to find it?"

"Maybe..."

Mandy went on. According to her, it wasn't Wally Eager who was mad. It was Dad. Wally Eager was just in Dad's imagination.

"Anyway," Mandy said, annoyingly now, "this isn't a diary. It's a novel. Lots of novels are written like letters or diaries. Like 'Bridget Riley's Diary'. Or 'Frankenstein'. It's called 'epistolary'."

I'd heard of 'Frankenstein'. Dad had it on video. Dad's notebook WAS like a story, but I was sure there was something under The Hill, beneath the bowling green. I was sure that the something down there had MADE that ball turn the wrong way.

Later, I asked Mum if Dad ever wrote any novels.

"No, only began them."

So I was right. I understood it now. There were two Dads. That's what 'them' are? Our Wally Eagers, our other ones. The bits of us that are missing from us. I had to organise a search party to find the other one of my Dads. The bits that are missing one – and that would lead us to the one we knew. Because the other would be everywhere the one wasn't.

Chapter Six ~ The Machine

> They would take a few provisions and go to the open hills,
> disappear for the whole day, sometimes for weeks and
> months. They often didn't have a particular destination. To
> go on a *sarha* was to roam freely, at will, without restraint.
> (*Palestinian Walks*, Raja Shehadeh)

I'd arranged to meet Mandy in Prison Lane. It was a special
occasion – the first time I had fibbed about anything important
to Mum. I told her I was going to the shop.

Mandy is allowed out anyway, but I'm not. She's a year older
than me, and she says her reading age is five years older than
average. I don't know why I like her. It's not because she's clever.
Mandy says she likes me because I am different.

When I tell Mum I'm not clever she says "O yes you are!" but
the 'O' sounds sicky, a talking-to-a-baby 'O'.

It was dark. The cctv camera on the big wall fidgeted like a bird.

If you push yourself hard against the wall the camera can't
see you. Not just because you can't see the camera. I'm not that
stupid. I haven't thought that since Year Two, cramming myself
into the door frame whenever I was sent out of class.

"I'm going to go and look for Dad. Me and Ben are going.
We've packed special bags and food. And umbrellas and as many
clothes as we can wear so we can sleep outside at night."

"Because of your Dad's story?"

No. It wasn't just that. Something else had happened. Of
course, we would have gone anyway. Just because of the story,
and The Hill and the inside-out city. But now we knew Dad
WANTED us to.

The day before, after Mandy had gone home, we had had tea.
Mum had cleared the table, and I realised what it was that she
was clearing. Dad's things. They'd been in the middle of the big
table when Dad disappeared. And each day Mum had moved
them further from the centre. Then they'd been put on a chair

back. Then on its seat. Finally they'd jumped back onto the very end of the table. And now Mum was propping them against the side of one of the green recycling bins. All through chicken in breadcrumbs and paprika potatoes I'd kept sneaking looks.

"Alice, what are you doing tomorrow for your rehearsal? Alice? Dreamer! Come on, I'm running you a bath, Ben. Alice, go and get your pyjamas on."

When she'd gone I grabbed the pile of Dad's things. There was a plastic bag with nothing in it, an old jumper full of holes, a lumberjack shirt, a shoulder bag (again with nothing, unless a pair of gloopy batteries counted). Dad must have emptied anything important. Like he knew he was going away. Like he hadn't had an accident.

Finally, there was a plastic sandwich box with some dry crumbs inside. It smelled like the end. I shook the box and the crumbs rattled softly. I hugged the old woolly shirt. Something in the shirt crunched; the same sound as snow makes when you walk on it. I turned the shirt around. In the top pocket I felt a papery lump; drawing it out I unfolded tickets and notes and shop receipts. Dad had bought socks from the Army Surplus and Bombay Mix from a health food shop. There were really old train tickets from when we were visiting friends. Something from a bank. On lined paper was a list of things to do:

do shopping list
oven (couldn't read)
fire alarm b's (couldn't read)
snacks

It was written in scratchy handwriting. Dad's. Had to be. Then, in pencil, but in the same writing:

Dread. (Place of pan-ic)
Hub.
Superfluous.
Accidental Museum.
Dreamscape.
McCurdey.
Geometrical Space.

New Menhir.
Revolutionary playgrounds.
Wormhole .
Z World.

(Then, in the same pencil) **get batteries AA**

"Mandy, I think they're all places."

"Why?"

"Well... playgrounds are places to start with, OK? And museums are for sure and the first one says 'place'... 'place of panic'. '**Wormhole**', a hole is a place, even though it's not there, it's the missing bit of a place. '**World**' and '**Space**' – those are places? '**Dreamscape**' could be like a landscape, except in a dream. I don't know about the others. Maybe '**McCurdey**' is a village. Squeeze in a bit more against the wall."

"Why?"

"Because."

"My Daddy says never to do anything anyone asks you to do unless they can explain why."

I took a big breath.

"Everywhere there will be people with phones who can report us, or take pictures of us and email them to the police. Even if 'them' are not everywhere, 'them' have people who will be. Mum is working for 'them' and maybe all parents are – all teachers, all Brown Owls, sweetshop people. And students, even ones in our street."

Mandy seemed to shrink.

"We have to do everything in code. Speak in code. Walk in code. Even though we are going to look for Dad we musn't actually look for him. We have to do other things to find him."

"What other things?"

"We have to find the places on the list."

I turned the list over and showed Mandy what I had found. On the back the pencil Dad had used had come through the paper leaving eleven holes.

"So what?"

"Eleven holes."

"Yeh?"

"This is a map of the eleven openings we have to find."

"Where's the legend?"

"The what?"

"The legend."

If it was George and the Dragon there would be a cave and that's where Dad would be.

"A legend is a box on a map where it says what the marks mean. There are only marks on your map – no legend – so how do you know what the marks mean?"

"Dad is my legend. I know what he means."

Even though it didn't make any sense she couldn't argue with it. Her Dad might be a solicitor who takes her to symphony concerts and teaches her bridge, but my Mum is a clinical psychologist.

Anyway, Mandy hated being left out of anything. I don't think she was ever allowed to do things like we did – exploring in the woods, or dressing up as pirate-murdering robots and using all the furniture in the front room to make a night club. When she came round to our house her face looked different to when she left. Mum would criticise her clothes, but I knew she liked them – they were all made by artists, whereas ours came from Next.

"She can name anything, but have they taught her to feel anything?"

I didn't really know what Mum meant, and Dad would tell her off for saying it.

"OK, when do we leave?"

"You know we won't come back until we've found my Dad."

"We'll have to come back at some time."

"You have to swear you won't come back except with our Dad. Even though you might never see your Mum and Dad again."

I could hear the camera creak. There were shadows crossing the bottom of the lane. And voices at the top.

"Quick."

"I'll think about it."

"No. Either you say 'yes' now or you can't come."

She was angry, but I could tell she wanted to come.

"How do you know I won't tell my Mum?"

"Because you're not one of 'them'."

Mandy's eyes grew so wide I thought the whole world might drop into them. Then we would never have an adventure. Then there would just be nothing, only swimming about in her huge thoughts.

Two students appeared at the top of the lane. Drinking from beer cans. At the bottom the only old lady left in our road appeared, pushing her shopping basket.

We ran past the students and crossed the road back towards home.

Mandy whispered breathily, "What's code for 'yes'?"

"Just don't do anything. Just wait. Something will happen."

And we ran up the street and she seemed to smile even though she was puffing.

"Thanks," she said, as she rang on her bell. That was code.

Somewhere on the street a student was practising the saxophone. In the upstairs windows faces were lit by computer screens. Someone groaned behind dirty curtains – and in every house I knew there would be thinking, reading, watching strange films, making up songs, learning lines, drawing graphs, writing stories. At night the grown ups planned what happened the next day.

Chapter Seven ~ Packing The Kit

Stumbling needs to be thought of not as a loss of footing
but rather as a finding of one's feet...
(*Social Choreography*, Andrew Hewitt)

My kit:

– *Dad's list of places (obviously).*

– *His map on the back of his list (not much of a map –
Mandy's right.)*

– *Cloak of Invisibility. Mary Poppins's umbrella. Willie
Wonka's last golden ticket. Legolas's bow (I think he's
sexy). A rabbit-proof fence. Permission for an endless
sleepover. (Wouldn't it be brilliant if you could take anything
from movies that you wanted – in your head you can.)*

– *Chalk (in case).*

– *Compass (maybe we can fix it).*

– *Camera.*

– *Food – carrots (we can clean in a stream), pepperami (not
the very hot one), rice cakes (no – Mum will notice they
have gone... yes – Mum will notice we have gone first).
Chicken bits saved from plate (in silver foil, looks like
something nuclear, maybe we shouldn't carry anything
metal?) Lettuce (clean in the same stream as the carrots –
Mum says the people who wash it are treated badly and so
don't care too much about washing their hands after going
to the toilet.) Chocolate digestives, big packet (bad luck,
Mum). Apple juice... orange juice, Ben doesn't like apple.
Water (Mum says you die from thirst before you die from
hunger). Sultanas (easy to disguise as rabbit droppings).
Flaked almonds (difficult to disguise as anything... perhaps
fingernails of torture victims, but that's more suspicious
than flaked almonds...)*

- *Notebook and pencil. Collecting box for 'interesting things'.*
- *"Not too much" (Dad's advice).*

Ben's kit:
- *Large spiderman (changed by me to small spiderman).*
- *Dalek keyring (he's got the idea.)*
- *Book of castles.*
- *Book of trees.*
- *Book of the seashore (who knows?)*
- *Felt tips.*
- *Book of Barbara Hepworth sculptures – (he did it at school and Mum took us to the gallery in St Ives).*
- *Book of... (no more books and he has to carry his own bag.)*
- *Woolly hat, woolly gloves...*

Ah! I'd forgotten about clothes.

I put on three lots of tights. Changes of knickers in my bag with my special kit. Usual things. Fleece. Extra fleece, wellington boots... walking boots are better – in case the places weren't near. I hadn't really thought about the distances between the little marks of blue ink. I'd looked very closely at the paper to see if there were any clues in the way it broke, or in the edges that were left. The marks all seemed quite close together when you looked at the whole piece of paper, but when you put your eye right up against one of the holes you realised that the page wasn't flat at all, but was full of mountains and valleys and plains in between. The peppery pencil-edged holes looked a long way from each other when you were up close. I couldn't tell if there were seas, but maybe the holes were even in different countries. Dad kept all the phrasebooks in his loft. To explain we would have to draw pictures. Pack extra paper. Maybe it was going to be a bigger explore than we'd thought.

I made Ben put on two extra layers. Even though it was warm

now, we might still be looking after Christmas.

Mandy was packing too, but we didn't know what. I tried to tell her, but she said she didn't need 'patronising', so it could be anything.

Ben said Mandy shouldn't come because whenever Mandy and me play he always gets left out, then he cries, then he bangs on our door, then we push him out, then he kicks us and then he gets sent to his room. I said it would be different this time. There wouldn't be any doors.

Ben said he wanted to bring his own friends. Who? He said he'd make a list:

- *A zombee.*
- *A dalek. ("What about in the woods?" "It levitates.")*
- *Mum's bst frend woh is a fizsist. (Takes him to fireworks).*
- *Gost. Unkl Frederick.*
- *Zac, Tom, Nola, Afiz, Betty. From schol.*
- *Djaq the chmizt frm Robn Hood DvD. (Actually, a scientist WOULD be helpful. Mum's friend the physicist only knows about tiny, tiny things. She says you have to specialise. I bet Djaq knows about everything from her time, and she is a boy and a girl. She IS everything.)*
- *Frnkstin – the monstr.*
- *Pirate wit ocptus hed.*

"OK, that's enough. You can't REALLY have all those people coming along. What if the zombie starts eating everyone?"

"Then I'm not going!"

"Well you can bring them in your head. I'm taking Mary Poppins's umbrella in my head. Just the idea of it. So, if we do need to fly or if it does rain, then we can still think we're dry, or we can think of a way to get somewhere else."

I thought he would say "it's not the same", but he said "OK".

"You can take other things in your head if you want?"

"What?"

I didn't know. I had to make it up.

"... ideas. You can take an idea you want and then you can use it when you need to."

"OK."

I didn't really know what I meant. But I thought it was a good plan. So here is my list of ideas to take with us on our exploration:

Look both ways before crossing the road. You may have forgotten what country you are in.

Shadows are things too.

You can make anything into sculptures.

No one can ever do nothing.

Exploring goes on forever.

The sky might be a painted ceiling.

Someone is watching.

Do everything in code.

I realised I needed to add another thing to my kit. It's a sort of a mix of an idea and a thing. *It's a bus stop that you can carry with you and whenever you put it down a bus comes, so you can always be moving.* That's idea number 9).

10) *That you can put more things on your list of ideas as you go along.*

And also I added Ganesha to the list of people – because he is the god of getting over problems. And of sweets, and Mum wouldn't be there to provide those for a while.

Chapter Eight ~ Going

...to let chance and the town take charge of you, for the
world we travel in is more wonderful than human plan or
idle heart's desire.

(*The Gentle Art of Tramping*, Stephen Graham)

"So, it's like we're on television the whole time?"

I hadn't thought of it like that, but it made it easier to
understand. I think even my little brother understood. Because
he had his serious face on. Mandy looked pleased with herself,
which was the only bad thing. She better not try to take charge.

The top of our street doesn't go anywhere. It's a dead end.
Only the people who live here ever come up our street. Maybe
some people who are stupid and don't notice the signs find it by
accident. It isn't an alley, quite. It doesn't have a name. And if
you clap your hands the sound in it is something like that on old
Doctor Who videos. (Maybe Dad's trapped in time?)

It wasn't even proper dark. It was teatime and we'd told Mum
we would play with our scooters on the pavement outside. We
wouldn't go far.

We put the scooters in the gap where our front window sticks
out. We'd already hidden our kit bags there – rucksacks Mum
had bought us for taking things on planes. Dad never liked going.
Which wasn't nice of him because it was our holiday time
together. He would say: "All the time it's a holiday, why do we
need to go so far?" He stopped saying that, because it made Mum
angry. I bet he carried on thinking it though.

We took the rucksacks from their hiding place. Up the road I
could already see Mandy coming out. She had her rucksack on.
She was going to ruin it.

"Did your Mum and Dad see you with your bag?"

"Sure."

"Didn't they ask you what it was for?"

"They never ask me anything."

At the mouth of the alley, we stopped. We could still turn

43

back now, but not if we went any further. The gap ran just a
short way before it turned to left and right, but we couldn't see
the turn. In the streetlights the bricks looked plastic. Like we
were about to walk onto a giant gameboard – 'Find Your Dad' –
with little blocks for houses and green stand-up things for trees,
like the towns they make for cowboy films. In the houses, the
windows were plasma screens, nothing behind.

But if we got to the other end of the alley, the fronts would
run out, and we'd come out in a desert or back streets in America
and car chases. I don't think we were scared, we were happy. We
didn't want to move in case we spoiled it. I wished that we could
take the mouth of the alley with us. Like the *bus stop*. Both an
idea and a thing. And use it whenever we wanted to get behind
the front of anything.

My little brother clapped his hands as quietly as he could.

"Boing... Boing... Boioioioioinggggg..."

At the end of the alley we turned right into the darkness.

Now it really was night. The time on the clock was probably
just a little bit past where it was when we got to the mouth, but
people and things had moved on since then. There were different
people and things in the night.

There was no desert and no car chases. Dead twigs poked at
us from above and stinging nettles leaned on us from the sides.
There were no stars in the prickly tunnel, but we knew where it
led: we followed by touch the tall wooden fence, past the new
house that was never quite finished, and onto the valley path.

We'd come down here lots of times, even with Mum
sometimes. And I'd come on my own. With my big cousin. Once.
There was a park at the end of the valley, the other way you
could get to the middle of town. But now the path was leading us
into a different version of here. It was an odd place anyway – a
wood and a field with cows right in the middle of a city. Mum
said it was only there because the university owned it and they
would build on it one day. Tonight it was weird times two and
then maybe times two again. It shouldn't be there and one day
wouldn't be. A wrong version of somewhere that would soon not
be at all.

Orangey lights beamed hard against the valley path. We went

down the mud steps and into the orange. A year ago they'd
tarmaced the path. It had been green with old grit poking
between the grass blades and you weren't supposed to cycle
there. It was stupid to put up lights, Dad said, it would turn the
place into a dangerous one. Without streetlights there'd only
ever been one murderer caught there, since we moved in. And he
didn't actually succeed. Dad said they'd made it like a motorway
and he wouldn't take us down there again.

We followed the winding stripe of shiny tarmac for a while ,
and then, even though there was no one else on the path, we
decided we had to walk in the trees. There are plenty of animal
tracks through the wooded bit and we took one of them, passing
some old skeleton Christmas Trees. Someone always dumped
their Christmas Tree in the same place, piling up dead years.

My little brother was leading us, because he could duck under
the branches. He told us to watch out for things – some tins of
beer – "that was bad" – and "a dangerous thing"; it was an
injection syringe with a needle. The orange was getting darker
the more we got away from the path. Darker moon too. Black
silvery. We couldn't see the whole round wheel of it, but it was
up there, big and in bits. Soon there wasn't much but dark to
hide in.

"Here's one of those things."

To my brother everything is a 'thing'.

Thin black and white trees cricked and cracked and when
they shook their leaves it sounded like silver foil crumpling. In
the trees some birds were fighting. Magpies probably. I'd seen
two of them attack the big street cat that sat on our back wall.
They got either side of it. One would peck its tail and when it
turned to defend itself the other would peck. Since then we
didn't get any poo in our garden. I liked the magpies.

The thin black and white trees came to an end and there was
a space with just a couple of big shapes. This was where the
kingdom of 'things' began.

Someone had used branches, fallen off during the storms, to
make the 'things'. They were a bit like insects and a bit like huts.
Insect-huts. Scratchy little homes that moved about on thin legs.
They could catch you food and chew it into smoothies for you.

That's another one for the list of things: *a mobile home like an insect*. Maybe it could fly too? I'd read a book about whole cities that were like that. They stormed around on mechanical legs eating each other up. But I didn't like that. Why does everything have to be for a reason in stories? Why can't things just float around because that's what they do? Chill out.

Even though we had only just set off I knew already that we would never find Dad by looking for him. How could we if we didn't know where he was? We had to look in code, to look without looking. We had to be out here, being, hanging, that's what would get us to Dad.

One of the 'things' had a big, thick, pronged head – a root maybe or where branches had sprouted. Ben was tugging at one of its legs, trying to pull it over.

"Don't do that. It'll fall on your head, stupid!"

Which made him pull harder. I hissed at him. "It's a sculpture!"

He stopped pulling. My little brother is more scared of art than doing in his own head! That's sick!

At the far edge of the gap, we stopped to see our way back into the trap of thin black branches and sharp white twigs. We looked at each other, wondering why we were looking at each other and not going in. Something was changing. I couldn't make out what it was. Ben was looking hilariously serious again. Mandy had hardly said anything since we left the street. She looked like she might never speak again. Ah. *That* was it. No bird fight. No crinkling leaves. The whole tiny wood was soundless. We turned round together. In the gap behind us everything had got really 'thick'. The shadows were gloopy, the trees shone like big black polished pillars. The wood shuffled into the shape of a burned palace. The air tasted of earth, with moles in it. Moles dying of shock. Ben trembled. Mandy was stiff like a lolly, face like a telly with the aerial out. Only the jerking Ben moved, the rest of the plasma world was stuck on 'pause'. Then one of the insect huts, the one Ben had been pulling at, lifted a leg and stepped towards us. I wanted to run. My legs refused. The thing shuddered and turned its horned head, its black-brown eyes were hungry, all its legs lurched at once. The insect tried to leap, but missed its footing in the grass, its legs shot in different directions and its head bounced on the silvery grass and rolled off towards the field at the bottom of the woods.

I wanted to blame my little brother because that would explain everything, but I couldn't because the trees on the other side of the gap, the trees out of which we had just come, were taking shape. There was a thin sound. A pipe in a house creaking or breath in a tunnel. Something squeaky escaping from an iPod up on the path. Perhaps, but I didn't think so. The sound made everything very sharp. An evil duvet was being wrapped round me and tied up with belts. It all seemed real because it was obviously not.

We were behind the front already.

We were only a few yards off the tarmac path. I bet with myself there were students up there walking home hugging their laptops. But I knew that even if I screamed they wouldn't be able to hear me. They weren't in this.

The trees on the other side of the gap juddered. The sky went slippy. Each line shifted like iron filings on a magnetic face. In place of the field of black poles there was now a picture. Of someone. Huge. In a long grey coat, buttons shining, smeared with a kind of dust. The thing wore red boots with designs like claws. Between its mac and its chin there was a bush of black hair. It was the same between its sleeves and its fingers; it poked out like from men's shirts when they don't look after themselves properly. Mum says. It looked stuck on.

I knew I was going to have to look at its face.

It was so round I thought it was the moon at first. Sort of greenish. Its eyes were craters and its teeth dark seas.

Mister Binns.

My poor little brother was now shaking so much that he was knocking against me and Mandy. Mandy seemed to be taking it all in, a computer downloading stuff. I knew she would crash if I let her run on much longer. And my brother would wet himself and we would have to go home.

"Run!"

It was as if we'd been waiting for a word. We turned and dashed through the twigs, scratching our cheeks and eyelids.

Leaves in our mouths. Roots against ankles, slipping on the curves of cider bottles.

The trees had been waiting too. They let go their breath in one great howl, shrieking and bending. The whistling pipe shouted in reply and we screamed back.

We burst into a new gap of dead grass and big trees. Running either side of another insect hut, we headed fast for the scratches ahead of us and disappeared into the sharp tunnels, knowing that behind us the woods were already forming up again into those hairy arms, long coat and wide, light green, empty smile.

We scrambled over heaps of dead flowers and grass cuttings. We passed a stile on the field side. The woods were narrowing now, and the trees further apart, shrinking away from each other. We could hear cars on the university road and we ran towards the sound. We were going to make it now. Ahead was the wire fence, the old iron gate had been tied up and a new one put in. Once through that we'd be safe.

Chapter Nine ~ Everywhere

"Square de Missions Étrangères may be used for receiving visitors, for being stormed by night and for other psycho-geographical purposes."
(*Square des Missions Étrangères*, Michèle Bernstein)

"What was it?" my little brother wanted to know.

I don't know why I bothered.

"It was an animal, and a man, and a thing, and a bit of the moon..."

Mandy said: "No. It was everything. Everything."

Which is what I was trying to say, but she had to make out she was saying something new. I was naming the bits first. I knew it was 'everything'.

"It was just the woods, then?"

A purple light shone from one of the student flats. Traffic lights changed from red, through yellowy orange, to green. As if the colours in our world were rebooting.

A blue bus pulled up at the stop right next to us. And we got on. *9: a bus stop that you can carry with you and whenever you put it down a bus comes, so you can always be moving.*

"Please can we have three... those things... is it 'day riders'?"

"'Explorers'?"

How did he know?

"Well, he", the driver pointed at Ben, "don't need a ticket. And, you two – where you going?"

"Next stop..."

"Just go sit down."

He waved his hand in a nasty way, probably trying to be kind.

We sat down and the bus jumped forward, the harsh lights of the bus shutting out everything outside, a moving waiting room. People doing nothing till their lives started again. Staring into their shopping and their work bags, no one spoke to anyone. With a hiss the bus pulled up and we pushed Ben down the aisle and onto the pavement. Mandy had to jump before the swishing doors caught her. The bus levered itself up and pulled away.

I knew where we were. Dad would bring us here. Lots. It was one of his favourite spots. I wondered if the bus driver was maybe an agent for our side, pretending to be miserable. There was something about his voice.

"Russian," said Mandy.

"Really?"

She nodded as if she had been there (probably) and was personal friends with all their bears (hmm).

Ben said he felt sick.

No one could get travel sickness on such a short ride.

"Maybe he was poisoned?" Mandy suggested. I was really pleased she had, because I could call her stupid and mean it. Even really clever people are stupid sometimes.

Ben was sick. Nothing serious, because he immediately wanted to start on our supplies.

At last we stopped arguing and throwing up and looked around.

Beyond the low wall that Ben had just been sick down was a miniature field, full of long grass, too high to be a park, but not high enough to be a jungle. An in-between. That's how people treated it, people who spent their time in it, in-between people. They'd wear strange hats and have picnics, drink beer from big plastic bottles, or make speeches. They had dogs that looked nervous, that could see bad things their owners missed. On the other side of the grass was a row of houses covered in twirls and knobs and curly bricks. Dad had said they were "Victorian". They looked like they might be haunted. The scariest had a castle turret bursting through its roof. The turret was sharp like a spike and it had a window into a small round room. Dad had said that this was the house where a fantastic mathematician...

"Magician!"

"Mathematician, actually, Ben. It's different..."

...but I'm not sure about that, because this mathematician also did tricks. When he was a small boy, the mathematician would throw himself to the tops of lampposts and whirl round them in spirals. At university he would hang by his feet from famous buildings.

Dad had said that the mathematical boy later discovered that numbers were really shapes and that one, two, three was a kind of map, and that there were other numbers that were like arrows... for getting to places... and not just in our heads. Numbers were "out there". And that the boy got all this from whirling round lampposts – because everything in the universe has to whirl round one way or the other.

Ben began to whirl round the lamppost below the turret until he felt sick again.

Mandy had nothing to say because I'd been talking like she does. Bossing everyone with what she knows. I hadn't left any space. Sorry, Mans, but tough.

I felt that we were all about to decide to go home. But then Mandy became a hero.

"Maybe that's why we're here?"

"What?"

"If the man who realised that numbers are really space, discovered that everything moves around something else, then maybe this is the something that everything moves around?"

We all looked at the lampost.

– *10: the lamppost everything moves around.*

At the top of the road was the Spiritualist Church where they call up the dead, opposite was the Church School where the bell hung outside a little tower, down from that the mosque where on Friday there were always little queues of chatting men, some with hats like cake tins. At the top of the road was 'Water Street', because there was a well and a beautiful lady had refused to do something – give away her father's sheep or pay taxes or something – and anyway, they'd cut off her head with her own scythe, she'd picked it up and everywhere her blood fell foxgloves grew. Mum says that she's not really a Christian saint, she's a Celtic water goddess, but what's the difference as long as it's true. Pilgrims came to drink the magic water, Michael Jackson tried to heal the whole world at the football ground. If you put your ear to the pavement you can hear the stream. They buried it after the cholera and maybe the magical mathematician saw them do that?

That was just the start of all the things that revolved around the lamppost. There was a cinema where Nanna's favourites, The Beatles, played (Gramps said she screamed and became historical) and next to that the chapel that took ages to build; there was always a joke in the panto when Gramps went: Sleeping Beauty would wake up after a thousand years and say: "Haven't they finished that dome yet?" That was in the theatre where they all died. Just up from the lamppost. It burst into flames, but the doors opened the wrong way. The theatre was full of poor people, dreaming about being gypsies. But which way were we supposed to go?

"How do you know so much?"

"They're not school things. Dad told us them. Maybe because this IS what everything whirls round?"

"Which way?"

"Uh?"

"You said everything in the universe has to whirl round one way or the other."

"That's just tiny things."

"The water in the bath has to whirl round the plughole one way or the other."

For the third time we looked at the lamppost and then at everything else. On a noticeboard the moonlight glistened from the winding patterns left by snails. A painting over the café window showed a sun rising above the edge of the world. Behind the glass were faded posters of pyramids. We'd gone there with Mum (to the café, not the pyramids) for a sweet goo called Baba Gamoosh. Though that might be the fat one from Star Wars... Next door the newsagents had closed down, the last headline propped against the window: 'Dog Eats Local Man's Shed'.

Just after Dad disappeared all the birds had begun to fight. There was a war for different layers of the sky above our street. Herring gulls fighting magpies. Crows tearing apart pigeons.

I looked up into the dark layers. There was someone in the turret of the magical mathematician...

WHOOOP! WHOOOOOOP! WHOOOOOOOP! WHOOP!

A fire engine, the colour of blood, came roaring out of the night! We always loved to see them go by. The station was close to our house, so we would see the fire-fighters in the front pulling on their clothes, as if they were becoming something else. Sometimes it was Dad changing. I looked to see if he was in there, but there wasn't the usual scramble. Sometimes, it looked like there were animals and men, fighting to become each other, things wrestling and ghosts dressing in uniforms.

This time there was only a reflection of the street, as if the cab was full of still, black water.

WHOOP! WHOOP!

The engine slowed, its flashes darkening the sun over the café. It curled round the in-between space of long grass, heading back the way it had come. I hadn't realised until then that the waste-park was a triangle.

In the fading bursts of purple light, I saw a young boy stood in the window of the turret. He was looking. Not at us, but at something far away. Towards the prison, back near our house. When he was alive he must have been able to see the hangings from there. Swinging one way or the other, round the thing everything revolves around.

Dad wouldn't walk in the park by the station because that's where the crowds once came to see the murderers die.

The boy in the window leaned away. He seemed to be wearing a dark Puffa jacket. He moved as if he were cut out of black paper. He put his fingers to the window, but his hand was back to front, its fingers were on the wrong way round, like an arrow, pointing beyond the café.

The fire engine clattered around the distant corner and headed back towards the fire station.

When I looked again at the turret, all the blinds in the mathematician's house were down.

"He pointed this way." I jabbed a finger at the town. "The boy from years ago, he was disguised in modern clothes."

We walked once around the lamppost and then followed the magical mathematician's back-to-front arrowhead fingers.

Up ahead were the lights of the High Street and the Christmas crowds. I knew there was nothing for us there, nothing at all, but that felt right. Nothing. We had already seen Everything. Now, we had to find Nothing.

Chapter Ten ~ Nothing For Good

Q) What is un-space?
A) It is the labelless car parks, crawl tunnels, disused attics and cellars, bunkers, maintenance corridors, derelict industrial estates, boarded-up houses...
Q) Who are the Un-Space Exploration Committee?
(The Raw Shark Texts, Steven Hall)

We were somehow following Dad's list, but I wasn't sure how. Our jumping on the bus – even though it had all been a mess and a panic – was the right thing to do. We had shot down one hole in the back of the list and reappeared out of another.

Now we must be heading towards the third hole, in the middle of town.

Sure, town was a strange place to look for Nothing, being so full of things it seemed to push you out sometimes. My brother was always getting knocked over by a pushchair or a shopping bag. But somewhere among all that stuff there must be gaps.

I quite liked the crowds. Dad had taught us to ignore them as actual people and see them as waves breaking on the pavement.

"Autons!" Ben would shout, pointing at the dummies in the shop windows, but I pretended Ben meant the people. The people were robots. And one day they would turn really bad, their hands would fall away from their wrists, hanging backwards... I'd already seen that tonight.

I worried now. What if 'they' had got into the magical mathematician's house? Didn't the backwards hand point towards the full up town? What if the ghost boy was sending us the wrong way? Or calling other automated things?

I remembered this feeling. Like I couldn't do anything to change what was going to happen. But I had never stopped when I had felt like that. I actually wanted to carry on doing what I didn't want to do.

Were there really rays?

My little brother tripped on a piece of broken pavement and I reached to catch him. As we steadied ourselves, Mandy asked if we were "OK?" In that moment I felt something like a ripple. As if a large fish had swum past. Or a horse galloped in a deep stream.

Far ahead a small group of shoppers were moving in a beautiful way. They were more attentive than ordinary people. They swayed like dancers, but they weren't dancing, they were walking. I couldn't see their faces, there was nothing special about their clothes. I couldn't tell their age or whether they were men or ladies. Their walking was a kind of camouflage to look like everyone else, but they glowed as if they were powered by the stores. Then they were gone. Somewhere into the town.

We were going that way, anyway. But when we got to the point where they had disappeared, there were too many possibilities. An alley, a door, a house, a pub, a staircase. Another empty space, full of nothing happening.

There was something. Not much to look at. Some steps that must once have led somewhere but were blocked off now by a concrete wall. I quite liked the funny feeling that hung around places like this.

"Why are we stopping?"

I made up a reason. So we didn't have to face the robots. So we didn't have to die of boring things.

"It must have been a shadow."

"There aren't any."

Mandy was right. Though the place was tucked down the side of a dried-blood building with horrible bricks all cracked and angry like sores. Though it was crammed in by a pub and a set of flats. Though it was back from the road. There were no shadows. As if there wasn't enough of anything there to cast one. The streetlamps lit it with a wash of light and it had no shape at all. Streetlamps round which all things and nothings whirl.

"What's behind the wall?"

Mandy bent at the knees as if she was measuring the space with her eyes.

"I don't think there is anything. They built the steps for something but they never built the something. They put the wall in to stop people falling off into nothing."

I shivered. It was getting cold.

"I think it's for ghosts," said Ben.

None of us believed in ghosts.

"They come out of walls."

But we believed in these ghosts.

"How come we never noticed it before?"

"Why would you look at it? You can't even sit there – the steps are too... sharp."

The edges were thin like knife blades. Mandy could feel the place even better than I could.

But only I could *see* the ghosts.

They weren't ghosts of people. They were ghosts of a place. Useless place. Unloved place. If things had ever happened here they didn't now. The space was changing like old people do when they stop getting visits. Ghosts are hungry things.

I can't really describe them, because I could feel them as well as see them, a sort of mixture of both, and that was confusing. They were a bit like people, but they weren't. They were a bit like things, but they wanted to eat. They couldn't hurt us like people could.

"Can you see them, too, Alice?"

"See what?" I pretended. O why did the robot thing in my brain, the big ray machine that they probably kept in some house nearby, why did they always make me say stupid things like "no" when really I wanted to say "yes"?

Mandy looked like someone had just concreted over her.

"I'm sorry," I said "I mean 'yes' – yes, I can."

My little brother screwed up his eyes and stared at the concrete, his head slowly dropping onto his right shoulder.

"O, yeh," he said, unconvincingly.

"Why don't we go down there?"

I'd not realised that it was 'down', but there was a sort of concrete ramp leading to the beginning of the steps. A shallow dip in the town. A pool where puddles of spirit collected. The ghost of all the lonely places in the city had dribbled and run and gathered in this concrete sink. The smart new buildings next door were attempts to cover up what was there, as if they'd knocked down some really lovely old building. But they couldn't get rid of its ghosts, rolling up like fog every night, expecting to feed on the atmosphere, always disappointed. When it snowed this would be the place where the snow lasted longest. There wasn't even litter here. Probably even cats didn't come to wee.

"OK."

We half slid, half stumbled down the slope, steeper than it looked.

At the bottom, in the sink of spirits, we stood very close. We didn't want the ghosts to get between us. We would let them feed on the edges of us. It didn't hurt or anything, they weren't vampires. They were just sad corners, nooks. It was rather nice being snacked on by a place. Like being nuzzled by a dog but without the wet nose.

Even so, they were taking something away.

"We shouldn't stay here too long."

But we were getting something back.

"I think we're invisible here."

Without shadows and in the wet light of all the street lamps, no one in the passing cars looked at us.

"They don't even see it. That's why the ghosts are here. It's not *for* anything."

Ben began to study the place very closely.

"It's... ours, then."

Wow. Genius. Yes. Could be anyone's.

And I wondered how many more places in the city were like this. And I knew partly. Because I was thinking of a patch of grass by an underpass and some steps down to a locked door by the little swimming baths and a piece of roof that the grass grew on and a big iron gate where brambles had locked it tighter than chains and a place behind wire with islands of kerb where there'd once been a petrol station. And I knew there'd be ghosts and explorers collecting in those places too, slipping there by force of loneliness, longing to visit or be visited.

All those places could be ours.

We could have our own kingdom of nothings. It would run alongside Queen Elizabeth the Second's one. We'd slip between kingdoms and keep our own subjects fed with bits of ourselves.

Wow. We had swapped *something for a whole world!*

"What do you think you're doing?"

Chapter Eleven ~ The White Tunnel

So long as the temples and churches are full the entities are
happy. Once the congregations start to drift away... then
the entities are no longer fed. After ten years or so, they
begin to hunger, then they start to manifest themselves as
an apparition and feed off the reactions of the observers... If
the reaction is not enough... the animal mutilations and
chupacabra attacks begin: then there is a reaction to feed
off!

(*Psychodemiurgics*, Gilbert Nelson)

We ran like crazy.

He wasn't frightening like Mister Everything in the woods
was frightening. He wasn't frightening in a way that was scary
but good. He was scary *and* nasty.

The moment he spoke the ghosts shoved us out of their
concrete den. They could tell he wasn't part of our expedition.
He was grown up horribleness. And the ghosts didn't want to
lose us to that. They were pushing us out of danger.

Up the ramp we ran, passing either side of the man coming
down the slope, him slipping on its smoothness. We didn't know
which way to go and milled in confusion at the top. But Mandy
pulled us and the ghosts pushed us and before the man could get
a footing we were running along the pavement, the traffic
flashing by.

We ran in a single file. The orange street lights half-alive in
the damp road. We ran through a sea of Fanta. Mandy at the
front, looking over her shoulder. I was at the back jabbing my
little brother. The pavement narrowed and I heard the rattle of a
train underneath. Perhaps we should catch one, it had worked
with the bus.

The man hadn't followed us. Maybe he was just a caretaker,
but I didn't really think so.

We stopped at a Zebra Crossing. Mandy, dressed all in black,
flashed on and off as she crossed. Each black stripe was an oily

layer she might just slide into, each white stripe a light that might evaporate her; both were magpie layers that peck through the whole city but only surfaced here, same as the ghosts.

I looked at the drivers, but they weren't really looking at us. It wasn't late enough for it to be strange for us to be out on our own. We could catch the train and no one would question us.

As we followed the road around, the big jail rose up over a garden wall. We were heading towards home. We'd be at the bottom of Prison Lane soon. But I didn't think the ghosts wanted us to go home. I didn't think Dad did either. It wasn't time to complete the circle. Not even the boy in the magical mathematician's turret – even if he was more plastic dummy than person – wanted that. Not even Mister Everything-Binns – he hadn't frightened us just to run back to Mum. I think they were *all* pointing us to somewhere else.

Except the caretaker. And we'd escaped from him.

Further down the road there was a way into the station. A sort of back way. Ben was very excited: "Train! Train! Train!" He loved trains. Mandy was sensible: "They won't let children on, not on their own." I asked her how she knew, and she said she was only guessing.

And so we came to be sitting in the bright, eye-stinging train, with the darkness sliding by outside, thick and dark like chocolate.

It was a lady who came to see us about tickets. She had a big smile, one tooth bigger than all the rest. It danced about over her bottom lip as she chuckled away at us. Ben didn't have to pay and Mandy and me bought tickets for "the end of the line" which made the lady chuckle even more. "The end of the line" was Mandy's idea, she blurted it out. The lady looked at our rucksacks piled on the table, almost impressed.

We were becoming something else – a sort of unit. Not a gang, but something that was more than three kids. A kind of force. Because we were organised, felt everything and had a good reason.

I looked at our reflections in the window. Mandy was thinking hard. Ben leaning on the table, sleepy. I looked through the glass. White and brown waves were surging up to the train.

"We're in the sea..."

Mandy and Ben climbed over to the window, Ben hitting his nose.

"We're not in the sea, we're by the sea."

The train was running alongside the water. The tide was in and the winds were blowing the water into big waves. Spray spat along the glass.

"Ah!" Ben jumped back as a large handful of sea water hit the window, spreading like octopi over the glass, then winding rapidly off towards the back of the train. I felt things slow.

It wasn't the end of the line, but we got off anyway. We wanted to be by the sea. There were always empty buildings near beaches. Places where old people sat. Sheds for boats. Beach huts Mum said she wanted to buy, and Dad would suggest renting, before they both would go off the idea. Places where people brought along those who couldn't look after themselves. The seaside felt like another waiting room. We would be out of the wet and nobody ever checked those sorts of places, did they? Places where nothing happened. Or we could find a cave. There'd be no caretaker there.

The train pulled away and the lady ticket person looked at us from the frame of the last window. Her big tooth was scratching at her lower lip. Her eyes were working. She was filing us away, downloading our faces to her memory stick, wondering if she should have done more. The rounded square of light disappeared under the cliff.

Dad had said once about a tunnel. Three tracks went into it, but only two tracks came out.

Over the white pointed stick fence, far out along the cliff, a little apart from it, stood a big red pillar of rock. It was supposed to be a man who was turned to stone for taking directions from the devil. Next to it was another pillar; his servant. But why so huge, bigger even than Mister Everything-Binns?

We were a kind of lost, even without the fog that had trapped the two stone men. We knew stories about this place from Dad, but what if the stories were about going deeper and deeper into bad kinds of space? How would you know that? Did Dad know where he got his stories from? None of us knew what the real code was. All we could do was avoid what things actually meant, in case they were the devil's directions.

The cave was too wet. The shelters too busy. Even coming up to winter, with the night damp and the sea throwing up a thin spray, still there were people out walking dogs, reading newspapers, nosing around and breathing the air. No one was under the pier, but the tide was coming in and we would have rusted away to red under there.

We climbed the stone steps up from the beach. The coloured lights strung between the lampposts were dead. I could just hear the beep beep, ring and crash of the games in the Entertainment Centre. Just smell the vinegar from the chip shops. But there would be people there, on guard, watching the little bits of money changing hands or loading up the foam punnets with curry sauce.

We went the other way. Towards the darker part. It was starting to drizzle. We walked close together and against a high wall.

The wall stopped suddenly and we were hit by a gale of wind and spiky rain. Ben held his face and cried. It was all going to end.

"What's up there?"

The gap was an opening for a long driveway that looped back towards the sea. Just above this driveway a mist was falling, a grey sheet of scratchiness. It covered the distant building like a rug over a poorly person, but we could still see what a warm place it must be. As if a different part of the universe had taken off, flown through space and landed here.

Through the top of the mist two towers with tulip roofs poked at a rare brave star. Along the edges of the roofs were shapes lifted from some kind of holy world, shapes we'd done in school – from Egypt and India and 'The Arabian Nights'. In the middle the building was like a shiny biscuit tin, round and pretty, with oval wings. The light inside was the colour of Lucozade, the windows like half sucked barley sugars. It might have been a temple made from elephants' tusks and diamonds and washing up liquid, and at any moment priests in long red robes and pinnies might have come out of the spray.

"It's a hotel. They won't let us stay there."

Ben cried some more. Mandy was too clever for our good.

"We have to try."

I led them up the driveway, through the grey mist, towards the white temple. The nearer we got the warmer the building looked. Magical, even if it was only a hotel. There was a sign to say it was. But it wasn't the kind of hotel we'd ever stayed in. Mum and Dad took us to hotels that were just like people's ordinary homes; the people lived in the back and we stayed upstairs and ate in the front. This wasn't like the home any ordinary person would have. It was like someone's heaven.

"We can't go in there."

My little brother's eyes were filling up with rain and tears.

I led the way up the mouthy stairs. Pushed the glass doors. A sign on the desk said "Reception". There was no one there. A man in a red wine uniform disappeared into a corridor, but he hadn't seen us. Another sign said to "ring for attention", but we didn't want any.

"Come on."

We dripped on the beautiful carpet, its patterns the same as those of the building outside. Inside as outside. Like nowhere I'd ever been before, but of course, Mandy would have, so I didn't say. Another wine-coloured man appeared and disappeared. We slipped into the nearest corridor. I tried to picture the whole place and where we might be in it; whether we were heading for the biscuit tin or the oval, and where would be the least people.

On the wall there was a painting of the building, but without its name. And it was red, all red.

We kept going, the corridor bent and we were in a bar full of people. Dad had taken us into bars. A line of people were leaning on the shelf where they served the drinks, others were sitting at little tables. A man in the hotel uniform looked up and saw us. In his hands he continued to polish a glass with a towel. Beyond him was the oval room. There were people in there. Dancing in pairs. The ladies sparkled like the building. They turned in curling patterns across the oval floor. Outside, inside.

The hotel man glanced over his shoulder at the dancers and

then quickly back at us. He was putting the glass down, without taking his eyes off us. It slipped from the edge of the bar and there was a crash. All the people in the room turned and smiled, they laughed out a friendly cheer. The ladies shook and the sparkly things on their dresses jingled. The men swayed and glinted like knives. The bar man fussed, grabbed a dustpan and brush; his eyes still on us, his smile for everyone else. He disappeared under the bar for a moment; when he came back up his eyes were already searching for us.

Music skipped in, quick and jerky. It knocked Mandy and Ben out of their dreams. They shuffled. The man behind the bar put down the dustpan and brush and began to move round towards us. He wouldn't let us stay, he would call someone important, they would call the police, we would be taken home and have to explain why we had caused everyone so much worry and trouble and what did we have to say for ourselves? That we had Dad's list? That we'd taken a six-year-old boy and frightened him and put him in danger? That we were nine years old and ten years old and should know much, much better and were very, very sorry? That we should have achieved much, much more?

A laughing, clapping man in shiny shoes danced to the bar and took the bar man by the shoulder, interrupting his beeline for us. The bar man laughed, as if he had to, and the top of his head became red under his thin ginger hair.

"Quick!"

As the bar man turned to take a big glass from the shelves behind him, I grabbed Ben and pulled. Mandy followed.

Not the way we came. Never go back the way you came.

Beyond a table of glowing men and watchful ladies was a little white door. "To The Beach". The group were in such a world packed with themselves, that we were invisible. We only had to squeeze through the white door. As I shut it I could see its outline curved like the roof outside. It was part of the pattern.

The tunnel behind the door was also white. It stretched out of sight, sloping downwards. At intervals along the ceiling were pale green lights. The floor was dry, but the walls closed in like a cave's. The colours and hum and music of the bar were all gone. Not even a tiny, muffled version survived. We walked as quickly as we could and then waited to see if the door to the bar would open.

Two minutes. No one came.

"He didn't see where we went, did..."

"Look at that!!!"

Ben's finger was close to something on the curved white wall. A miniature prehistoric beast, a tiny version of something that the telly was always "Walking With". About two centimetres long. Greenish grey against the white, it was armoured like a flexible knight, its pointed feeling-things fingering the white surface; half-tank, half sensitive.

"There's more of them."

"They're OK," said Mans.

"Are they real things?"

"They're called Sea Slaters, actually."

Mans always knew.

"Why do they look like they're from another time?"

"Because they are – haven't changed in millions of years."

"All to be here?"

But that applied to everything. We looked around us. Like being inside a worm. At the end of the serpent were two doors. To the right a big iron one. From behind it came the hiss of waves. The door to the left opened into a tiny roundish room. It had no windows, just the same white walls as the tunnel. The brain of the worm was empty except for more Sea Slaters.

Mandy touched the floor.

"IT'S NOT WET!!!!!!!!!"

Mandy's words clattered and clanged. We laughed and the room made every gulp 'boinoinoing' and ring. Like the alley but mega.

The alley. That seemed a long time ago. It wasn't though. Just that the night had been more full of things than usual. Maybe we could always live like this.

We put down our bags and emptied all the clothes. None of us wanted to go outside. Something horrible was waiting for us beyond the iron door, we knew that. A giant Sea Slater churning the waves with its antennae. Something like that. We used our rucksacks to make a kind of mattress on the floor. Then we piled everything on top and each found somewhere in it to get as warm as we could. We didn't talk again. We were too tired. And, anyway, we didn't know what you were supposed to say.

Ben and Mandy were both deep asleep when I heard the door to the bar whine.

Then the lights went out. The door complained again and there was a rattle. Then silence. We'd be OK till morning. And I could fall asleep.

Before I did, I saw, creeping under the iron door, a dull yellowy-brown light. The sea outside thumped harder. Full of Sea Slaters trying to get in.

I had tricks to help me get off to sleep, like pretending I was in a deep sea diving bell, going down and down and down...

Chapter Twelve ~ Looking For The Accidental Museum

A society of *fugueurs* dedicated to forging new and unexpected pathways through city and countryside alike. Freewheeling psychogeographers intent on uncovering the hidden, the forbidden, the derelict and the *subterranean*.
(*Philosophical Transactions of the above Company of Glasgow giving some ACCOUNT of the present undertakings, studies & labours of the INGENIOUS in many considerable parts of the world VOL 1*, Company of Vagabonds)

Ben and the crab were facing off. The crab's claws were held high, Ben swished a lollipop stick. They circled back and forward, then around each other. Ben was being told off by Mandy. Maybe she was telling off the crab too.

The light from under the iron door was now lemony and bright.

"It's weeing!"

I scratched bits of sleepy dust out of my eyes. I'd never woken up with a crab in my bedroom before. I started to crawl over to it, but the stone floor was cold, so I rolled onto my heels.

"It's not weeing," said the know-everything. "It's trying to breathe. Out of the sea it can squirt water round its shell to re-oxygenate, then suck it back in. It takes its own little ocean with it. It's a Shore Crab."

The brittle green thing on the floor seemed suddenly important. Setting a good example.

"Let it go."

We all stood back and the crab started for the iron door. Mandy tried the rusty handle and the door creaked open, letting in waves of bright sunlight.

"Quick. Pack the bags."

The Shore Crab scuttled out onto the red beach. The water that had been knocking all night was a long way off now.

Mans made us share our different bits of food ("for a balanced diet"). Ben gave us each a slice of ham, I'd brought buttered bread, Mans had carrot sticks, "washed" she said, so we wouldn't need a stream. Then we put on our rucksacks and slipped out.

A long way off a stick figure threw a dot to a dog.

The sand was soft and damp and difficult to walk on. Each step broke through the sandy crust and stuck in the liquid mush underneath. We stumbled at every stride. In the corner of my eye I could see that a group of people were suddenly nearby. I couldn't work out where they had come from on an almost empty beach. I didn't see their faces, but they moved like the sculptors on a dvd Mum had got me from the library, after I'd asked about Dad. I didn't much like the things they made, but it was neat to see how they moved. As if their bodies were full of eyes. By the time we'd got to the top of the beach and onto the prom, the sense-people had gone.

There had to be a good reason for the train ride. We knew there was for the bus ride. That had taken us to a place Dad liked. It might have been number two on his list, the '**hub**'. A place everything swings around. And the empty, haunted place might be '**superfluous**', number three?

So what were we meant to find by the seaside? There had to be a museum in the town. But would it be "accidental"?

We used the toilets on the sea front. Mandy showed me what she'd packed, including a makeover kit. For disguise, she said. And then we walked. We passed the sickly coloured rides outside the Entertainment Centre. A moon-faced mechanical fortune teller, that for a moment reminded me of Everything in the panicky woods; it boomed, wanting money. Ching ching, omp omp omp went the machines. The air smelled of old chips. The sky rang with screaming. What were the birds always so angry about? What if that reason was a really good one?

The atom bomb shadows, where the summer flowers had been, spelled WELCOME faintly. A grey, cut-out paper head watched us with beady eyes from a window of a small hotel. Mandy said: "Basil Fawlty". He looked faded too, one more bored

ghost. The waves bashed at the end of the pier. We looked back
at the sea. I felt it try to drag our eyes out to everlasting greyness.

"Come on!" badgered Mandy.

We couldn't take the train again.

We wound through the flower beds, and against the flow of a
stream that ran in a wide concrete channel. On its brown waters
sat a black swan. I thought that was impossible, but Mandy said
they brought them in from New Zealand. A laundry sign: "We Do
Do Duvets".

It began to rain. We walked as close as we could to walls.
Mum must have rung the police by now. The TV would be
showing pictures. I wondered which ones Mum would give them.
Me and Ben on a beach in France? Or jumping off rocks at one of
the Tors? We had to make ourselves look different.

"Put up your hoods."

We scraped along a pink grapefruit wall. Above it the clouds
peeped purple and black. Morning felt like evening. Time was
upside down and inside out. Rain began to thump down. On an
arch a sign: 'Open To Visitors, 12pm Till 6pm'. But it had hardly
gone breakfast time. Even so, one of the huge wooden doors
beyond the arch was part way open.

"What is it?"

The main part of the building was shaped like one of those
spinning things from a game. Or a stone flying saucer, but with
lots of corners. On top was a smaller version of the whole thing,
like a cockpit with windows, somewhere it could all be driven
from.

We hadn't a choice. Ben would have to go home if he got any
wetter.

Inside was cold and damp too. A big placard: "DANGER.
BELLS UP." It leaned against a wall, as if it didn't really mean it.
A tall wooden ladder, thick and uneven, stretched all the way
from the stone floor to the ceiling, miles up. Hanging on the
white walls were black wooden boards, covered in lines of golden
writing from olden times. Outside, the rain whacked on the
graves. I began to pull at the sticky bronze handle of a stiff
padded door.

"Let's leave," said Mandy.

"We don't know what it is. It's the wrong shape for a church."

I went through the door. It closed behind me and I was in a little wooden box, the size of cubicles at the swimming baths. There was another door so I pushed at that and it opened with a sigh.

The building was the same shape on the inside as on the outside. I counted eight sides; it took me three goes. It was dark inside except for a violet light coming from the roof, where the building narrowed like a funnel to that cockpit on the top. No one was driving. Weak light dribbled down the walls and piled up in the shadows. Around the floor were things; a map, some signs, old cases, a small ladder that didn't reach anything, an iron box, shelves of books, shells on a table, white statues of men with twisted beards trying to grab something. It was as if over millions of years all the emptiness in this big eight-sided hall had slid down to the floor and turned into fossils.

It was an **Accidental Museum**.

The door sighed again and Mandy and Ben came through.

"It *is* a church – look, there's God!"

Ben pointed to a coloured window, thick with dark reds and blues. A white man with a calm and untwisted beard. This figure was outlined in thick black lines like Ben's drawings. Though Ben didn't usually draw God.

"It's our museum. In the wood we saw the scary man and we panicked, so that's **"Dread (Place of pan-ic)"**, then the triangle where we got off the bus, with the grass, where the roads go off everywhere, that's a **"Hub"** and then ... Mandy, what does **"Superfluous"** mean?"

"Something no one needs."

We all looked up at the white man with the stiff white beard in the window and the black lines around him began to thicken and grow. The stick rain that had been quietly drumming on the roof, paused.

"You shouldn't be in here, I'm afraid."

The door sighed and we all jumped twice.

An old man with a large red head was standing just inside the door. He had sprouts of thin bluish hair smoothed back across his skull. He was dressed like a jumble sale. He tried to smile in a way that wouldn't be scary.

"I do beg your pardon, children, but the church isn't open this morning. I was just setting up for a funeral. Were you interested in the church?"

"Alice thinks it's a museum."

Thanks, Mans, tell everyone our names.

The old man laughed, but his laugh was sad.

"Yes. Yes." He was trying to summon up the energy to disagree. "Some people would like it to be. No, quite right, young lady - it is a church. There are services here, matins, evensong, mass, we have a lovely new lady vicar..."

"Why's it not the right shape?"

Mandy sounded weird and angry.

"Ah, I don't - really - know – the tower is very, very old, but in here it was all rebuilt, you see..."

"Why?"

"O, I really wouldn't know. There is a little book somewhere." And he began to search around on a table covered in leaflets. "I think it was to get more people in. I can't find it. But I do know there's only one other church like it in England."

"What one?"

"O, I wouldn't know that, my dear. Isn't it something to do with the temple in Jerusalem? Everything else is. Eight sides? It's a mixture, isn't it – a circle and a square. The square is the shape of worldly things and the circle is the shape of..." and he waved his hand through the air, the ends of his fingers were caught by the light and sparkled as they cut through the emptiness of the hall.

"In an eight-sided shape..."

"Octagon," said Mandy. She couldn't help herself.

The old man bent over the table and took a piece of paper. Resting it on the table he folded part of one end and then ran his thumbnail down the crease. Slowly and carefully he ripped away the end part and held up the remainder.

"A square, approximately, yes?"

With trembling fingers the old man bent the sheet of paper round until two of its edges met. The square into a tube.

"Remind you of anything?"

"Toothpaste?"

The red faced man mugged around the building. What had he done with the ghosts who should have been here?

"Give up?"

"The pillars!" shouted Mandy and there was a dull echo.

"Just so. Now. If I were to peel open one of the pillars..." He allowed the paper tube to uncurl. "...the tube would make a perfect square, and yet the pillar is round. It's both circular and square. You see, the world and the..." and he waved his hand again through the light "...are always together, both in the whole shape and also in each of its parts. But I have to lock up... you don't want to trapped in here with a funeral."

The man nodded his big red head and clapped his old hands and waved us towards the door. It groaned as Ben pulled at the handle, as if it didn't want to lose us.

"Why does it have two heads?" I asked.

"S – t. N- e –c – t – a- n," read Mans from under the statue.

"O, that? Saint Nectan. Two heads, yes... well. There *is* a Saint Nectan's Church not far away. In one of the villages. They sometimes come down here for their services. None of us has a vicar to ourselves, you see. Come on, now. The funeral party will be here any minute!"

The big head shooed us out of the church. The rain had stopped.

"If you want to get to St Nectan's you'll have to take the bus. It's right over those hills. Only three miles, but too big a climb for children. Ask to be let in. Say you're doing a project and Patrick from the pink cottage sent you, they'll know who you mean."

He laughed and locked the door with a giant key. With a wave he was gone, crabbing behind his pink wall.

We weren't pathetic children who couldn't climb a hill.

"Why do we want to go to St Nectan's?"

"It's code, isn't it?"

We followed the old road, the hill soon hurting inside our legs. We passed one big house set in wild gardens. We climbed over the little wall, not sure why we had. A voice shouted "oi!", but no one came. We carried on up hurt hill. The houses got smaller. A picture of a hovering stick man said "Danger Of Death". I wondered if there really was, I decided 'yes'. We pressed our faces to the wire hoping we could see the danger. An invisible choir was rehearsing among pillars and discuses, power more magical than church.

The houses disappeared and it was definitely countryside, but disappointing. I'd thought there would be nothing but wild. I thought it was only in the city that everyone was bunched up, but it was the same here. First a wall, then a fence, then a field with a sign on the gate – a shouting man with a tiny head and a huge flat black hand. The field had big cows in it and we decided the road was safer. What if the farmer with the tiny head and the big hand saw us?

We walked under crackling electricity wires and crossed a busier road. Mandy looked one way, Ben and me the other. **Idea no. 1.** The flat ground on the other side turned out not to be a moor, but an airfield. Closed years ago, I suppose. A great big levelness with a few tarmac strips. At the side of one of the runways was a wooden control tower, an Insect Hut that might one day get up off its foundations and start to stab with its splintered wooden frames and broken glass. Someone had painted rude shapes on the runways, the size of planes. The wind blew hard and dry. Our coats crackled as they were whipped against us. Ben's cheeks glowed red like a devil statue.

"Are you OK?"

He cried and I decided I would not ask him again.

In the middle of the airfield we stopped. We could see in all directions, but that didn't help. Obstacles were useful for deciding things. On one side was the sea, a long slope up to a jagged Tor on another and then there were thousands of dark trees. We headed for the trees. Before we could reach them, the ground dropped away and we began to slide down the side of a choppy hill. Halfway down, we climbed a stone stile; a brown metal 'Public Footpath' sign had slipped off its screws and jabbed its arrow at the ground. "The Path to Hell", said Mans. Ben said everything was melted underneath the earth and we would be evaporated. Piles of gorse were heaped like rubbish. Sheep nagged at each other. The rain started to slap again. The forest in the distance misted over. There was something at the bottom of the hill.

I'd already seen a thing I hadn't dared tell Mans or Ben about. Just before the freaky signpost, three bushes had formed the face of a man, powerful and creepy and arrogant and sad, an anxious green face. I hadn't said anything because I was always seeing these things and every time I pointed them out everyone else claimed only to be able to see wood knots or cornflakes.

The 'something' was ruined. One wall standing. The sign said: "10th Century Chapel".

"That's the gloom wall," said Mandy. Which might have been very clever, but not very nice. Inside the railings we found a horribly wrong place.

The floor of the roofless chapel looked like it was still indoors. Made of pretty red tiles, patterned like a carpet in a living room. I tried to stop thinking that the missing walls had still been there until just before we'd climbed over the stile and that they would spring back the moment we were gone. The only bit of the floor not like a living room was the hole. This was round and full of black water. Mandy got a long twig and poked through the surface. A huge paw reached up and grabbed her face, pulling her down into the... no, that didn't happen, but it ought to have. Because the twig didn't hit anything, so Mans fetched a branch that had fallen from one of the trees. It was longer than her, maybe longer than me and her put together. The big branch didn't hit anything either. Even when Mandy began to put her whole hand and then her whole arm under the surface.

"Don't, Mandy. Pull it out!"

"It's fine," she said, and two hands covered in weed grabbed her neck and pulled her down towards a bright green troubled face that was rising up to meet her... No, that didn't happen either. But when Mandy finally gave in to my screaming and pulled out the branch she gave her own little cry. She said something tugged at the branch as she lifted it out. The end was crumpled, but it might have been like that to start with. Any spookiness was ruined in the arguing and we trooped off through the iron gate and into the trees.

Even here there were fences. They forced us on to a small road that spread wide through columns of very tall trees. In between the pillar-like trunks were low mounds, stumps of something once grand, amputated long ago and smoothed over now. We passed under a high garden wall. For the first time since we'd set off down "boing boing" alley, someone (mentioning no names) said that we should go and tell a grown up what we'd done. Well, there was no way. We hadn't found Dad. Mandy (because it was her, obviously) thought that then we should at least spy on the house to see if the people there might be the kind of people we could tell if we needed to.

Mandy cupped her hands for me to put my foot in, and began to lift me up the extra couple of feet to see over the top. If I didn't want to call, why was I looking? I jumped down and cupped my hands, and Mandy stepped up. Straightway she jumped back down, shook her head, and we walked on.

I had caught a brief look; a tower not a house, though there were chairs by a lawn, in the drive one of those big square cars that Mum says should be banned, and in the middle of the lawn a bronze model of the Earth torn into strips.

We passed large broken greenhouses, a weird cottage where deckchairs were cemented into the garden, and a field of dead maize with a spaceship-shaped hole in the middle. We took a path that felt ancient, floating on the footsteps of hundreds and hundreds of years of travellers.

"The council probably made it for the Millennium."

Saint Nectan's didn't look very special on the outside. And it wasn't open. There was a notice saying where you could get the key, but I didn't think Dad would be hiding in a church. You were supposed to be able to hide in churches if you'd committed a crime, but Mandy said that that wasn't true anymore.

We did the hand-cupping thing again, with Mans balanced with her feet either side of a stream of brown water that ran under the church. Inside it was old and white, except in the little curtained area where they kept costumes for choirboys. Through a gap I could see a small banner, done by someone our age, or made to look like it; a man was having his head cut off. I was glad Mum had taught us about Celtic water gods so I could turn the horrible picture into an idea and it didn't hurt anymore: Dad had somehow led us to places where people could carry their own heads and this was a clue for how we could find him; by looking from just to the side of where our eyes would usually be.

What began here as a brown trickle ended at the sea floating the impossible.

"...anyway," I said, "at least we know we're on the right track."

Mandy pretended to examine the wall of the church, mumbling something about New Zealand.

Chapter Thirteen ~ The Big House

> ...reality erupts within the spectacle, and the spectacle is real.
> (*The Society of the Spectacle*, Guy Debord)

We knew that the lovely world of dark woody dark and Hearties couldn't last forever. 'Hearties' were what Ben called the huge anthills of pine needles that dotted the forest floor; "like the fat man from 'Laurel and Hearty'". It ended at a low wall on the edge of a field, in a corner of which lay a dead sheep, inflated and stiff.

The forest had been damp and soft, but real. The field was different; here there wasn't much of anything to rely on. It hardly had a surface and underneath was almost certainly not there at all. Not even lost gloves or inside out statues like under Wally Eager's city. The countryside was less there than town.

Ben was the first to fall through, up to his knee. Mandy caught him and we pulled him out. Nearly losing his boot. We couldn't walk without boots.

At the bottom of the field was a farmyard. Very, very carefully we picked our way across the thin skin of grass. I was scared that if we fell through we might go all the way under. I didn't tell that to Ben and Mandy, but I made them walk so carefully that they got more scared than if I had. We reached the farm before the crust could give way. The farmyard was muddy, the buildings old and crumbly, barns patched up with what might once have been bits of the gloomy chapel.

I waited to get bitten by the farm dog. It didn't come. Nor did the farmers. With their little shouting heads and huge flat black hands. Nor the farmer's wife with a kindly something made from hot milk and cheese or something. No one came. A hen pecked around. The only thing human was the music. The sort they played on 'Strictly', but not the pop. It'd be an old farmer in his barn, milking the cows by hand, listening to his cassettes. We hadn't met a person since the red faced man from behind the pink wall. Now we were going to tell this farmer that we had run away from home and that our parents were already very worried about us and could they please ring the police to come and fetch us. And I knew all that because Mandy was marching off towards the music and I couldn't think of any good words to stop her. We'd done all we could. It was only now, giving in, that I realised how cold and ill I felt, how muddy Ben was, how scared Mandy seemed; perhaps because she could see the things that Ben and me were missing.

Mandy stopped in the doorway to the barn and I pushed past. No farmer. Just music and the long faces of hundreds of sheep, their eyes weird with fascination, bright with mad fear, as if we'd arrived with news of a star or a magical baby. "Well?" they seemed to say, "Who's coming this time?"

We ran. Out of the farmyard and along a lane. Another dead sheep beyond a hedge. We kept running until Ben had to stop because of a stitch. I told him that the best way to get rid of one was to keep running. When he tried to answer back he was sick.

We wiped Ben's face with a leaflet he'd picked up in the eight-sided church.

We'd hardly set off again, when a small, old car, with mud halfway up its sides, drove by. Fast. A family jammed tight inside. Big red faces turning angry as they saw us. Fury bulging out of tight smart suits and under big sky blue hats. The lane had started at the farm, so we had to have come from there. They could blame us for anything. As their car squealed around a corner we climbed a gate and ran across a ragged green field back to the edge of the woods. From inside the trees we could hear the family in the farmyard shouting, see the car setting off back down the lane. It passed the gate that we'd climbed and headed further down the valley towards a big house of silvery stone, long smooth grounds and rows of giant tents.

At the next stile we started to spot the security guards. They were sweeping across the fields just below us, a line of four of them, with others on the road. We knew what they were. We'd seen them in town. The uniforms that weren't real. They carried scratchy walkie talkies and touched their ears.

For a while we avoided the guards by walking closer and closer to the hedges. Three times we dashed across little fields, but then when we tried to cross a fourth we had to dive back. At each end were security men guarding the only gates.

Engines purred. We crawled to the middle of the hedge. Through the twigs we could see people stepping out from big bright cars, in clothes that only people in magazines wore.

"Oi! What are you up to?"

The first thing I noticed about the security man was how wide he was.

"You'll miss the ceremony! Come on. From the farm, are you?"

We had come from *a* farm...

The second thing was his name tag – E. Binns. Something like that. Everything Binns. A wall in a fake uniform. A giant kid with sharp creases. His eyes bulged and all the time his face worked as if there were angry beetles trying to organise themselves under his skin. He loomed over us like a wave about to break, but his eyes were on distant things. All the way to the horizon was under the control of Mister Everything Binns. The marquees flapped together, the expensive cars parked in even lines, the metal sinks bubbled and stank sweetly with the same food, men folded towels over the same arms. The people in designer suits and dresses had been lined up by Mister Binns to make channels and arches and rows. The same tune was piping everywhere.

Mister Binns spoke into his lapel as he marched us around the edges of his order and towards a big marquee. His earpiece crackled back like one of the angry beetles burrowing through earwax. He stopped us at the door to the tent, the throbbing plate of his face wrecked by moon craters. The other walls in fake uniforms began to shift out of the pattern and move towards us. Binns looked at us as if only now seeing his mistake.

Inside the marquee were hundreds of people. The men carried pillar-shaped hats and skin-like gloves. The women wore blue and yellow headdresses. We disturbed a ripple of faces.

At the back of the marquee was a table covered in shiny material. They were going to do some kind of secret magic.

Binns pushed us back from the door.

That's why there were no cameras. This was where these magazine people did their secret things. A scream. The uniformed walls that had been closing in on us were broken by a new disturbance. The slice of audience that I could still see inside the marquee turned to the door, all the beetles under all their faces swarming. And even though everyone was powerful and dangerous I could feel the anxiety in their movements, like model solar systems tripped over by a clumsy teacher and now trying to get back to their old orbits. Everything to the trees went choppy and upset. A smaller car was drawing up out of line with the others. Guards stiffened and tried not to stare. The chatter in the marquee jerked and broke down.

The pretty woman who got out was about Mum's age. Sort of like Mum really. Mum is pretty. It's just that she's not famous so nobody cares. Except me. And Dad, obviously. Ben doesn't know what beautiful is yet. He only knows about insects and daleks and things like that. He thinks they're beautiful. Which they are. But not in the same way as Mum. Or this lady. When I saw her, unfolding in her lightning blue dress and shining like the magical cars, her long hair free, I knew that she would live somewhere like the hotel that was built like a temple; it would be just for her. Everyone in the slice of marquee was looking at her now from out of narrowed eyes.

She didn't go to the grown ups. She bent over three children standing opposite us, on the other side of the marquee door. The boy was dressed in a miniature version of the suits, with the same gloves and pillar hat, circle and square in white and gold. A fake man. The girls were dressed as princesses, scratching at their arms and legs. A woman, their Mum probably, knocked their hands away. Behind them the rest of the family, big and shifting, were almost popping out of their best clothes, just as overexcited and uncomfortable as they had been in their muddy car. Nodding and bowing, they pushed the children forward. The boy cried. One of the girls dropped the flowers she was offering.

The beautiful lady smoothed down their hair, picked up their flowers, held their hands and made them laugh. The big family all laughed too. One of the guards bent over them all like an umbrella. He translated whatever the beautiful lady said, although everyone was speaking the same language.
"Are you from the farm too?" She turned away and spoke generally. "How lovely to have so many children in the ceremony..." then back to us: "you look absolutely famished, have

you come straight from the fields?"

There was a jangle of laughter all around. When I looked up there was a crowd of helpless faces behind the beautiful lady. And behind them the mixed up bodies of the angry farm people she had abandoned. Her words were like tiny pieces of glass falling into a cup. Her eyes were piskie eyes.

"Now, come with me and you can have some food," she said, bending her knees and crouching over Ben, brushing flakes of dried mud from his hair. "I know we shouldn't start until after the ceremony, but no one will mind if we fatten you up! They won't start without us!"

She was the smiling face of all this. Later they were going to eat us.

"Yes, please", said Ben, "I'm bloody starving."

Mr Binns, out of control, lunged at Ben and was waved back by the other walls.

Ben was copying Mum. She always said she was "bloody starving" when Dad did the cooking. Something had happened a long time ago, and when they said these words they remembered it, and they would laugh and hug. And now Ben had sworn in front of the most beautiful fairy-lady in the whole wide world and the most powerful and dangerous people in the universe.

"Goodness me, then we must get you some 'grub' right away!"

She led us, hand in hand, to another big tent, where there were rows and rows of tables. She commanded the waitresses to lift the silver lids.

Chicken legs in an orange sauce. Vegetables curling on pieces of toast. Millions of things on biscuits. Bowls of tiny eggs and tubs of wet, salty, black seeds. Big pieces of flaky meat.

Mandy whispered to only eat the healthy things.

The moment we tasted the food the beautiful lady was gone, as if we'd broken a spell. I thought the servants would pull the food away from us, slam the lids shut, straighten the tables. But the fairy had left powerful shadows behind, like the ones left by bombs.

A helicopter landed in the field next to the cars. Shouting and hurrahing, the people swarmed out of the marquees and towards a rope held by the guards. They moved like wolves, cleverly pushing each other aside.

"I think they *are* going to eat us," I said.

Joke music from the speakers bounced off the hills. The pack of dangerous people stopped pushing and fell still. The swollen farm family were at the door of the food tent, pointing at us and shouting.

"Quick, let's go!" said Mandy.

And we squeezed under the wall of the marquee.

"Round the back!"

Still stuffing our mouths with unfamiliar tastes, we raced between flapping walls of canvas. No one else seemed interested in us.

Behind the tent were more tents, bigger and bigger, hung with bunting and triangular flags, a castle of canvas and empty stands round an arena prepared for jousting, horses and knights already impatient for action. We slid through the gaps, ignored by people who would have been posh in our world, but were actors and servants in this one. Behind the tent castle was another castle, one of stone, quiet and moody, annoyed at being swamped. Keeping close, again, to its silvery walls, we crept around to the back. It was nothing special there. A car park full of caterers' vans. We ran between them. From the back of one a vicar was dressing in white robes, behind another a group of sniggering men waved cigars at a laptop. On the screen was a strange foreign city with a skyline of spike-shaped buildings and below it the smaller buildings from our own High Street. The vicar did not see us, but the giggling men turned together, like a swarm of starlings shifting direction, fingers tightening around their cigars, lips sharpening, eyes sinking back around their heads. They could catch us if they wanted, pushing off from the ground, circling and swooping, but cold as dinosaurs they let us slip away along a ditch, over a stile, and then through a hole in a hedge into a field full of sheep.

"Don't like sheep," said Ben.

"Don't be silly," said Mandy.

We ran with our hands on the ground, using the sheep as cover. No one followed us. Maybe they were going to sacrifice someone else.

"Where is Dad, then?" asked Ben, as the woods began to thin out, the sounds from the speakers already gone.

"We haven't found everything on the list, Ben..."

We could have walked along roads, but now we liked trees and fields, hedges and gates. Ben had realised that sheep weren't like piranha, they didn't hunt in flocks.

Aching and shivering we walked field after field, wood after wood, until finally we saw our big river between the trees. Grey mud like alien sick stretched to the opposite bank, a snake of blue in the very middle. A blurry group of marines were running across the dank mud in shapes, leaping from one line to another, stamping their regimental number into the yuck. They did that every day, and every day the tide washed it away, and the stamping would begin again. I'd thought the number was always there, but Dad had explained. I hadn't believed him until now. Dad was always telling you things.

The railway track ran alongside the river. It wasn't hard to find the station. The man said that our tickets were still good for today so we didn't need to buy new ones. He asked how we got to be so muddy, and not to put our feet on the seats, thank you very much.

Ben told the man that we'd been to see a church in a field. Which was an odd enough thing for the man not to bother with any more questions. Ben was asleep by the time the train drew into the city.

Chapter Fourteen ~ Dad Again

I realized then that other people thought about the city the same way I did, that others saw it as a seemingly infinite and mysterious place waiting to be explored and discovered.

(*Stroll: Psychogeographic Walking Tours of Toronto*, Shawn Micallef)

We turned into the High Street by the big store shaped like two boxes. Mum says it was voted "ugliest building in the world". Like they know. "It's clone city", Mum says. The shops that is, the people are autons. (That's my joke, Ben.) I wanted to go home. Mum was going to tell us off and it would be cringey, "so let's get it over with". Get back to normal (minus Dad).Mandy said our Mums wouldn't get worried again until it started to get dark. Which was clever to realise. So we went for a look round the shops.

Autons come in waves. Their eyes are shiny like fire engine windows, and you can't see who's driving.

In the window of a bright store, walking towards us were the reflections of three children. Copies of us. I forced myself to look directly at the approaching things, but nothing was there. Looked back to check. The things were still in the reflection, exactly like us, almost on us, back-to-front. I saw myself flinch as they disappeared into us – but they didn't come out the other side because when I looked back, hoping they'd be disappearing in the opposite direction, they were gone. We'd passed the whole window so when I next checked for reflections it was in a brick wall.

"Something just got in us."

"What?"

"I just saw three robots, looking exactly like us. And we walked into them and they didn't come out the other side."

"Do you think it will help?"

We laughed at Ben's weird question. Crazy laughing,

hahahaing out the last bits of our energy.

What are you supposed to feel when you've just become part robot? That it might not be so bad?

We walked on and I checked the windows. And I saw it happen all over again.

"How come *you* can see them and not us?" asked Mandy.

The city stretched like a cat made of straight lines.

"Maybe only their reflections are visible?"

"That's us, you idiot. You get two reflections."

Mandy walked to the corner of the window and her reflection split in two. Then she shuffled so she was exactly half round the corner and half still visible. The half of her and its reflection looked like a whole person, but symmetrical, unnatural. Mandy lifted arms and legs and hovered, a gingerbread girl in the middle of a leap.

Ben was delighted. "You can fly!"

His misunderstanding fitted everything. There was nothing special about this. Missing people, codes, lists. It was all desperate. The same world as the thin ladies with scared eyes and the men with plastic bags who didn't join in with the waves. We'd been lucky. Children who made a mistake and got away with it.

We slipped back into the crowds and went with the currents. They were disturbed by now. Still plenty of autons, but something inside them had come away and was flapping about, angrily, like injured birds. Dad said we would be the first children to be poorer than our parents, but I couldn't see any Mums and Dads in designer labels pushing starving kids with no shoes. The disconnection was somewhere else.

Past what Ben calls "Marks and 'Spensive" was the entrance to the new shopping centre. Mum doesn't like the new shops. We get a box every week from a farm and when it arrives, Mum goes to Mandy's Mum to find out what half of it is. Dad says we shouldn't be in the car so much, but we have to go to so many shops – the baker's, the butcher's, the fish shop. Mum lets him call at the cheap beer shop, where he disappears into glass canyons and brings back bottles with strange labels: eagles, bees, bombers.

I said to Dad once: "Everything's a code, isn't it?"

"I hope so, Alice. Otherwise, how will we understand each other?"

The new shopping centre is mostly glass, perfect for disappearing in. No one sees anyone else in the light, all in their own white tunnels, hypnotised by prehistoric lice. A maze of thousands and thousands of unconnected holes, each with a life at one end and a till at the other. But people did glance at us, probably the mud, so we started to attach ourselves to women on their own. Then to couples. Just hanging a metre back so everyone would assume we belonged to them. When our adopted 'parents' noticed us we'd break off quickly and find new ones. That way we were invisible, even though Ben saw our photos on the front of the local paper in one of the shops.

The new shopping centre is called The Ziggurat. The idea is, Mum said, that the escalators take you up to the place where the gods live. So we made up a way of getting higher and higher, by attaching ourselves to different people. But the building is a trick. Each time you are about to reach the spike at the top, the escalator ends in one of the shops. It only *looks* as if they go all the way to heaven; really they churn everyone around and around inside. We kept trying for ages, each time turned back to home cinemas and kettles and shampoos.

The plasma screens were full of fire. Bonfires in strange cities.

"Osiris Security".

People on the High Street seemed more panicky than hypno-tised. Maybe they just wanted to be home eating sprouts. It was colder and darker now, getting nearer to Christmas minus Dad.

I stumbled and all the world jerked. A band of people in big coats dashed by as if racing supplies to an emergency. They looked back and one of them, a lady, nodded as if she knew me, as if to say "it's ok". A tall, graceful man with orange hair and dark skin swept the street with wide searching eyes, nodding at each shop name. Two men walked across us, one with short white hair and a bent stick painted in large red and white stripes, and the other with a straggly black beard dropping off the end of his chin, diamond eyes behind his glasses. Their heads swivelled and examined every gutter. They were talking about "ordinary angels" when they disappeared into the traffic. I tripped again, nearly going over on my ankle. The world jerked a second time, and when I tried to show Mandy the hurriers, noting man and examiners there were only panicky robots. Something had slipped away from us.

Mans wouldn't come: "it was *you* wanted to come back?"

"We were too far away before," she said. "This is where I wanted to run away to."

"To the *shops*?"

"Why not?"

"Mum says..."

"'Mum says'!"

Our Mum says: "Only stupid people want labels."

"Maybe I *want* to be stupid?"

"You'll end up like... *them!*"

A man stroking a muzzled dog, his face cut and scabbed, grinning under his wounds, was watching us.

I saw Mandy take a sweet dark pleasure from this.

"Didn't your Mum teach you not to patronise?"

I don't know what 'patronise' means so I couldn't say anything. Why weren't you allowed to say 'them'? Who else *were* they? They were different to us.

Mans was enjoying my silence and I couldn't think how to break it. Her eyes grew bigger; black magnets sucking in all the High Street. They weren't the only dark attractions – the muzzled dog had black eyes. And so did a baby, watchful in its pushchair. And a woman in a motorised wheel chair, basket loaded with small bags. The face of a stand-up cardboard author in a bookshop window and a herring gull screeching from a roof. The street was guided by their pools of darkness and Mandy wanted to slip in.

"Because they're... unhappy, Mans!"

"I'm unhappy."

"No you're not. Please. Let's go home."

"Why? That's WHERE I'm unhappy! I didn't come to look for your mad Dad!"

It felt like I was in training for later, when boyfriends would leave me, and people I loved would let me down in really big ways.

Ben's eyes opened up like huge taps. We were all falling into the darkness of the eyes. Want to, not want to.

"Please, Mans. We want you to be around. To play."

Mandy snorted.

"Dad says grown ups should learn how to play."

" 'Dad says...'! Your Dad's... gone..., Al. Sorry.... but didn't you notice?"

"He's gone to find..."

"Find what? Go on. Find what?"

Say it.

"Find out what is beneath."

"What are you talking about?"

I was falling into the darkness. I was only just hanging on to the edges of her eyes. I might as well as let go.

"Beneath everything." Which I could only get out accompanied by a shrug.

"O yeh. Well, actually, there isn't anything under everything. Everything is already under everything... there's no space for anything if it's everything. Everything is all there is and it's already there. There isn't any room for an underneath."

The big black eye opened and we all dropped in. Plop. Dad had run off to find something that did not, could not, exist.

Black eye opens again. Dad drops in. Distant plop.

"See," said Mandy, adding more sticky dark gloat, "your Dad's no different from me."

All the High Street stood fixed in the grid of black eyes.

"Yes and I love you both and I don't want you or Dad to die."

It had popped out.

"Huh?" said Mans.

"Die?" Ben was back.

And the High Street hiccupped back onto its beat. The black eyes misted and narrowed. Mandy cried a little. The dog curled, the baby's pushchair disappeared into Marks and 'Spensive', the herring gull took off, the woman on the wheelchair sliced through robots and disappeared into The Ziggurat. The black eyes were gone. I helped Mandy wipe her tears. Her eyes were light brown, with green flecks.

"How can I go home!"

"Blame us!"

I was remembering all the things we learned in our buddy group – about how to help people. But I had to stop myself doing any of them. Because Mans would know straight away that she was homework. How were you supposed to do the right thing and not let other people know that that's what you were doing? Did everything good have to be done secretly?

"There are bad people, Mans. In the countryside we hardly saw anyone. But here, there are lots and some of them must be... you know. And if they you know... they'll latch on to you. But you're a good person."

What I'd said about "love" was true, but as I said it I'd felt it end something, something dark and scary that might have been more important.

Mandy sniffed. "I was horrible about your Dad..."

But she looked scared. Not thinking of my Dad now. People were beginning to notice us. Across the street a man with half moon spectacles on the end of his nose leaned his head towards us. From behind a café window a man in a large black coat, thin hair slicked back over his pale head, shot us a glance.

How do you get people to un-notice you?

On the other side of the High Street, among the jerking, excited people, was a walking man, speeding along the street, leaning forward at an impossible angle, a black swan, brushing people away with his black wings. He had the face of Dad. The mad walk of Dad. He was wearing the mask of Dad.

No.

No...

No!

That's Dad!

I managed to remember the buses that are allowed on the High Street, even though 'Dad!' was filling my brain almost to the top. Something was still sensitive to accidents (on the list, **no. 4**). I held my little brother's hand and looked both ways (**no: 1**), waited for a dirty bus to pass, and ran to the figure pacing along the opposite pavement. Mandy was older. She could cross safely on her own.

"Dad!! Dad!!"

He didn't turn round. His walk was faster than our run. He began to leave us behind. I let go of Ben's hand. I was going to lose Dad!

Ben ran as if he was wild. All arms and legs. An animal in the woods. He caught the man's leg.

The man stumbled and almost fell. He turned to see what had almost brought him down. He looked puzzled. A question mark scribbled on a school jotter. There was nothing in his eyes. Ben was a piece of pavement he'd tripped on. He looked around as if he saw the High Street for the very first time.

I saw the world that Dad now saw – a boiled, wet, empty city. I chewed the same cellophane he chewed. Was revolted by the same nothing, the same boredom, the same useless haunting. I saw him, a limping sprinter, a knight with all his armour broken, a shamed celebrity on the stage of an empty theatre, a foreigner standing, waiting beside a machine in a closed factory, an over-made-up chav stacking shelves while a supermarket burned down around her. Dad. From the Book of Revelation. Silly beast.

Ben opened his mouth, but the word 'Dad' didn't come out. He couldn't even do that. He backed away.

I ran to stop the man moving off.

"You're our Dad!"

He looked worried.

"I have to be somewhere... "

"Dad, don't you recognise us?"

"Are you on television?"

What?

"He doesn't want to be our Dad."

"Dad, this is us? What's wrong with you!"

I looked hard at his eyes. Like watching for fish from the sea wall.

"Why won't you talk to us like you're our Dad?"

"Now look, my lovely..."

"That's what you call us!! "Lovely"!"

The man stepped back, but the fish did not shift.

"I called you "dear"... I have to be getting on." He glanced around him.

At his back was a huge silver fang, five times his size. The

Riddle Spike. On its uneven surfaces were questions, puzzles. The answers were on the backs of large silver balls at its base. Why bother people with questions about things you already know?

The man was reading the clues.

"Do you remember these, Dad?"

"I've never been here..."

"Dad, this is where we live."

"Uhuh..."

"... this is your list!"

I felt in my coat pocket and pulled out the words:

Dread. (Place of pan-ic)
Hub.
Superfluous.
Accidental Museum.
Dreamscape...

"You left this on the kitchen table. It's a map to find you."

I turned it over to show him where his pencil had scratched through to the other side. He held out his hand and I gave him the list. What if he ran off? I wasn't sure I could remember all the words.

The man ran his finger over the back of the list and handed it back.

"I don't recognise it."

"It was in your shirt! We think it's a route – code for a route... and that the list is different places... or different KINDS of places... but where's the last one? Here? Is this the destination?"

The man pulled a face at the word 'destination', as if it made a bad smell. Unnerved, he looked about him.

Mandy had joined us. All in black; her black hair like the dot on an 'i'. Dad looked at her but didn't seem to recognise her either.

"She's Mandy. She's not part of our family. She's from across the road."

He looked across to the other side of the High Street. He

didn't understand anything.

Ben said: "We went to the woods, Dad. Down the lane. We saw a man who was a million miles high and he wore an old coat and his head was a moon and his feet were boots like claws and his teeth really old and bent."

"He was like Mister Binns, Dad."

The man shook, the jerk running through his whole body. I thought something had hurt him, that he'd brushed against something sharp on the Riddle Spike.

"Like in your story."

Ben was nodding like one of his little model footballers with unnaturally big heads.

"I saw him too," Mandy added from a distance.

"Here?" He looked about, puzzled.

I'd kind of hoped that Dad's illness would make him even more interesting, but instead of that, the leaning and pacing and wild-eyed speed was the jerking of a dead muscle, a ghost connected to the street lighting. He was as uninterested in us as before.

Ben giggled. Dad didn't seem to think it was funny.

"Hey, it's the kids who lost their dad!!!! Durrrr!!"

Three boys from big school. They always picked on us if they caught us in town. They had a secret name for themselves. They'd even made fun of Mum to her face.

"You're so gross he ran away!!"

They laughed like frogs.

"Actually," I said, already unsure, "this is our Dad!"

They turned to Dad like a chorus full of eyes.

"No," he shook his head. "I'm on my way to... um..." Then he scratched his nose and the frogs croaked with joy.

"You've got a weird dad!"

"No, I'm nothing to do with them..."

"Yes, you are, Dad!"

He tried desperately to explain himself to the frogs.

"I've been travelling. Sometimes to islands. I found an extraordinary piece of wood behind a café..."

He smiled and looked so pleased with himself. The frogs thought that this was the best thing and they swelled up with sarcasm, letting the darkness open up for Dad.

"Wow. That's really... good."

"Good wood, 'Dad'."

"... it was full of promises... each plaque was a promise..."

"'I promise to be a loony'!"

The frogs hopped up and down in excitement at their brilliance.

"...to give blood, to give away cat food..."

"Cat food!!!"

Croak, croak, hop, hop.

"... but the placque had been thrown away, left behind a wall. Don't you think there's a poetry in that? A plank full of promises left behind a wall..."

"No, we think you're weird and we'll tell the police if you keep talking to us, because we're children."

Dad looked at us and then at the frogs. As though they and us were the same thing. A switch clicked in his head and he turned and ran. The frogs jumped and clapped with joy. In a flash Dad had disappeared behind the silver of the Riddle Spike. By the time we'd stumbled over the small shiny worlds, he'd completely gone. All we had of him was the laughter of frogs.

"Was that really your Dad? He is such a mong!"

Mandy was looking at the pavement. Ben didn't seem to understand that they were laughing at Dad.

"Dad *is* going to come back, actually..."

Mandy looked even deeper into the pavement.

"Yes," admitted one of the frogs, "with a plank."

"He's a planker!"

Frogs had never had so much fun. They were fencing with flies. Their big cruel tongues lolled.

"Excuse me, you're the lost children, aren't you? Alice? Benjamin? Mandy? And who are you?"

The frogs jumped, unhappily. They were shrivelled by the policewoman's frown. They hobbled away.

"We're OK, thanks."

"I don't think you are. Your parents have been very worried about you."

Ben blurted out: "Have you found our Dad?"

Had Ben not realised that the man we'd just met *was* Dad?

"My little brother doesn't understand, Miss. Our Dad was just here. We were talking to him."

"The man here just now?"

"Yes."

"Where did he go?"

"There!"

But there was no one 'there'. Just the Riddle Spike. And the waves of anxious robots.

As the policewoman led us away from the High Street I looked back and saw something. More than a thing, actually. I saw The Thing.

Chapter Fifteen ~ Psychology

> I became sensitive to the mood or tone of a place... It was a
> question of learning how to move with the minimum of
> friction to provoke the minimum attention.
>
> (*Sunshine State*, James Miller)

When I told Mum about Dad not recognising us, she seemed
relieved. But that wasn't good, was it? I knew she'd explain,
though. She knows strange things about minds.

She asked us why we'd gone and I said it was because no one
else was searching for Dad. She looked a bit shocked and nodded
slowly, as if she was saving something up.

After extra kisses and cuddles Ben was put to bed. Mum let
me watch a grown-up programme, while she made lots of phone
calls. When that was done and I only had a little more awakeness
left, she turned the telly off and took the phone off its cradle so
that it beeped for a bit. Then she said I could tell her what had
happened. Over a cup of hot chocolate. Daughter to Mum.
Awake on the edge of dreaming.

Somehow, even dozy, I knew not to tell her everything. In
adults' programmes people are always careful about that, they
hardly ever say what they actually think. So, I told Mum as little
as I could about our journey. Only the route, really – the bus, the
town, the train, finding a dry place, walking past some churches
and houses, the countryside and then back and meeting Dad. I
saved up most of the truth for the bit with Dad. Except for The
Thing.

I wanted to bury The Thing. Maybe in that shrinking pile of
hedge bits in the corner of the sub-atomic particle that passes for
our back garden. Or under the loose plank in my bedroom floor.
Somewhere for The Thing to shrivel up and disappear. But it
wasn't that kind of an easy Thing.

Apart from that, I told Mum everything else I could about
Dad. How he didn't seem to know us, how he thought Mandy

was from over the High Street. Until the part when Dad disappeared into the crowds of clone shoppers and the policewoman found us. Then I had a cry on Mum. Because I suddenly felt relieved to be safe, and that it could all have been much more dangerous than it was.

I felt a bit better then. Mum asked if I'd like to know what she thought was going on.

Maybe Mum already knew...

"It's a 'fugue', I think...," she said.

What's that?

"A kind of breakdown... a 'fugue' happens when someone's mind is so full of things that it has to have a rest from real life. So it takes a holiday from reality. For some people that holiday can be terrible and they find they're stuck in a horrible nightmare, seeing a world full of ghosts and monsters..."

I didn't tell Mum that ACTUALLY the world *is* full of ghosts and monsters. Especially if you counted the things the caretaker takes care of. And Sea Slaters, of course.

"...the unlucky ones hear voices, get frightened of the smallest things, sometimes of everything. Not a nice holiday, eh? But for the lucky ones... running away from your self is a better kind of holiday, a journey."

Dad doesn't know who he is, but that won't upset him. He won't really know why he's on his journey, except that it's really important. His mind can't deal with anything as complicated as reasons, so it'll just have a good time. All Dad really knows is that he needs to keep going, buy tickets, order meals. Do all the things he does when he's well – but he won't realise that he doesn't know who he is.

"When a person runs away – do they ever come back.... in their head?"

"O yes! Of course, darling! Just as soon as that mind is ready. Rested and ready. The same as... better than before, in fact, because their mind isn't full of things getting them down."

"Why didn't you tell me before? We only went because we didn't think anyone was doing anything."

I didn't remember thinking that, but it seemed like a good thing to be angry about.

The room jerked.

"I really wasn't sure that I did know. Until just now, what you just said about Daddy. And I didn't want to tell you certain things, because I didn't know what those things meant. I was very worried about what they meant... But not now. Look."

Mum opened one of the cupboards high on the living room wall. Her shadow was more real than she was; it was all black and white now. She took down a big grey box. She opened the lid. The box was full of startlingly bright letters and printed-off emails, and pages and pages of white lists of numbers and dates.

"These show where your Daddy's been using his credit card. Here, see – London, Manchester, and little places – these are towns round here, some are further away... Paris, Munich, Isle of Wight, Jersey... Dad's been on such an adventure!"

"Why didn't you tell us?"

I knew there was something that Mum wasn't saying.

"I wasn't... sure that it was your Dad who was using his card. I thought someone else might... might have stolen it."

"And poor Dad wouldn't have had any money?"

As soon as I'd said it, I knew Mum had been worrying about something much, much worse.

"But look, I got this, just before you went."

Mum showed me a fuzzy photograph. It was obvious that the man in it was Dad. You could see where he was going bald.

"It's from a cashpoint. Dad's fine. You've seen that for yourself."

"You should have told us."

"I didn't want you to think that Dad had just run away from us. But I didn't know why he'd gone. He's not to blame, Ali, you mustn't blame him. Ever. That's what happens in a 'fugue'. They're really not unusual."

You disappear without warning from your home and you don't know who you are or what you've done - surely that's what "unusual" is?

"Why don't you fetch him, Mum, if you know where he is?"

I waved the papers at Mum, really – not pretend – angry now.

"He doesn't stay anywhere long enough. He's elusive. If he stops too long in one place his mind starts catching up with him, doing all that work that made him poorly in the first place, so he moves away. He is always one step ahead of himself. So, maybe we don't want to find him too soon? Don't want to spoil his holiday? Anyway, he hasn't done anything wrong. He's not in danger. As far as the Police are concerned he's just someone who ran off. They're not interested in him. He's our problem."

"But he's a grown up."

"O, they run away too. It's something that happens... like twisting your ankle..."

"Twisting his brain."

"Exactly."

"You won't tell anyone at school?"

Ribbit. Ribbit.

"Not if you don't want me to."

"How long before Dad comes back?"

"'Fugues' can vary..."

I saw Mum's face scramble, like the digital telly does sometimes. I knew she'd seen something in my eyes.

"Let him stay out there." I sort of shouted it out.

I couldn't help looking out of the window, into the black sky above the houses opposite. Mum still hadn't put up the new curtains. I forced myself to look back. I mustn't let Mum see what I was re-seeing.

"Wait till he... remembers." I said. "That's best - you said."

"The best thing we can do for Daddy is to keep going, do things as we normally do."

Mum fetched out more boxes. She'd taken time off work to drive round looking for Dad. There were legal documents, to help Dad with his hearing. The smoke had affected his ears as well. She'd made a map too. There were no countries on Mum's map, no edge of the world, only Dad's route. Mum had done drawings of buildings and taken cuttings from the newspapers of things that happened on the day Dad had been in certain places, of puzzling figures and phantom trespassers. Mum said the map helped her work out what Dad was thinking, what might make him choose his next place. It was a map of his mind's journey, she said, and, making the map meant Mum was sort of taking the journey with Dad. That was the idea.

I asked if she'd tried to find *us* just as hard. She laughed at me like she would have laughed at a grown up, laughter that was hard. She stopped herself. I saw in her eyes a map of us as big as Dad's.

Mum said lots more things, but by then I was only a quarter listening. I was another quarter realising and the rest planning. We must not change too much, we'd get too far from Dad. We must get back to the routines. School. Brownies. Choir. Painting club. Extra help with maths. Forget exploring, re-wind the tape, act like things hadn't happened.

I didn't mention Mister Binns or the magical mathematician, the haunted well or the bighead in the oddly shaped church. What was the point? I knew none of them had been real. They were pretend characters from the crazy holiday that our brains had been on. And they would only worry Mum.

I told her that I wanted to be a clinical psychologist when I grew up. That made her happy.

For a treat, Mum opened one of the boxes of chocolates she was saving for Christmas. When I went to throw away my sweet paper under a 'healthy pizza' box I found hundreds of leaflets with photos of me and my little brother. It was the one in Torquay. Embarrassing! Mandy's was her school photo.

That night in bed I decided I would not speak, even to my little brother, about the things we'd thought had happened on our journey. Let alone The Thing. In the morning I still hadn't thought of a good place to hide it. I knew I couldn't leave it where it was. It was growing there, on the edge of a scummy bit where things I couldn't stop thinking about overlapped with making my mind up. It was pushing on a sore bit, irritated by not doing something I knew I should. Love everyone. Eat more fruit. That sort of Thing.

By the second night back, The Thing had its own heartbeat. Bump-bump, bump-bump. It was fast. The Thing shivered with excitement and it had a Goth wardrobe. A mouth had opened up in a part of it. It was building up to telling Mum that Dad was a fake. So I killed it by writing it down, drained all its black blood into a few lines of code, folded it up seven times, and hid it by the water pipe under the wonky floorboard in my bedroom.

Inside its paper maze I could hear it trying to puzzle itself out. But the folds always led it back to the start, like The Ziggurat. Hee hee!! Thanks, Dad. Now I had my own Secret Monster.

Dad told me once about something he thought he saw from a train. It was at night. And impossible, of course. He was going off on a training course. In the window of a grotty social club, like the one Gramps goes to, he'd seen a big dirty old room with a dartboard and a snooker table and a stage. On the stage three people were teasing a rotting, biting, living-dead zombie. Dad said that even though he knew he'd seen it wrong he was angry at the three people, and sorry for them too. They were bullies who would eventually slip up. Everything is 'eventually'. And 'eventually' is a really scary thing. Eventually always gets you. Like a cheesy zombie, it wanders around really slowly, for ages it's miles off, and then suddenly it's right on you.

After our journey, I didn't see Mandy for a very long time. Days and days. I was too busy putting everything back to where it had been. When we did play, almost two weeks later, neither of us even mentioned Dad. Maybe we knew our Mums would be spying. But I don't think we wanted to, anyway. Mandy was doing her Brownies 'Cultures' badge and I had the biggest part in the Christmas school play.

Chapter Sixteen ~ Routine

> In spatial *détournement*, a rambler reuses elements of a
> known territory to explore a new psychic space with a
> different meaning, often one beyond the boundaries of the
> "original"... maps of outer space are folded into maps of
> terrestrial space.
>
> (*The Bodmin Moor Zodiac*, Nigel Ayers)

Mum was going to take me to an art gallery. Not the type for old
art, this was for completely new things. No one even knew
whether the things in it were any good.

First we had tea at our favourite café. Ben and Mum and me.
I'd been rehearsing my part as Scrooge in 'A Christmas Carol' and
Ben had brought home a note from his teacher about his
Snowball costume. It was nearly Christmas and there hadn't been
any snow. The whole world was going to burn. I had my usual
Turkish salad, which is nothing like English rabbit food. And Ben
had what he always has: sausage, fried egg and couscous. As
always, we were kissed and cuddled by the owners, and treated
to syrupy round cakes with almonds in the tops. Ben drew the
owners a picture of a dalek and they blu-tacked it to the counter.

After our journey my legs had ached for days. But Mum had
decided that Ben should try to get a special star for walking to
school, which meant we all had to walk. She said to make it a
game; that way the journeys would go quicker. So I decided the
route, and Ben decided what kinds of things we had to look out
for. Mum decided on how many points for each thing. It was a
game she got from Dad. Before our Dad disappeared I always
took us long ways round so we'd find strange bits, things to ask
questions about, odd places that got the most points from Dad.
Now I tried to find the most boring and uninteresting ways. The
mega-dull. Anyway, Mum always gave the biggest marks for the
most boring things. The obvious thing was to do the same route
every day. I wouldn't even need to look where I was going. Mum
never noticed anyway. She was interested in people.

Still tasting the tang on my tongue, I kissed my little brother and we dropped him off at his friend's. Dad was always getting at Mum to arrange for Ben to spend more time with his friends – because Dad didn't like speaking to the Mums in the playground – and now she'd started to do all the things Dad had nagged her about. She'd even put the curtains up! All this and doing all the things she normally did. We'd gone back to old routines times two. Most days we didn't get back home until it was almost bed time. I hardly watched telly anymore. Anyway, Dad liked telly much more than Mum.

After dropping Ben off, we went to the gallery. It was smaller than I'd imagined it. All the pictures were completely new and all of them had been done by the same person! They don't stay up on the walls very long, even if people do like them. The man who made the pictures was actually there! And they weren't just paintings. Mum said I could meet the man if I wanted to, but I didn't. I did see him though.

There were two kinds of pictures. One lot were very big and fuzzy and made in warm glass (I touched it when no one was watching), the other lot were small and not very well done, in the sorts of colours we had in squeezy bottles in the art drawer at home. Mum said the big ones were actually photos taken by the man on his mobile phone then 'blown up' (made bigger, not exploded – though some artists do explode things, Dad says). The photos were blurry, but I could make out a factory and some flowers. If you looked for long enough you could see other shapes too. Not things, but shapes. And you could see the 'blowing up' itself.

I didn't need Mum to tell me how the second kind were made – bad painting, but she said it was on purpose. It was 'child-like' because you need a little humility (not being too big for your own boots) when you're painting the universe, Mum said. The bad paintings were all of galaxies and clumps of stars; the idea was that you noticed that there was a difference between the ordinary things made fuzzy and the huge big things made badly and the art was the gap in between. But I didn't see people looking at the gaps. They first looked at the little card by the side of the picture, then at the picture, but after a while they mostly looked at each other. They were more interested in people. Like Mum is.

Dad would have liked to have come here, because the pictures were about different kinds of space. He would have seen their secret gaps.

Once we'd been round the rooms, Mum got us drinks and talked to lots of people, including the person who did all the art. I could see she must have understood his pictures because he didn't get angry at all. Mum even made him laugh. I was glad she didn't introduce me to him, though, in case I said something stupid. Mum said it wouldn't matter, but even a kid can hurt an artist, I think.

The invitation card had said this was a 'private view', but it wasn't very private. Lots of people came. Everyone asked about Dad. I tried not to listen to them, but I could see Mum thought I was being rude. So then I tried to listen, but the pictures on the walls were distracting me. I could wander off into their blurry places where voices became gurgly and the gallery began to fall down baby spirals of badly painted galaxies. I could listen to the grown ups just enough in case they asked me a question, not so much that I had to leave the children's universe.

At home we just enough had time for Ben to have a bath and me to practice Scrooge with Mum. She got me to think about what Scrooge felt inside, why he was so mean to people, why he wasn't happy, why he suddenly started seeing ghosts. I thought ghosts just turned up! But Mum said: what if they were things that his mind was making, because it couldn't cope with all his meanness? He never gave anything away, everything he had ever had he kept locked up, especially his feelings. His mind couldn't cope with all that collecting of those many, many Things, all that hiding away under the floorboards of his brain.

Was she really talking about Dad? It didn't quite fit.

After Scrooge I got changed, brushed my teeth, had a wee and got into bed. No time for reading tonight. A tap in the bathroom was still hissing. I got up and tightened all of them. But I could still hear something.

I got back into bed and tried not to think that it might be The Thing down there, whispering the answers to the code, working its way out. I pretended I was in a tiny submarine. It must have worked, for a while anyway, because when I woke up again it was much later. Everything in the house was still, dark and quiet, except for the whispering. That was a roar. A furious hissing that seemed to be coming from everywhere. I got up and went to tighten the taps again, but the whisper was howling under the bath now. The Thing had almost escaped, but couldn't quite puzzle out the last clue. It was thrashing around, still snagged on its paper maze.

Slap! Slap!

That was new. Part of it had escaped from under the floorboard and was hanging down into the kitchen. It was thumping something in its frustration.

Wap! W.... WAP!!

Something big had fallen. It must be slithering in huge bits from under the floor, down through the ceiling and into the kitchen, an oily string of ugly truth. Truth was supposed to be beautiful, wasn't it? But from what I could hear, truth was a treacly thing. I had to check, before I could wake Mum. Maybe I could clear it up without her ever knowing the truth?

In the dark kitchen a shape was reaching from the table to the ceiling. It was twisting like a wet eel and it made a sound like a giant being sick.

Uhhh. Woaaarr. Ssssss. Thwap, thwap.

The glistening Thing smacked something again and again onto the big table, opening its sticky wings like a collapsing curtain.

A groan came from just behind me.

The tip of something sharp speared into the room and flicked the light switch. In the big splash of brightness, before Mum flicked it off again, I saw the water pour out of the ceiling and the light fizz sparks onto the family table.

Mum couldn't find the secret tap that turns off Everything, so she rang Dad's old work and, just like after Dad's accident, our house was full of grinning men in uniforms, clumping about.

Ben woke up and made everyone laugh by complaining about there not being enough fire. No one laughed very long though. They soon started thinking about what was really missing from our house.

The next day we walked the same way to school as we'd come back the day before. I tried not to look at things, but someone had put a traffic cone on the head of the big soldier on the horse and I couldn't help thinking that that was worth at least one point, and remembering that Dad had told us that the horse's bottom was pointed towards the soldier's village, because they never liked him there – six points. Next time we'd avoid the soldier.

At school we did 'rivers'.

No rehearsal today, but there was football and I won the little bronze medal (it's actually painted plastic) that the man who comes to the school gives out at the end each week. I am the champion, and I was the only girl there.

On the way home, I avoided the soldier, going the other side of the church, and if I hadn't seen a Star of David on one of the gravestones and had to ask Mum about it I wouldn't have noticed anything at all. Getting better. But a Star of David. That must be worth at least seven points.

My little brother whined all the way home about my medal. In the end I gave it to him to put on his wall. Mum said I was "kind", but I think I was "just ready for something else".

The house was strange now. The folded paper had gone. Maybe the firemen took it. Or perhaps the water man who came to change the pipes took it. Maybe the house ate it. Spies have to eat their codes.

Down in the kitchen there were big driers, like miniature jet plane engines or the hairdryers of gods. They blew all day and we were always thirsty. At night the air tasted fake, like somebody was making it up.

In bed I wrote a list of things to get for not leaving home:

- *Subscription to First News.*
- *Chocolate fountain.*
- *Gold pipes and taps.*
- *CCTV for Dad's loft.*
- *Sound-soak-up wallpaper.*

- *Hooks from ceiling of hall for shoes.*
- *Daily delivery of bagels and cream cheese.*
- *Wi fi for when I know how to encrypt.*
- *No bananas.*
- *No yoghurtt umj.*
- *Nnn rhnnn...*

The last bit was code from the edge of the bit of my brain that I go into when I fall asleep.

Next day, I decided to concentrate as much as possible on the walking itself. One foot in front of the other, not thinking about anything we passed. The problem with walking is that it isn't very much to do with one foot in front of the other. It's more about the mind bobbling about on the top of your neck.

Blue plaque for famous writer on landscape – eight points.

Alien-shaped sweetie staring out of hole in wall – three points.

Writing on road next to lamppost says "move" – four points.

Toy policeman peeping out of shed window, very funny – ten points.

Routine wasn't working very well.

I asked Mum if we could go to the proper art gallery. After all we'd been there lots of times before and that's what routine is. But that wasn't the reason. It's not just a gallery, it's also the "museleum" - Ben's word. Inside it has all sorts of old things, but first you have to get through the front door without looking at the outside. It has a skin of interesting stones. Sandstone made of deserts three hundred million years old and Aero Chocolate Bar stone made in the volcano that went off under where the Arts Centre is now. Its outside is a map of what's underneath it. Thousands of people drive by it every day, hardly any of them notice. They don't have a Dad like ours. And now, nor do we.

A man at the top of the stairs opened one of the double doors to let us in. His hand left a fatty mark on the brass handle. Statues tried to tell us off but we were too quick for them. Upstairs were the new exhibitions, but I wanted the old pictures.

The one I had come to see was of three beautiful ladies from olden times, in big bustly dresses and coloured hats with ribbons. What I like is that the old fashioned ladies, who are not so beautiful when you really look, are firing arrows from bows. I don't know why I like it really. Maybe because I'm the only girl who turns up for football. Maybe because I like the dresses. Maybe because most of all I like sport in dresses!!

This time, however, I didn't feel comforted by the picture at all. Instead, it rattled my teeth and shook me around like I was jelly. First thing, the picture wasn't dead anymore. There were lights on in the big house in the background. I'd remembered only dark windows before. And now I recognised the house. It was the one in the valley, by the angry farmers and the haunted ruins, behind the tents. And the lady in the blue and silver dress pulling back the arrow I was sure was someone I saw, far, far off near the big house, as if she was in the picture twice, or at different times. Only she had been dressed in modern clothes. It was only paint, I knew that, and a really dim memory even though it was just a few days before, but something ugly and awful was happening in the picture. And we had to get out. As I pulled Mum away, I realised that neither the beautiful lady at the house nor the old fashioned lady in the picture were really so pretty; or at least prettiness wasn't really what was important about them. They were huntresses. Killers. Sports in dresses. But now there wasn't anything left for them to hunt any more. Even so, the lady in the picture had drawn back her arrow, like a dancer but more dangerous, the points of her body like a grid, or a map, the angle of the bowstring and finger exactly the same as that of her back and shoulder and elbow. The same angles as the house. They were all part of the same plan. They glowed, but I could see nothing in them, they freed the light from the darkness.

One last look back from the door; I couldn't help it. Behind the house, there was the wood we had escaped through. And behind that the hills, tors and the empty airfield. But I couldn't get to them. The picture was thick. There was no way beyond it.

At the weekend Mum drove us out to revisit some of the places we'd found on "your own little fugue". I quite liked that, really. It meant we were getting closer to Dad. But we didn't find him at any of the places. I knew we wouldn't. Not if we LOOKED.

What we did discover was that we'd probably got the route in the wrong order. The hotel was the **Wormhole**. We'd got each of the first four on the list right, **Dread. (Place of pan-ic) Hub. Superfluous. Accidental Museum**, Mum reckoned. But taking the train had thrown us out of sequence.

We were sitting in the car, rain flooding down the windscreen. On one side of the road was the empty airfield. On the other a golf course we hadn't noticed at the time. The players leaning forward into the wind.

"I know that hotel very well. Your Dad's definitely been there – he took me for a drink one afternoon. Full of old fogeys. We didn't spend much time in the tunnel, he was more interested in the prayer steps, and there's a minaret, isn't there? Or there was. I think your Dad said it was based on three or four buildings, Islamic buildings, in India. A Colonel in charge of engineering for the Army in India built it... his job was restoring Indian monuments... whatever that means. Anyway, he's supposed to... according to local legend, the sort of thing your Daddy likes... he's supposed to have had a secret Indian wife – the Colonel that is, not Daddy!! Hence the tunnel. It's a wormhole to India."

India? I had thought there might be other countries.

We'd gone to the ruined chapel, and to St Nectan's – Mum fetched the key, it wasn't any more interesting inside. Mum said the ruined chapel was super creepy and that there were stories about it, but she didn't want us to hear them. We drove past the tower and through the tree cathedral, which Mum said was "lovely" and "neolithic". The eight-sided church was locked and I didn't want to tell Mum that we knew where the man with the key lived in case she was worried that we'd been talking to strangers.

Ben was playing with his pirate figures in the back – one with the head of a hammerhead shark, another with a squid instead of brains, a third with a crab's claw for a hook.

"What's a wormhole, Mum?"

"Physics. I'm no expert, but if space is curved it's quicker to burrow like a worm from one bit to another rather than go all the way round on the surface. Supposedly. But mostly people mean it as ... an imaginary thing, it just *feels* like you could do it, it *feels* like you're closer to India."

I didn't believe that. Just *feeling*, that was all? Surely there were more to it than that? The corridor under The Hill in Dad's diary and the third railway track. I wondered what other beach we might have come out on if we'd been brave enough to open the iron door straight away, instead of waiting till morning. The gaps weren't there all the time. Wally Eager had got through, but later, when Dad was in the cupboard, the wormhole had closed up and the bricks were back. I wanted to ask Ben, but he was living dead and under the sea, walking with the slimy bones of sailors and duelling cutlasses with a barnacle-faced ghost.

"Has Dad ever been to India?"

"No."

More lies.

Ben looked up from Davey Jones's Locker, then sank back into the depths.

"Maybe he'll go to India now?" I said, to worry her into explaining.

"It doesn't seem to work like that. His journey is..."

"Mad," said Ben.

Chapter Seventeen ~ "The Room We Never Use"

They soon realised that 'archaeologists' and 'historians' were involved in the cynical creation of a false 'place' called 'England'... They worked on the hypothesis... that the very matter of place was mythical... that the landscape itself was fabricated. Late one night... Barney – stripping to the waist – ripped into the chalk with his mattock. Within minutes their theory was proven, they cut through the made geology and discovered the hollow 'heart' of England – that place they called the *underchalk*...

(*The Listening Voice*, The Newsletter of the Equiphallic Aliance)

"O, I hate what the supermarkets have done to our farmers, Nancy, but unless *someone* educates the children they eat nothing but junk."

I don't like junk. OK, I like pizza, but that's not junk. Not 'Healthy Pizzas'.

"I don't know how you cope, I honestly don't. Dear me!"

"Not since Paul's gone..."

"Well, you know we're praying for you, don't you?"

I don't reckon Great Auntie Beryl and Great Uncle Tony ever go to church. And the idea of the two of them getting down on their knees on the rug in front of the telly and praying for us was a bit scary. It could only make things go even more wrong. It was one of those Things from an old comedy movie – supposed to be funny, but actually it made you feel bad.

Great Uncle Tony appeared in the door to the kitchen nodding very hard at us and itching at his little moustache.

Great Auntie Beryl and Great Uncle Tony are our Only Remaining Great Relatives. We had lots of them when I was a baby. There's a picture somewhere of me being held by Mum, surrounded by a great crowd of Great Aunts and Great Uncles.

(Actually they were Mum's Great Aunts and Great Uncles, they were mine and Ben's Great Great Aunts and Great Great Uncles, but once it gets to Great you get the point.)

Except for Great Auntie Beryl and Great Uncle Tony, they'd all died – even Mum's Mum and Dad had moved to France and dropped dead. That wasn't anyone's fault though.

Now, because it was just before Christmas, we were having to pay our visit to the Remaining Great Relatives. The trouble was, that's all they did: remain. Our visit was a kind of test we had to pass before we were allowed into the grotto.

They weren't really, really horrible, I suppose. And actually, if you listened carefully to what they said, they could be quite funny, but by accident mostly. They had got stuck somewhere in the past and were only going through the motions in the present. And they went through these motions "with a vengeance" (Mum's words). Every tiny little thing was turned into a battle or a speech. A crisis would develop around it, an exorcism performed on it. It took hours to make a pot of tea. You daren't ask for anything. Even when something was offered it came with so many questions that you were soon too sick-of-the-whole-idea to enjoy whatever arrived. Eventually.

"I don't mean to be rude, Nancy..."

Great Uncle Tony always says this when he's about to be rude.

"O, don't take any notice of him, Nancy... she won't understand you, Anthony..."

Great Auntie Beryl could say different things at the same time.

"He doesn't know anything about television. The dvd player is still in its box!"

I looked. There was no dvd player under the tv.

Ben asked: "Do you have digital, Auntie?"

"O, yes, dear, but I've made your Uncle set it to the old one. He gets confused with the digital, you see. That's how we suffer! Now, crisps, everyone? Are you allowed crisps, dear, or is that another thing that's now politically incorrect? "

She looked daggers at Mum, who looked confused, guilty, and furious with herself all at the same time. That was The

Power Of Great Auntie Beryl.

"Do they teach you Hinduism at school, dear?"

"Yes!"

I perked up. I really liked religions where there were lots of gods. Great Auntie Beryl stamped her foot and marched into the kitchen, hitting Great Uncle Tony with her oven gloves as she passed him.

"What was that for?"

"You know," came the reply from the kitchen. Great Uncle Tony didn't look much of a Hindu to me. Great Uncle Tony went through the three expressions. Great Auntie Beryl knew how to get to people.

By now Mum was furious and was already gathering up all our things ready to leave, but, seeing the danger, Great Uncle Tony swooped after Great Auntie Beryl and rebounded from the kitchen with a huge tray of tea and cakes which he crashed down on the glass table in the centre of the living room.

"Don't do that, you buffoon!"

Great Auntie Beryl poked her head around the kitchen door.

"And don't stand there looking like an early Christian martyr!! Nancy, I've only just replaced that glass! He dropped the poker on it! We don't even have a fire! Can you believe it? What were you doing with the poker? Help yourselves, don't stand there like lampposts!"

And the rest of Great Auntie Beryl erupted into the room, with a larger tray, full of hot snacks: mini-pizzas, cheesy things, sausages, duck in pastry. All mine and Ben's favourites. Mum had to put all our things back on the chair and let us tuck in. Great Auntie Beryl clapped her hands and marched back into the kitchen to get the sweet things ready. As the door swung back I saw her feeding supermarket packaging into her bin. Mum watched her, and then quickly turned away as Great Auntie Beryl lifted her head, pretending to be interested in the living room. It was a very clever place. Everything was very bright and startling – there were jugs with scrunched up faces wearing old red uniforms or rainbow headdresses, wooden Africans with spears, miners made of coal, paintings of green and blue people who Great Aunt Beryl and Great Uncle Tony didn't know (I'd asked) standing on beaches they'd never been to (ditto). Mum said it was "jazzy", but it had got stuck, playing the same note over and over again.

The Remaining Great Relatives only ever ran out of Things to offer, mess up, go and get ready, confuse, brew, heat up, cool down and criticise after at least two hours; more than four episodes of 'The Simpsons' or two 'Doctor Who Christmas Specials'. Finally, Great Auntie Beryl cleared away and Great Uncle Tony seized his chance to complain about the roads and to quiz Mum about her movements at Christmas, suggesting various short cuts and sensible precautions. He had heard of something called 'car-jacking' and Ben became very excited about that. But it turned out to have nothing to do with Torchwood, nor Djaq from Robin Hood, nor Captain Sparrow of the Black Pearl.

It was a strange house. Ben fitted in there like nowhere else. He became the quiet little person Mum always really wanted him to be (though she says he's "full of beans" and that "that's great.") At the Great Remains, Mum *tries* to get him to misbehave; she tickles him, asks him to tell jokes and show off his Cyberman march. But Ben just looks serious and the Great Remains eye him like he's one of those weird vegetables from the box we get.

Outside, daylight was fading. Great Auntie Beryl had heard some of Great Uncle Tony's motorway suggestions.

"He doesn't know what he's talking about! He's hardly had that car out of the garage in the last two years!"

"I drove you to Bridge Club last week! I don't recall you complaining then!"

"I was too terrified!! We nearly came off at the bypass!!"

"Every time we go round a corner you think we 'almost came off'!"

"Take no notice of his short cuts, Nancy. I doubt if any of those roads still exist!"

I hadn't thought before that roads might one day not exist.

Great Auntie Beryl retreated into the kitchen and we had to listen to Great Uncle Tony's rushed instructions – the letters and numbers of roads, where to turn, how fast to go, where the hold ups and speed cameras would be... (Ben woke up, but it wasn't 'hold ups' as in highwaymen.)

"I can hear you whispering, Anthony. He gets lost on the way to pick up his pension! He thought 'looting' was an airport! And for thirty years he thought Danny La Rue was a woman! I wondered why he was so keen! I always wanted 'Morecambe and Wise'.... you're not going to tell me they were lesbians, are you?"

Inside my head I could hear all these people trying to eat my life. It smelled like tyres and sounded like grit.

When Mum had been my age, shortly after the asteroid made the dinosaurs extinct (only joking), there had been lots of Great Relatives. And they had had such great times. They had weddings and anniversaries where they sang 'Dear Old Dutch'. Mum taught us all the words to sing along in the car:

> *"We've been together now for forty years,*
> *An' it don't seem a day too much.*
> *There ain't a lady livin' in the land*
> *As I'd swop for me dear old Dutch."*

They had brilliant Christmas parties, with great, huge glasses full of whisky and gin (one looking like liquid leather, the other like a ghost in a glass) and bowls full of salted peanuts. Then it would begin, the stories from the hilarious history of Mum's family: Great Uncle Fred's war wound from falling on a beer bottle hidden in his shirt, an after hours police raid on the William and Mary Club (what *is* that?) when Great Uncle Charles was arrested for replying "Good evening, I'm a fitter" to "Good evening, sir, I'm a policeman". I still didn't know what a 'fitter' was, but Ben and me knew it must be about the rudest thing that you could possibly say to a policeman. Our other favourites were how a bird did its business in Great Auntie Brenda's hair just as she came out of the hair salon, and how Great Aunts Celia, Brenda, Beryl and Charmaine all dived for cover from the bombs, lying face down in their best party dresses in a big puddle and laughing as the explosions went off all around them. In these stories no one ever seemed to get hurt; even Great Great Uncle

Stan's attempt to hang himself was foiled due to the huge length
of rope he used. And then, suddenly, they were all dead. Great
Auntie Beryl and Great Uncle Tony might as well have been. Life
passed them by like lost tourists. "I don't let him watch it!!"
shouted Great Auntie Beryl. "He gets it all from the newspapers!
He doesn't know what he's talking about! Never seen it, have
you?!?! I won't let him!" She finished wiping her knobbly fingers
on the tea-towel, folded it over a rail, and waved Mum, who had
thought she sensed a chance to leave, back into her seat.

"Don't be going yet, dear, I've hardly had a chance to talk to
you - stuck in that awful kitchen. He's been promising to re-tile
it since the year dot."

"I tiled it last year."

"He doesn't have a clue. Come in and look at this, Nancy! Not
you, children, you stay with Uncle Anthony. Very hot things in
here! Look, Nancy – does he listen? I asked him to re-tile it and
he goes off and buys imitation bricks that make my kitchen look
like it's part of an ancient monument!!"

"Auntie, they're very..."

"I don't care what they're "very", my dear - they make it look
like an old barn!"

"Well that *is* the idea, darling," Great Uncle Tony offered.

"I don't want ideas in my kitchen!! We don't have them in the
rest of the house! Can you understand why I get my migraines,
dear?"

Great Auntie Beryl shut the door, like a spider closing its trap
on prey. Mum would be kept alive, but all her inner bits would
be liquidised.

Great Uncle Tony jerked slightly, realising he was stuck with
us. Ben tried to interest him in a Doctor Who magazine, but
Great Uncle Tony pretended to suffer an asthma attack. Ben
waited for him to run out of wheeze and tried again. This time
Great Uncle Tony pretended he didn't know who Doctor Who
was, but Ben caught him out with a clever question. Then he
tried to pretend that he hadn't understood, but made himself go
so red that he *did* have an asthma attack. Great Auntie Beryl
refused to come and told him to stop showing off to us children.
It was all quite interesting.

After ages, Mum managed to fight her way out of the kitchen, looking for where Great Uncle Tony might have hidden our coats. But Great Auntie Beryl still had some moves.

"We've been thinking about you, Nancy."

"Yes, you said..."

"Ah!" Great Uncle Tony waved his hands happily. "Something more prac-tic-al than prayer." He made another great sweeping move with his hands that ended at Great Auntie Beryl, who had begun, slowly, to unclip her handbag.

"It's in your other one, Beryl darling."

"No, it's not."

"I think you'll find it is, dear."

"He swaps them, you know! He goes through them. Our own 007 – except he combines it with fingering the mince pies, so he leaves fatty clues!"

Great Uncle Tony was ordered to bring the second bag. 'It' wasn't in there either. Round the flat, our only surviving Great Remains coughed and wheezed, turning out secret drawers, all the time shouting at each other. Mum checked the bag Great Auntie Beryl had had in the first place.

"Auntie Beryl, are you looking for this envelope?"

"Of course, that's it, dear! Anthony! I said! What a waste of time!"

"She doesn't look!"

"He doesn't listen!"

From the brown envelope, Great Auntie Beryl withdrew a piece of newspaper.

"From the Express, my dear. We both thought it would help you with your work. Now you're the only..." she looked at Ben and me. "... source. How *are* you getting on?"

It was Great Auntie Beryl's big mistake. She leaned forward as if about to sink her beak into a small hairless chick, and suddenly realised, too late, that she was falling into the trap of a very clever spider. I saw my Great Uncle's face freeze and his eyes dash back and forward, as if hypnotised by the different thoughts crossing in front of him. And as each opportunity raced by and disappeared into the distance, Mum talking quicker and quicker about her work, his eyes raced faster and faster, searching more and more desperately for a gap between ideas.

Great Auntie Beryl was less frantic in the eyes, but more tense in the body. She seemed to have pulled every muscle she had; ricked and bent like a bow. When I got up to leave the room I saw her try to shoot me a glance, but her neck was stuck, caught in the angles of 'the plan'. Mum had her fixed. Like mongooses do to snakes in encyclopedias.

I waited outside the door. One of the Great Remains would surely follow. But they didn't. I meant to go to the bathroom. It would be easy to pretend I wanted a wee. It didn't really matter what the excuse was. Just to be away from everyone for a bit. I didn't care if they made their usual remarks about 'waterworks' and 'worms'.

I didn't get as far as the bathroom. Between the living (ha ha!) room and the bathroom was the door to "The Room We Never Use". It wasn't creepy or anything. I'd been in there before. Dad had accidentally gone in there once thinking it was the living (it's not even funny) room: a small box with a couple of chairs, some suitcases, a cabinet full of old crockery and piles of magazines. In the corner was a sewing machine that had been partly dismantled. And that was it. The sewing machine was as near to a skeleton as it got. The titles of the magazines – 'Golden Memories', 'Home and Heritage' - as close to treasure. No hints of a concealed tunnel, no peculiar patterned wallpaper with hideous messages, no safe in the wall behind a green lady. Just unnecessary and unwanted things in separate piles, a smell like stuffing, a place fading to nothing, hovering somewhere between useless and unwanted. Exactly where I wanted to be.

I sat in one of the unneeded chairs.

Most places belong to someone – it's 'Dad's attic' or 'Nanna's kitchen'. Even the grotty ones you can get into trouble for hanging about in; there are caretakers. But this was nowhere.

I did nothing.

Me and it didn't belong to anyone.

Just by sitting there, I was a space and it was a space. Unowned, but not exactly free. Hovering, at least, in between other things. That's how I sat for almost all of Mum's speech. Floating in a space of unwanted things. I didn't feel bad once. I didn't think very much – that I noticed, anyway – but I did wonder if I could visit all Dad's list of spaces just like this, from a chair in nowhere.

Mum said I should have been in the living (don't make me throw up) room, studying my Great Remains, learning how to understand what had happened to people like them. But the feeling in "The Room We Never Use" was better than football. It *looked* small, but if you closed your eyes it was a desert in a Wild West film or a tiny ship on a huge sea. Or the top of green hills, staring down on three ladies from Victorian times, firing arrows across a chequerboard lawn. At each other. There were no targets in the painting, I realised.

I knew it was all about spaces now.

After we got back from Great Auntie Beryl and Great Uncle Tony's, I went round with Ben to see Mandy and I laid out the new plan for them.

This time we wouldn't make a great expedition of it, with rucksacks and raiding the fridge. Instead, we'd sneak off when no one would notice, just as I had at the 'Great Remains', and then sneak back. This was what 'splorin' was really about: most of the time you should live your life just as if it was normal and then, when no one was looking, you'd slip into 'splorin', and then straight back again into normal before anyone had time to check you hadn't gone. It wasn't about going anywhere, it was about the space you were in.

Ben didn't say anything because he was watching Mandy's new dvd. Mandy said she understood what I meant, of course she did, but she didn't want to be normal most of the time. And also she had had a long talk with her parents and they'd all decided that Mandy would from now on be allowed to do strange things in her room, and that it was her free place where no one except Mandy would decide what happened, and they had bought her a new dvd player and a whole lot of dvds including 'The Lord of The Rings' big box which up until then had been too gory for her. And three new black dresses. Mandy said we had to make up our minds; either we grew up and went 'splorin' properly for the whole of our lives or there was no point in going at all.

I said: what was so special about being weird in one room?

And why did she need three dresses the same colour? Which were silly things to say because Mandy only got annoyed. And nearly cried, which made her even crosser. And said that she didn't want to go 'splorin' again ever and wished she hadn't in the first place if we were only going to play at it like kids.

That wasn't so bad, though, actually. Because I had already really decided not to do any more 'splorin', either, actually. That was true. But I'd wanted to test it out on Mandy. Because of the funny moment at the Great Remains in the room they never used. I'd just wanted to just make sure, a hundred per cent, that I shouldn't give it one last chance. It was a '**Z World**', wasn't it? Like on the list. I knew that's what Dad meant, a small place that could be a whole world, ready to be messed with, with its own species and jungles and brains. I'd accidentally slipped into one of those parts of Dad's planet that was poking up into ours.

But it was just as easy to see it from Mum's and Mandy's points of view. As it was all in my head.

The room at Great Auntie Beryl and Great Uncle Tony's was my little escape pod, my way of floating off into my own outer space, and I could do that anywhere. Mandy could do it with her orcs and elves. Ben with crabs, maybe. I didn't really *need* "The Room We Never Use". Nobody needed it, even for its unnecessariness. From now on I'd stick to places that I didn't need. Doing things I didn't need to do.

I left it as long as I dared before I went back to the living dead room. Mum was just coming to the end of her story, at which she leapt to her feet, clapped her hands, shouted "o no, the oven!", grabbed us and dragged us to the door shouting "thank you, thank you, Beryl, happy Christmas, Tony!", while Great Auntie Beryl struggled to her feet waving the newspaper clipping and Great Uncle Tony floundered, arms and legs kicking like a crab on its back. Mum levered us skilfully out of the room, pushed us down the corridor, out the front door and into the car, belting us up, revving and driving away. Great Auntie Beryl and Great Uncle Tony watched us from their kitchen window; elderly versions of the frogs. Yeh. The frogs were old people in kids' bodies..

I tried not to look back. Couldn't help it. In the window the two huge frogs with massive football eyes were still there. And the eyes could speak through their pupil slits and they said: "we'll get you next time, you'll have to come back next year, and then we'll have you and keep you here, keep you here forever."

Chapter Eighteen ~ Scrooge

...the fugueur was no average man on the road. He was
sober, clean, respectable, a member of the working poor...
(*Mad Travellers*, Ian Hacking)

The thing about Scrooge is that he must have been good really,
otherwise he couldn't have changed, and yet he's horrible and
mean to start with. Which makes you think about how people
are. I couldn't help putting a bit of Great Auntie Beryl and Great
Uncle Tony into Scrooge. They'd changed, Mum said. They'd
once been fun, just as much part of the hilarious history of
Mum's family as the other Great Aunts and Great Uncles. So you
could change any way, not necessarily good. Which made doing
Scrooge very slippery, because what were you supposed to base it
on if people can become anything?

At school we were still doing 'rivers' as well as the Christmas
Play and the two got mixed up. Because 'rivers' change too,
they're never the same. I had to ask Mrs Thornborough what it
meant that 'you can't step into the same river twice' and she said
that it was because the water that was there the first time would
have all gone by the time you came to step into the river a
second time. So rivers – even though they have a name, like
people – were never the same thing from one millisecond to the
next – like people. That's why the Great Remains were like dead
people. Because they *were* now the same from one year to the next.

Scrooge's river had got itself all dammed up. Fallen branches
and trunks and bicycle frames were trapped in its rocks and
more and more stuff was building up, less and less water was
getting through. The money and the work and the business had
collected and none of it was moving much. Meals hung around
in his stomach. I didn't think he had a poo very easily. His house,
his coins, his insides - all stuck and stinky. That's what the spirits
were – the stink of stuck things. Only when the whole thing, all
his life, his whole body, collapses, only then does the dam give

way and the farty pus comes roaring out, and he gives stuff away and he laughs... the laugh that's been stuck for years. And the moment when that starts, when everything he is begins to collapse, that's in the cemetery, next to the grave of Tiny Tim, with all the Cratchits crying and saying how wonderful Tim was, and how strange that he should be buried alongside "him"... and I would suddenly be terribly frightened, no, no, and I would hold out my hand, and feel my way toward the words on the gravestone beside the fresh gravestone of Tiny Tim, shouting for the Ghost to tell me what it read, and my fingers reaching out to it and feeling along the words and into the carvings – E – B – E.. and then they slip down to the next line – S – C – R – O – no, no, please, not... G – E! O, it is! And the dam breaks and I'm nothing but things and coins and pens and papers and dead leaves... and at the same time I'm moving, EVERYTHING shifts, and races and pours and I cry and I'm alive, I'm still alive and I'm breathing and I can speak and I can sing and I can laugh and I can give presents and I can order things for others and give money to the poor and I want to do everything, EVERYTHING!! I want to make up for all the time I've wasted, stuck!

Except, this afternoon, I haven't quite got to that moment yet. I'm still at the bit where I'm reaching out for the words on the gravestone. My fingers wriggling to feel the cardboard stone. This is the last time we'll do it. The third performance, if you count the dress rehearsal that the Nursery were allowed to come to. I want to make this the best one – so I wriggle and stretch my fingers a little more, hold my body a little further away from the grave, pull myself a little harder in different directions, about to let the dam break.

Tom is Mister Cratchit and he's saying "Oh his laugh was as strong as his heart was weak, oh Tim, my poor, poor child." And I say: "Oh Tiny Tim! I won't let this happen!" Mrs Cratchit (it's Ivonna) turns to the audience. And I look out at them, and there's Gramps and Nanna (Mum's already been twice so she's let off today) and Mrs Turner, our head teacher, mouthing all the lines, and I remember that we're not supposed to look at the audience except when we talk to them and that I'm forgetting to act, and I'm losing my balance, wobbling not between the name on the gravestone and discovering mine, but between Scrooge and forgetting my lines.

I hear Ivonna speaking the words before I say "Say the name! Say the name!" I know exactly how it goes and exactly what I have to say, but I'm losing my way, I'm being pulled apart too early. Ivonna says: "Then let's be happy, let's think of others less fortunate than ourselves! As Tiny Tim would have us do! And, maybe even spare a thought for the man that lies alongside our little son!"

There's a big pause and I can feel myself falling down into the middle of it, the light in the middle of the hall is drying up. I can't swallow. Mrs Turner is mouthing the words over and over again. "Say the name! Say the name!" I'm reaching, I'm reaching for the words. At the back of the hall, I see above the heads of the back row of the parents the tops of the doors swing apart. And Mum comes in. And she stops. She's watching me. Waiting, waiting to see where we are in the play, how we're doing, whether it's OK this afternoon. And I can't let her down, and I reach towards the grave and feel the name. "E – B – E..." and then "S – C – R – O –..."

... and over the heads of the back row I see my Mum wave to someone outside. Waving them in. Like there was a giant river out there. Like they were breaking the dam out there. And I see her mouth the words: "Come in. Come and see!" and she waves her hand again and then steps back, holding the door. And then the dam breaks and the river rushes and I say "no, no, please, not... G – E! It's me!" And Dad walks through the door and smiles. And waves (which is very unprofessional, I tell him later). And I hardly know that I'm speaking, but I'm smiling and giving away turkeys and kissing Mrs Cratchit and ordering plum puddings and giving sixpences to the poor and singing the final song and bowing and then running through the audience, who all turn their heads like a machine, and I jump at Dad and nearly knock him over and I feel his back with my hands, my fingers wriggling across him, feeling for the shape of his bones under his coat, and I know it's him, he's really, really there. And then I cry a big river right down his shirt.

Chapter Nineteen ~ The Fugue

Knowledge is only to be gleaned... from what exists or is
recorded on or in the earth of the work or remains of man...
(*The Old Straight Track*, Alfred Watkins)

When we got home Mum said Dad had turned up at her work.
He knew exactly who he was and where to go. And she said that
we weren't to worry, and that Dad wouldn't say or do anything
weird and that we certainly weren't to be frightened of him.
Although he didn't remember everything he'd done while he was
away nothing bad had happened to him, and it had been a
wonderful adventure and that when it was the right moment he
would tell us all about it.

"Did you go 'splorin', Dad?"

"I did, Ben, that's exactly what I did!"

And that was all we really heard of Dad's adventures through
tea time. He was much more interested in hearing what we'd
been doing. We told him about the play, about going to Great
Auntie Beryl and Great Uncle Tony's, and a bit about "our own
little fugue" which was mostly from Ben, because I didn't want to
say too much, just in case. And I didn't want to ask him about
when we met him in the High Street or about The Thing. He
recognised us now, and maybe that was the most important
thing.

After tea, me and Ben played at Crazy Frogs, then Dad took
Ben up for his bath. Mum said I didn't need to have a bath and
could get straight into my pyjamas.

When I heard Dad turn off Ben's light I shot down the stairs.
Mum had a beer ready for Dad. An all-time first. And she'd
poured herself a wine. When Dad came down I sat on his knee
and looked at his face. He didn't look very different, but he was
brown from the sun, and his hair was long. He'd been all around
the country and over the Channel – he'd been on trains and
ferries and he'd walked. Nothing was different from what he'd

told us in the High Street. So it was all true. It was the same story twice.

He just forgot who he was, he said. And needed to be on the move.

My brilliant clever Mum. She was completely right. It had been a brain holiday. Nothing else.

Dad told us how he'd sometimes met up with others who seemed to be on the same journey. That there were lots of people like him, 'splorin'. He could remember meeting Ben and Mandy and me and how our meeting had affected him. Part of his mind knew who we were, and it started whispering to the rest.

"I started to get upset for the first time on my journey. Strange things started to happen. Up till then the journey seemed wonderful, but very... straightforward. Clean hotels, chatting to folk in the bars. Nothing felt odd till I met you. After that I kind of knew I was running away from something. I walked through the town, across Cathedral Green, then doubled back – I didn't know where I was going. I ended up at the bus station. I had to get away.

"I do remember catching a bus. It was getting dark and I watched the city slide past, and the bus turning off the main road and heading along little lanes, hardly anyone getting on or off. It was hot from the bus's heater and I was wiping condensation off the window. Things on the outside were bent by the water on the inside.

"The next thing I remember, it's light again, I don't know whether it's the next day or days later, and I'm walking down a road that I half recognise, but it's the kind of road you get everywhere. I must have been walking down this road for half an hour and my knee is starting to get sore. It's sunny though, and generally I feel fine, when I hear the sounds of a vehicle. It's a car and it's sliding all over both sides of the road, like it's being chased or the driver's in a fight with a passenger. Anyway, I start running for the trees and the thing comes off the road and starts to chase me! Cutting down ferns and bouncing over tree trunks, then – smack! – just before it flattens me it wedges itself between two saplings. Revving away like crazy. The motor cuts out and there's a bad burning smell. It's at this point in the movies that the car explodes, but nothing happens. Not even a hiss and clouds of steam!

"Next thing I know, there's a wild man standing over me and chuckling. Not threateningly, like it should be in the middle of nowhere, but like sharing a joke. I chuckle back. And point for him to see the big truck, in camouflage, pulling up on the road behind him. Soldiers in uniform hang out the back, ogling the wreck. The driver winds down his window.

""Need a pull?"

""We'm good," says the wild man, waving them away.

"I checked out his car. I could see right through one window and out the other. There was no one else. His "we" included me.

""You sure you're OK, mate? That was one hell of a shunt!""

(I got the feeling that Dad was changing the actual words, for my sake.)

"He looked down at me. 'Friend 'ere'll be sure I gets 'ome safely.'

"So now I feel like I have to get up out of the grass and show my face. I could see the army driver trying to work it out. He quickly winds his window up and the truck jerks forward and disappears. And I'm left in the woods with the wild man.

"He wasn't so bad, actually. And pretty soon things got a lot clearer and less crazy. The wild man found a stiff bit of branch and we levered up his car boot. Inside wasn't the body that I'd thought might be there, but the mangiest, dirtied, oddest Father Christmas costume you've ever seen!"

I giggled.

"Actually, at first I thought it *was* the body!"

I giggled again and Mum "hmmm'd" the way she used to when Dad let us watch scary old sci fi videos, because little kids can't tell the difference between them and documentaries.

It turns out the wild man had promised to be Santa Claus for his sister's kids. They were all going to go on a private steam train thing, a Santa Special. Anyway, the wild man doesn't want to let his sister down again.

"'Let's get you to this railway,' I say. But apparently there's no way by road. The wild man throws the Father Christmas things over his shoulder and heads into the trees. I had to race like hell so I didn't lose him. I don't know why I hadn't noticed until then, but his Father Christmas suit was green and white. No red in it. His cords were green, his shirt green and brown, his hair green in the light, he kept disappearing in the trees! And all the time we march, he gibbers on about how he hates his family, hates the things he has to do, hates the little town he grew up in, hates the yoghurt factory because they sold out to the supermarket, hates the farmers because they're poisoning everything, hates the animals because they're crazy with artificial hormones, hates everything. He walks like the wind and the trees seem to pull back from him as we race through.

"After about an hour we come out of the woods and we're standing on a railway line. He's done it. He's not going to let them down this time. Except he can't remember which way it is, up or down the track to the station.

"'There's a fifty/fifty chance', I tell him.

"'on't believe in chances', he says.

"He puts his ear to one of the rails. Which I thought *was* taking chances.

"I asked him if his costume shouldn't be red.

"'You'm want us a' look like Ol' Scratch?'

"I thought: what is that accent? He was a strange bird. Hopping from sleeper to sleeper. It was killing my bad knee. But I forgot all about that when I see where it is we're going. Because now the track straightens out, the trees opening up like fans, and we get a view up ahead for miles. Over and above us is The Hill.

The Hill?

"Not any hill. 'The Hill'. The one I collided with Wally Eager under. The one under the bowling green all those years ago, with tunnels to the back of the cinema. Of course, it isn't in the same place now. But it's exactly the same shape. And I mean *exactly*."

I think Mum had been quietly enjoying the story up till then. Now I could feel a serious engine inside her start up.

"The wild man rushes ahead and I hop after him, sleeper to sleeper. The Hill getting closer. On top of it is a fringe of trees, like there'd been around the bowling green. Below the trees The Hill is smooth and shiny green. Almost geometrical. A cone with the head sliced off.

"The wild man waves for me to catch him up. Up ahead, a group of old guys in overalls and hi-vis jackets are digging up the track.

"'What they'm buggers up to?' he says.

'And when they see him they all start shouting: 'We found it, Spike! Spike, come on! Have a look at this!!! You're never going to believe this!!!!'

"The old guys wave and jump as best they can. By the time we get to them, they're all kneeling, their hands spread like market traders. Down by the side of the track they've laid out a display of twisted metal, scraps of clothes, a pocket watch melted, looked like that old reactionary Dali had been at it, bones, teeth, spectacle frames, old NHS style. They were all watching the wild man.

"'You know what it is, don't you, Spike?' I heard one of them say.

"'I know what you'm want me to think it is', says Spike, and he stares at The Hill.

"'It's proof, Spike. Your father was telling the truth all along. This is from '47.'"

Mum takes a deep breath, but Dad hears the sound of her coming interruption, like he's got his ear to her steel track. I've seen him do this before. Just before she's about to tell him off, or put an end to something, he'll throw her by changing the subject.

"Cutting to the chase.... I ask the obvious question and I get some dross about a hush-hush place the railway used to supply, how after the War the track was sold off..."

Mum is easing herself forward.

"...but the army kept sending men to be trained on steam engines. Long after steam trains had been replaced. I ask them what for, and they say they've signed something. Doesn't seem to stop them telling us about the big crash of 1947, though, a fire so fierce it burned all the evidence – train, bodies – and of something on board that shouldn't have been. Spike's uncle had been on that train, but Spike's father didn't start talking about it until thirty five years after it was supposed to have happened and before that no one knew Spike's father *had* a brother.

"The wild man's really upset: 'No kiddy thinks their Dad

knows everythin', he's saying, and he's heading for one of those trucks with two handles that you get in comedy Westerns, shouting. 'Not when they'm fourteen, not even when they'm ten. But when you'm six and you don't believe a bloody word he'm says, that loosens your roots – know what I mean?'"

I don't know if Dad had noticed that there might be something about us in his story, or that the fire on the train and the 'something that shouldn't have been there' wasn't so different from the fire that had stopped him being a fireman. And that maybe his story of the wild man was actually his own.

Mum tried to stop it.

"Are you sure about this, Paul?"

Dad wanted to finish.

"Anyway, the wild man starts kicking seven bells out of the cowboy truck. The sky's getting darker behind The Hill and I'm thinking, o my god, I'm in the middle of a forest with a bunch of conspiracy nuts and a green Father Christmas. But it changes. 'Here they come!' shouts one of the diggers and the wild man's suddenly not so wild anymore, climbing into his Green things, as the group gets nearer and nearer to what I'd imagined they would look like..."

Mum exchanged a glance with me, and then I saw she wished she hadn't. She'd let me see that she didn't believe. From then on she fixed her eyes on the yellow walls that look like Nanna's skin.

"His sister's dressed in expensive clothes, red coat, velvet mittens. The kids are just ordinary kids. Behind them comes Spike's Dad. He's a hole in the world. The sister's furious about the filthy Green Santa costume, but she doesn't even need to say anything. The kids stand around the display of old things, oohing and aahing. Spike's Dad hardly gives it a glance.

"Then, there's a shout: 'We've got more!' One of the enthusiasts, embarrassed by all this family wreckage has wandered off into the woods. We run to him and he's tripped over a rusty piece of track sticking out of the fallen leaves. The others start hacking at the ground, finding more of the same stuff as before: a shrivelled cardboard square of something, some black wood, the remains of a wallet. Every now and then a 'ching!' Or a 'hunk!' as they strike metal. Pretty quickly we find the path of the steel tracks and deeper and darker we go. The sister dances out in front, red riding hood stamping the forest floor for wolves' teeth. The children flit about, not finding anything. The enthusiasts carving out the route. Up above us the day has given up. I don't know what time it is, but it feels hungry…" "Paul, maybe we should carry on with this story tomorrow…"

"I won't remember it tomorrow."

I wasn't really listening to the story now. I was watching Mum and Dad. Wedged in between them I got the movements in their bodies. Dad was relaxed. His breath rolled out of him, his heart beat next to mine. Mum was going weird. Her skin felt as soft as ever, but underneath she was a crazy machine. Tiny parts moving at incredible speeds. Computers looking for combinations. Nothing was matching.

Dad had said this thing. That he wouldn't remember tomorrow. How do you know what you're going to remember tomorrow? There was a long pause, Dad shrugged and carried on. Mum's hands were stiff. I could feel a cold wet on her arms.

"Anyway… that brought us to The Hill, big as a block of flats. And the track runs straight *into* it. Now each blow is answered by a sound from somewhere else."

Mum couldn't stop it now. It was like that time that baby Ben climbed the loft ladder. She couldn't shout, she couldn't jump to grab him..

"The empty man takes a spade and taps it on the ground. First there's a quiet 'ching' and then, way off in the distance, another. The wild man grabs the spade off his Dad and whirls it around, slashing down the stems of the ferns and a green stink rises. We're not going to climb The Hill, that's clear. We're going inside it.

"The sister in red is reciting the 1947 tale. She's very keen on the evaporation of her uncle, how the fire was so fierce even the train disappeared. But what are the specs and the cardboard, then?"

Mum, now, is made up entirely of CCTV cameras. I can feel her, frozen like peas; stuck together so they can't get out of the corner of the packet. Dad thinks he can remember what's coming and Mum thinks everything important has already happened. I want to slip between them into the darkness.

"We were pushing back the ferns, we could touch the roof of what is obviously a tunnel. 'This be no cave, friends', says the wild man. And we all feel the smoothness of tiles under our fingertips. The enthusiasts produce a couple of torches. The ferns run out and we see the whole track, sleepers and rails. There are signs and numbers on the white tiles. It's colder and I realise I've been worrying about bears . Someone shouts: 'Light ahead!'"

As Dad says 'Light ahead!' I tune out, turn on an imaginary iPod and pretend music. I still catch bits of Dad's story... about squeezing through a bent metal gate, into a soupy grey cavern, huge shapes trembling in the low light of minty blue bulbs, something about an underground city.

"'Wow!! Wow!! Woooowwwwwwwwww!!!! WOW!!!!'"

Dad's waving his arms about. He's pretending to be one of the enthusiasts, going off on one about grey things in the murkiness. Dad, we don't care.

I know it's something about steam engines, but I'm falling asleep. Just as Dad's eyes are getting used to the low light, I'm switching the lights off. I'm sinking into a comfy mist. Dimly through it, trains are clumping, 'choo choo choo!' Mum's elbow, like one of the rods driving the wheels. I hear whistles.

"It's called the Strategic Reserve – a legendary supply of steam trains kept in mothballs in case of a national emergency..."

Mothballs?

I wonder if Dad means the trains are kept in a wardrobe?

"There was a man in there, among the trains, he was already there before us... there had to be, hadn't there? Lights. 'lectricity. Someone had to be down there. I thought at first I'd mistaken one of the enthusiasts, but I counted them all up and there was still one too many of us down there. As soon as the others were setting off back down the tunnel, I nipped back without them seeing. And, sure enough, there was still someone left."

Mum looked down at the arm of our sofa and bent over to pick off a crisp crumb. Like a heron on the estuary mud.

"Dressed in overalls. He looked up and saw me, Nancy. He'd really changed. You meet an old friend after a while, and it's not that they've aged, you expect that, but when they've become ugly, driven by dark things - he looked back at me, and I could see what an obsession can do, Nancy! It was Wally, Wally Eager."

Mum jumped forward and grabbed me.

"It's getting very late, young lady, you needn't worry about a bath tonight. Straight into your pyjamas and I'll bring your Milo up."

I was allowed to kiss Dad, a rushed and flappy Dad, suddenly hopping around trying to think of things he should do, goodnight, have you got your milk, pyjamas, and that was that. From the very start of the story Mum had been totally and completely right. It was all made up. Mum brought me up my hot drink and said not to worry about Dad, and the stories would go away eventually. They were just a kind of "theatre", put on to protect us from the real world.

Aren't they always?

Later, I could hear her downstairs. They were going over it all, again.

"Imaginary friends," Mum had said to me, with a silly smile. I could see Dad sat in his chair, in his head he would be building towers of words.

Chapter Twenty ~ Two Dreams

> In Italian *andare a Zonzo* means 'to waste time
> wandering aimlessly'... in the banal places of Zonzo,
> they defined... void as the *unconscious city*: a large sea
> in whose amniotic fluid we can find what the city has
> repressed...
>
> (*Walkscapes*, Francesco Careri)

The next morning the light was weird. The street was wet but it
hadn't rained. 'They' were watering it from machines. The roads
were normal. Houses. Hedges. Gates. The usual red window
frames. The usual green window frames.

And I am playing me now. I am the main character in the
street I am walking down ... down the...I can't even *see* the next
bit I am so scared. Then it flips and I can't think words, only see
pictures.

The ordinary road, the ordinary houses, red window frames
and green window frames.

In the middle of our road is a floppy periscope. Lolling over
one way and then the other, it slices through the street, around
the corner and into the crescent. Gone.

That night I had a second dream.

It begins like a kids TV programme with theme music and the
presenter saying "we're on a SEARCH FOR TREASURE!" Then it
jumps to the inside of a tumbledown castle. No roof, but a wall
and a door. On the floor are lots of pots and pans. There's a roll
of drums. In one of the doorways a curtain gets pulled back and
standing there is a skeleton.

I woke up in a sweat both times, each time so pleased it
wasn't real.

Mum's taught me that dreams are me talking to me about
me. So I reckoned the first dream was me telling me not to look
too hard right now. And the second was me telling me that if I
found anything... yeh, well...

Except that Mum wasn't always right, was she? I didn't believe her as much as before. The 'everyday me' maybe, but the deeper one that only comes out at night didn't, the part that had been there under the wonky floorboard when the Ugly Truth escaped, from under its wooden Hill.

So: the first dream was actually about me 'splorin' and the second was to do with the big silvery house. And I wouldn't get any further with getting Dad back just inside my brain. I needed to get out again and onto the panicky streets and the weirdy lanes.

Chapter Twenty-One ~ And And And

Move inside yourself.
    (*Stations: Places For Pilgrims To Pray,* Simon Bailey)

Dad went to see Nanna and Gramps. So me and Ben went along too, to give Mum a break. Nanna made us something from a packet that steamed up the windows while we watched the telly and Dad talked all the time to Gramps, who kept saying "it" was "a load of rubbish" and "fairy tales". Ben was cheeky to Nanna. Dad borrowed a big bagful of books about steam engines from Gramps, who said he didn't really want to lend them. He said Dad had to "straighten yourself out". When Dad got them home Mum made him drive the books straight back to Gramps. I know he only pretended to, though. Because, just after, Mum let me go to the shop for popcorn (there was a good film on and Mum lets us have popcorn at home for "good films, not rubbish") and I saw Dad in the next street sitting in our car, reading Gramps' steam train books.

When Dad got back, I could hear him and Mum arguing in the kitchen. I crunched my popcorn as loud as I could. Maybe Mum's found The Thing.

But even if she knew about everyThing, she wouldn't be able to help Dad. Because she didn't believe in Wally Eager. And we'd seen Mister Binns. And even if Dad was making up the stories, they were still about real things. Like Dad said: just because things are written down doesn't make them lies. What about 'Christmas Carol'? That's about The Ugly Truth.

I knew that Truth now. That the only way to get Things back is to finish the story and to do that we had to find Mister Binns and Wally Eager.

Dad was never going to be a fireman again.

I made a list: Things We Need To Do To Get Dad Back. There were 153 items.

Number 1: A new journey to find The Hill and with the help of Mister Binns to defeat Wally Eager and rescue the trains...

At school I've got a special teacher. Mum says that she's actually supposed to be less special than the usual teachers, but we think she's even better than them. She taught me how to read properly when I got stuck in the bottom group. Now she's in charge of our 'Buddy Group'.

"Mrs Thornborough, if my Mum and Dad argue, who should I agree with?"

"Both of them, Alice," she said, quick as anything. She doesn't make up answers like other grown ups.

But I'd already thought of that for myself.

"But what if what they say is so different that if you believed one you couldn't believe the other? Which one should I agree with then?"

"Still both, Alice. They're your parents."

Mrs Thornborough went off to referee in an argument between two of the boys.

I tried to think about how you could agree with two opposite things at the same time. I practised trying to force different opposites into my head. Fighting, spiky things. Tried to get them to laugh at each other's jokes. I tried it with different foods. Different smells. Different clothes. It worked with superheroes. I tried it with spaces. I closed my eyes and imagined being in two places at the same time, but still the same person. That didn't seem so difficult.

When I opened my eyes I saw the classroom was a kind of plastic model, like the 3D maps you get in 'museleums'. The desks were set out in a pattern, but because they weren't in straight lines no one had noticed it before. You had to imagine that you were on the ceiling and in your desk at the same time to get the picture. The children were arranged in shapes too: best friends and broken friends, outsiders and boys' gangs, top groups and push groups and mixed groups and bottom groups, the ones with problems and the ones with mobiles.

I was floating above the pattern. I was sort of in control, but I knew I would have to pull myself down soon or I wouldn't be. I was passing through all the connections and none of them were affecting me. I needed to *straighten myself out*. Things were all very close and a million miles away. I was floating away from best friends Mum had invited round for tea and then forgotten about until weeks later, by when I'd broken friends with them.

Mrs Thornborough told us to take out our writing books. Then our proper teacher told us to write a story about something real that we had done, but to write it as if it was an adventure.

I wrote about how I was going to find The Hill and save Dad. Not something that really happened, but something that was really going to happen.

Our Story

My Dad is a fireman, but he cant be a fireman now, because he was hurt in a fire and that's not just his body, its in his head too. My Dad has been on a great journey, but he hasnt got there to the end yet. So I am going to go instead for him.

My Dad went to a big hill with a wild man. They found a train that went into the hill. In the Hill there were more trains. The trains were more like shapes. But my Mum does not bilive my Dad.

I am going to go to The Hill the same way. To find the secret door and inside there will be tunnils, dark and wierd people. Then Mum will bilive my Dad. The people in the dark are weird and dont know about modern things. They only seem scary but they are just sad remaining.

I meet MR. Binns and he is cool, but bad and I meet Wally Eeger too and beat him. We get a train to escape. We escape back to town. I tell Dad the people still think that he told lies. I tell my Dad and he says the truth is inside him. I say if he did the things I now he did the fire engines under the Hill wuold come. That proves Dad is OK and good . In Town the three big boys pick on us and hundreds of bells ring and fire engines from under the Hill come along the High St and everyone sees my Dad is not a lier. As if Dad

called them from inside. In the windows of the big shop
people in town see Mister Binns like a giant making a thing
with his hand., the opposite of the lie thing. And even if
Dad is bad and he cant be a fireman now, still he is a scary
wizard who nows the real truth about things and he
becomes famous.

Chapter Twenty-Two ~ Back To Normal

> As she walked she never thought: "This is awful; how hot it
> is; how hungry I am." When matters became very bad she
> sat down under a hedge and quietly waited until they
> seemed better.
>
> (*The Gentle Art of Walking*, Geoffrey Murray)

That night Dad sat on the edge of my bed. After two chapters
from my latest favourite writer he folded over the corner of the
page and put the book on my bedside table. I had been waiting
for my chance.

"I know you saw me reading the steam train books," he said.
He'd seen me.

"I wanted to tell you that I've taken the books back to Gramps.
No more steam trains under weird hills, huh? I've been remem-
bering a lot more of my journey, and I've filled in most of the gaps.
So the important thing now is to look forward, do new things,
and get well. I need to get back to how I was in the fire service.
So I'm not going to be going off again. I wanted you to know that,
Al. Will you help me to get things back to how they were?"

I had to pretend. Not good pretend like Scrooge, but bad
pretend like The Thing. When would he tell me about The
Thing? Say that it was OK and that part of being grown up was
not telling people everything.

"We're going to set ourselves a timetable of nice things to
do," he said.

This was Mum, not him.

"We'll have a pattern, OK?"

Of course it was "OK". I wanted my Dad back. Pretty much
anything would be "OK". But this wouldn't do it. It was another
pretend, and it was stopping me moving. I had 153 things to do!!
It was eating up the things BEFORE I HAD A CHANCE TO DO
THEM!! We'd gone on the adventure to find our real Dad and
only a pretend sort of Dad had come back. I wanted my real Dad

who isn't normal. Normal isn't how things were.

Maybe it was best if Dad didn't explain The Thing right now.

The next day, after school, I found Dad's timetable pinned to the board in the kitchen. It wasn't a horrible timetable, there were nice bits. OK, Saturday morning was shopping and Monday was cleaning, but on Tuesday evening it was family swimming (because Dad was really fit from his 'fugue', compared to Mum anyway, even if the fire engine people didn't want him) and Saturday afternoon going to rugby or football (depending on which had the home game). And Dad had his own things. I thought he might try to do something with safety and stuff, but he'd 'boinged' all the way back to making things. He was starting classes at the university for people who aren't actually at the university. "Extra-Muriel", Ben says. Later, I saw him taking things up to his loft – special paper and expensive crayons that Ben and me weren't even allowed to look at, let alone borrow.

Ben got really cross about this and drew on a piece of torn out paper. It was a picture of all of us with captions. I was "lite grle" (light girl), Ben was "Ben", Mum was "big hrr" (big hair) and Dad was "bad dad" (he spelled that right). Mum thought it was very funny, and very sad, and said we should have it on the wall as the "family portrait". She put it on the living room mantelpiece until she could buy a frame. It moved from there to the little table with the phone. Then the back of it was used by Mum to make a note of someone's number. Dad took it upstairs to keep it safe, but he left it on the side of the bath and when someone had a shower big drops of water fell on it. 'bad dad' was OK, but 'Ben' went fuzzy like people look when they're behind glass you can't properly see through, Mum and me were just hollow splurges, the black had turned into red and purple, like coastlines.

As part of the Thursday early evening 'good for our minds' slot, I took Dad to the art gallery where no one has decided yet whether things are good or not. The same pictures were still up – the fuzzy ordinary places and the badly done galaxies. I'd thought he'd like it because it was about space. But the things he liked best were a part of the exhibition that me and Mum had missed. Boxes fixed to the wall, their insides full of red, blue, purple and yellow crystals. Like *really* looking into a universe.

Dad had to lift me up.

"Spar boxes," he said, holding me so I could put my face right inside the universe. "Collections of crystals from a particular area."

"Like our 'museleum' wall?"

"Like a 'museleum' somebody swallowed."

I began to think I shouldn't have asked Dad to come here and I pretended I was bored and couldn't we go and see the new cartoon at the arty cinema? He gave in, even though it would cause trouble with Ben. And next day he told himself off: "I need to stick to the routine, Alice. No sneaking off to the cinema when we should be doing something 'good for us'."

But the routine was spoiled, anyway. On the way home, Dad had suddenly breathed in deeply. Like he was about to say something important. We were by the statue of the soldier on the horse, a cone on the soldier's head as usual.

Say it!

Then he closed up and told me for the fifth time that the man on the horse had invented the concentration camp. The Thing crept back into the shadows of its cave. But I knew how near it was now.

From then on every bedtime story seemed to be about hidden treasure, lost secrets or forgotten prisoners. There was always something about to be discovered. Dad didn't seem to notice. I tried to ask him what the stories were *really* about but he said that Mum was the one who knew what things were *really* about. "I just float around on the surface." I tried to ask him again, but his eyes had drifted off to the book shelves. He mumbled something about "just being stories", then suddenly something seemed to snap into place, and he turned and looked straight at me, right into my eyes. And I could see right into the middle of the darkness of his. I'd never seen it so big. Just inside, hanging onto the edge, peeping out was The Thing.

Dad blinked and it went. He asked if I wanted a glass of water.

I hadn't noticed at the statue, but The Thing had been getting bigger. The more Dad didn't let it out, the more it was spreading.

Keeping to Dad's routine was as difficult as walking to school without noticing things. I had to stop myself from getting entertained. Concentrate on things that didn't connect. One foot in front of the other. But Mum was right about something. After a bit of not looking, you really did stop seeing things.

On our first Saturday morning shopping trip we had a bad moment, when a group of people came walking through the bushes at the back of the supermarket. The way they were looking, I knew they were on 'their own fugue'. Insect people. I pretended I desperately needed to wee and ran Dad back into the supermarket before he had a chance to notice the clicking fuguists.

One of the really good things about Dad's routine was that I didn't have to do the drying up any more. Mum had done a deal with Dad that he wouldn't do any dish washing if he did all the clothes. They were the one thing Mum had let slip while Dad was away. There were huge piles of dirty washing in the utility room, overflowing the green baskets. Mum only ever washed the layer off the top, so we'd been switching between the same two sets of things. Now, Dad was working his way through the backlog. My job was to go through the pockets. Dad would go mad if he found a 5p in the machine.

David Attenborough could have made a programme in Ben's pockets. In the first three washes I found a claw off the stuffed lizard at school, a plastic alien, five snail shells, a piece of cuttlefish bone, a 2p and the part of a violin that you twist to tune the strings. I made a little 'museleum' of them on the kitchen window sill. Mum told me to move them. I didn't, because they were a 'museleum'. Mum told Dad to tell me to move them, so Dad told me, and I didn't because they were a 'museleum', so Dad goes mad and starts screaming at me to go to my room, and Mum's screaming at Dad not to over-react and he's screaming at her not to undermine him and she's screaming back that he's only making this horrible to get at her for asking him in the first place, Dad says he's sick of her analysing every little thing that anyone does in this house and to leave her work at the office and thank god he never let her send Ben to her friends because they would have "screwed him up for life".

Yeh, Ben had been pretty weird. Making threats and saying he wanted to run away. I hadn't thought anyone was really worried. And I didn't think Mum and Dad would ever think of giving him away to their friends. I got rid of the 'museulum', but I made sure I screamed at them so they wouldn't know how scared I was.

The school holidays began and Mum was still working. So me and Dad and Ben made up a new timetable of things to do. Ben said: "Could we go and search for the Totnes Monster?" and that became another 'Family Story'.

I'd been trying to think what the timetables had reminded me of. Now I realised; they were like Mum's maps of Dad's journey. Because they were all about just doing things – taking money out of banks, buying tickets, going through pockets – never about the places. The timetables were Mum things.

There are two kinds of life. One is all about doing – buying things, learning, playing, collecting, loving. And the other is about places, about how to lose your way, forget what you'd set out to do and who you wanted to be... but we were supposed to avoid that now.

We went on the train to the big aquarium to see the sharks. Mum thought that we were "very weird" because we had fish and chips afterwards. That was the safe kind of "very weird" that we were trying to do now.

In the evening I had another treat. Dad had seen a poster at the football ground. There was an England Ladies Under 21 international. They never had real internationals at our little ground! It was only £2 to get in. My little brother didn't want to come because it was "girls".

We stood behind the goal, arriving just in time for the French national anthem, which Dad hummed for the rest of the match.

The match was a draw. One-one. Which was fair, Dad said.

The second half wasn't as good as the first. But I didn't want to leave. I liked the cold air and the steamy breath and the bright white-blue lights and the way the players played as if this was such an important thing. I wanted to be part of something like that. Something important. I loved just being near the feeling.

I suppose because it was so nice being out with Dad, I began telling him about "our little fugue", and that when our paths crossed in the High Street we weren't just out shopping with Mandy. Dad stopped me before I'd started on about our actual journey. He didn't want to know about that. Only about his list of places.

"I can remember just about everything, Alice – I know pretty much what I did once I got off the bus after seeing you. I stopped at a village, took a room in a pub that did B & B, I remember seeing the sign through the condensation. Everything after that is clear. It's sorting itself out." And he made a strange whirling with his fingers next to his head. "But I can't place this list you found. And I left it where?"

"In your shirt. On the table."

"Can I see it?"

"I don't know where it is. We showed it you in town."

"Did you?"

He was pretending not to know.

Was Dad in conspiracy with The Thing? I didn't want to doubt Dad, but I didn't trust him enough to let him look after the list if we found it. The Thing was everywhere now. It was more frightening than 'them'. Even in the misty breath above the football stadium it was there. It had been in the reflections on the shark tanks. And everywhere we went, I would catch Dad talking to insect people, always about the same Thing.

I caught a glimpse of him when he went to get the aquarium tickets, and again when he put our rucksacks on the luggage rack on the train, and later buying pies at the ground. It was The Same Thing as in the High Street that day we met Dad. I see it again and again and I want to turn it off, I try to stop it, to smash up the projector, but even though I wish, I'm always there, again and again, turning away from the policewoman and Ben and Mandy, and I see Dad do The Thing. He doesn't realise that I can see him. He's laughing with a group of insect people right there on the pavement next to the Riddle Spike – their eyes jerk about like they're on the ends of feelers - and Dad is pointing with one hand to the Riddle Spike and with the other, flattened, he's sawing up the air, making *our* sign for 'lies'. He *knows* who we are. He knows who he is and what he's doing. There's no fugue.

I haven't told Ben or Mandy. I can't tell Mum. Definitely not. Because the 'fugue' is what makes everything OK. If I take that away, what is there?

On the way home we bought spring rolls from the takeaway. They tasted of sharks' tanks.

On the rota next day, first thing was washing clothes. Dad wanted to finish off the dirty things that had been hanging around, so he put our recent stuff to one side and emptied out the last of the green baskets. They didn't really smell or anything, dried out by the huge aeroplane engines that had roared in our kitchen.

Some of the floorboards were still up, leaning over the broken clock, waiting for a water man to come and check if the shadows under the kitchen were dry enough for the boards to go back down. The table and shelves were clean now. But the ceiling still had a hole in it and the walls crawled with thin pink plaster slugs. Waiting for the decorators.

Dad sorted the dirty clothes and I went through the pockets.

At the bottom of the basket were the things we'd worn on our adventure, muddied up to the knees. Salty from the night in the tunnel.

In my brother's trousers there were wrappers and a stone. And some wood that had gone crumbly. In my jeans there were twenty three pistachio shells, a rock-hard raisin and the list.

Pretty obvious it would be there really, but I never think of washing as *actually* happening. Mum gets it out of my room, and then it disappears and then it reappears all clean, but I didn't think the clothes went to anywhere real in between. Like, where do emails go between computers? I thought the list vanished for a while like them.

Dad turned it over in his hand.

"It's something I could have written, notes from the reading I'm doing... "

He sounded doubtful. Had 'they' planted it? Forged it and put it where I'd find it? Or Dad had made it look like a forgery?

Dad took a pen from the table and began to copy 'dreamscape' onto the back of a packet of Grape Nuts.

There were wallpaper worms curling in the corner.

"Hmmm..."

Dad went to the fridge and fetched the blue notebook down from under Spiderman. He flipped it open and held the list against the writing in the notebook.

"It's mine, all right. It's a list of kinds of places. You're right."

"Was there an order?"

"What?"

"Were we supposed to find the places in a special order?"

"I don't think so."

"We thought there might be a pattern. Because there *are* these places."

"O, yes, but... What do you mean "are"? These are *kinds* of spaces, not actual ones. I noticed the same kinds of space crop up in different books I was reading..."

"Books?"

"Yes..."

"But not places outside books?"

"'Dread' places – I got that from those empty cities after everyone turns into zombies in... well, just about every zombie thing ever made - or every hillside in an Arthur Machen story..."

Who?

"Don't worry. Say, in 'Tom Sawyer' – the cave, somewhere that's too full of possibility – it's overwhelming..."

"But there are real places like that, aren't there?"

"The list's not about that ... look - "Geometrical Space" – there's a story called 'Flatland' that happens in a place where there are only lines along a surface, a place where there's no such thing as 'tall' or 'shallow'. The characters are mostly triangles... those are not real places, my lovely."

How could I check without him knowing?

"Flatland"?

"Or the shrinking doors in 'Through The Looking Glass'? Geometrical. It's from books."

He looked at the list.

"Did you find any of them?" he asked.

"We thought we'd found most of them," I told him.

"I suppose they're kind of universal places."

He rubbed his fingertip across the pen cuts.

"Places you recognise from movies and books."

He was still telling lies. Bad dad.

Chapter Twenty-Three ~
The Disappeared World

Because our cities are increasingly policed, militarised and
made banal. Because there is a conspiracy of boredom
against cities. Because the Great God Pan is long dead and
we still don't have the new myths we were promised.
(*A Sardine Street Box of Tricks*, Crab Man & Signpost)

Dad was very clever. I watched him all the time. He joined in
more with family things than before. But not so much as to make
Mum suspicious. She still complained about him gazing into
space at breakfast. There was nothing like the arguments they
used to have though. He was doing just enough to make Mum
happy and not too much to make her wonder why. It was all
pattern and pretend. I could see the shapes.

And just because Dad wasn't disappearing now in the way he
did the first time, that didn't mean he was really there. That first
time he had disappeared completely. This time he was going for
a few seconds and coming back again, or a few minutes, or a few
hours; fading in and out so no one noticed. Or so he thought. He
fitted his disappearances to what people in other families did. He
didn't have to lie because Mum always came up with an
explanation for him; the same way she had come up with the
story about the 'fugue' – because she always knew what things
really meant, rather than what they just were. He was "putting
out the bin." Or she'd ask him: "What did you get at the shop?"
or "How was the game?" And then he knew what to say. And
somehow he always had the key to the back gate to put back on
the hook or the match programme to give to Ben. Bad wizard.

Once I'd realised about his disappearing, I watched him
carefully. He did it all the time – a few seconds fetching a paper,
a few minutes tidying a room. Even just bending down to pick
something up, he could be gone for that moment. Or looking at

the wall or gazing into space – he wasn't there. Anyone can do this. I can do it. While people are thinking, "ah there's Alice, there's Ben's sister, there's our lovely daughter", actually I only need to be those things for a little part of the time, it only needs a small part of me to be in that space.

I started to experiment on just how short that time and how small that space could be.

Of course, I always made sure I had a reason. The only scary thing about it was that I might meet Dad in the world I disappeared to. I might see him with the Insect People or he might be 'having an affair'. I knew what that was. Some of Mum's friends from work had 'had affairs' and they talked about it to Mum in front of me. I know they're not doctors for your body, but did they think your ears don't work unless you're looking at them? And I could always guess which ones would have 'affairs' because they were the ones who were most luvvy-dovey with their boyfriends. 'Affairs' meant a lot of disappearing.

And what is the disappeared world like? No big surprise, actually – it's pretty much like this one, except the colours are brighter, the edges hurt more and little things look bigger. It's hard to go very far quickly in the disappeared world, you get distracted. It's like you've found the key to the spare room at the museum, or fallen through a stage into the costume store. It's the world we went to on our journey.

Actually, the only *really* scary thing is that I *never do* see Dad there, even though I keep sneaking off. So what *is* he doing when he's not here?

That's why I asked him if he would take us on a new journey to find The Hill. Not because I'm interested in The Hill. No. I'm not. But to find out where he really goes.

And I asked him if his Diary was true.

Chapter Twenty-Four ~ Gone Again

> Nadja commence à regarder autour d'elle. Elle est certaine
> que sous nos pieds passé un souterrain...
>
> (*Nadja*, André Breton)

"It's a story, Al, based on when I was a student, long time ago.
When I wanted to be an artist. I'm sure Mum's told you all these
stories."

He stopped at that, waiting for me to let him off having to say
any more. So I looked at him like he looks at my bookshelf. So he
had to carry on.

"I could see a hill from my bedsit, my little flat. I'd look at
that hill, and the bowlers on the bowling green up there, and I'd
make up stories about them. I could just about make out the
figures but I had to invent what they were doing. It's not about
anything that happened to me. I was confused when I got back
from my travels. I was still sorting out the real from the helpful.
The Diary was helpful, but not real – it's a made up story that at
the time I needed to believe. And we sort of made it real, didn't
we?"

"But what about Wally Eager? He WAS real. But now you say
he wasn't."

"Alice, even in my imagination I never asked the man under
The Hill his name. Remember? Wally Eager is the name of a
character – based on someone I knew at college. But that wasn't
his name. There are a lot of Wally Eagers in the world, just as
there are a lot of secret hills – if you look hard enough."

Yeh.

"But Wally Eager WAS real, wasn't he, Dad?"

"Made up. Nasty piece of work. I imagined how someone
would be if he turned really bad and then buried it under a hill
for a long time to root. Maybe on the journey I met someone like
him, I don't remember. Wouldn't be that big a coincidence,
though, would it? People always tend to think that coincidences

are far less likely than they really are. I just clicked on to 'Wally' for some reason."

"And onto 'Mister Binns'?"

"You saw a ... giant.... There was a man, weird guy, I knew vaguely who drank in our pub, I based Mister Binns on him."

He was telling me one thing to make me think another.

"In this street there are probably people like Mister Binns. For all I know there may be people like that in this street who are actually *called* Mister Binns. It's not likely, because I invented all the names, but it's not impossible. The world is always far more connected than people expect."

Then he smiled and winked.

Ah. Code. You never find anything if you look for it. Dad was helping by not helping.

I said: "I'm going to get a drink," and went down the stairs, shutting the kitchen door hard, then tip toed to the front door, and I was away.

The second journey began.

No lists, no kits, no one to get in the way.

Chapter Twenty-Five ~ Dialogue

> When I open the pages I'm off and away
> To the Land of Adventure and there I shall stray
> With all kinds of people, do all kinds of things,
> Hob-nobbing with brownies, and cowboys, and kings!
> *(Enid Blyton's Annual)*

I hadn't been down the 'boing-boing' alley since the night of the journey. I didn't bother with all the drama-queen 'stepping into wonderland' stuff, this time. I knew how to get there without playacting.

At the far end of the alleyway is what Great Uncle Tony calls a 'T junction'. I hate them, because they mean you are going to miss lots by not going the way you don't choose. And you never find out what that would have been. I went the way we went before.

The next bit of the path is like somewhere people's feet have scuffed into place, like the curve on a wildlife programme where the dolphin comes out of the water. There are bits of steps that aren't used now because people have trodden their own, and a fence held together by brambles. Sometimes cones and road signs are here, stupid students have stolen them. They're funny though because pedestrians don't need signs here. Pedestrians are signs here.

At the bottom of the steps is the 'motorway' path that Dad hates. I like it now that the little white walking men have begun to peel off the tar. You can get bits of them up and rearrange their bodies. The big white line down the middle of the path is more of a rocket trail than a dividing line.

I didn't run into the trees this time. There was no hurry. Just see what happened. Nothing happened. If Mister Binns was still there he didn't show himself. He might have been watching, of course, because through the tree trunks I could see people walking on the path. Someone with shopping, someone with a dog, a woman with a buggy, but none of them saw me. I was marked on a different map.

I listened for music. Trees creaked, leaves crinkled, birds were in their usual boring panic. Far off the trains rattled. Once, the air ambulance wooshed over. I imagined what it would be like if I could hear the movement of everything.

Someone shouted "help" in the park. A siren howled. A wasp buzzed.

I went very slowly from insect hut to insect hut. I knew Dad had made them. They were supposed to be useful, I think, to help people with changing the world. I tried to picture the layout of them in my head, but I couldn't keep the map still. Each time I got to the final sculpture, the earlier ones had gone. So, it wasn't meant to be that. I decided that I wouldn't leave the insect huts until I had puzzled out how each of them worked.

- *Number one hut: houses that could travel. (Was that what Dad was trying to do? Take everything with him?)*
- *Number two hut: one thing turning into another.*
- *Number three hut: backwards arrows. (Had Dad thought he was the first and others would follow?)*
- *Number four hut: sci fi bugs made of hippy art. (If anyone laughed at them, they fell down.)*

I sat in a small clearing where there were another three of the insect huts and listened to their conversation.

- *Tepee-grasshopper: The kid doesn't count. Thirty people have walked by since she's been here. None of them noticed her. She must learn to speak their language. They listen to music on iPods, they rush home to catch their favourite programmes.*
- *Alien bug-house like ours: Only one will understand. We are not everything. But one bite reaches all bodies. Eventually.*
- *Greenshield bug-snow lodge: She is learning that even*

superheroes, even those made by artists, are not drawn correctly in their worlds. Their maps should be more like burst pipes.

I listened for hours. They knew that I was listening, of course, because although they never used my name, they said things they knew would be useful to me. And they never properly answered each other.

It was starting to get dark. This had nothing to do with the sort of time that goes round the clock. It was about the lights along the path and the moon around the earth. The darkness switched on the lamps so I could follow.

I climbed up through the trees and bushes. There'd been some rain, the leaves were wet. I was shaking with happiness. I would step onto the rocket and ride it. But Mum was there with some of our neighbours, they were carrying torches. Were they going to burn the magical scientist out of his house? They wouldn't answer my questions properly. What is the matter with them? All they want to talk about is me. I am not important! I am not important! Can't you understand! Nor warm baths, warm bed, hot drinks! Is that all they think about, the idiots, just the same as the people who walk on the path and never listen to the sculptures?

I don't scream at them like I do when I don't want them to know I'm scared. I go quietly, so they think that nothing is wrong.

Chapter Twenty-Six ~ Prison Lane

A walk then, like a laugh, or one's handwriting, becomes a
signature, making our mark across space.
(*Slow Motion: stories about walking*, Andie Miller)

Today, Dad had another big talk with me about The Hill, the
Diary and the List. How we'd all been telling each other stories.
To help ourselves get better. Because sometimes we need to tell
ourselves made up versions of what is until we are ready to
accept 'the plain truth'. I knew which one he meant. Plain ugly,
he meant. That Thing was all stories, all true eventually, but
never yet. Until eventually it was all lies, disguising the angles,
hiding the fact that there was no plan, but that there will be,
eventually. It was all about being sick, of everything. How
everything *wouldn't* get better, but we would. And all that Dad
said I knew was a story made up by Mum.

I told Dad I wanted a hot drink. Dad said he would fetch it. I
said I wanted to fetch it myself. He said he would come with me.
I said I only wanted to drink it if I could fetch it myself. He said
Mum wouldn't allow that. I said he could listen that I didn't run
off. That was OK.

Down the stairs as quickly and lightly as possible. Open the
front door silently and leave slightly open. Slam kitchen door to
hall. Run to back door, taking back gate key. Race through
garden and undo lock on back gate. Run with key back into
kitchen. Dad shouting for me in the front road. Put key back on
hook. Through back door. Close back door carefully, quietly.
Through back gate.

They soon found me. I hadn't got very far along the back wall.
I had become so incredibly small that I could see all the dust on
the leaves and every drop of water on the moss. Mum said I had
been gone almost all day but I couldn't have, I'd got so little
done. I needed much more time to look at all the insects. I had
only touched the fringe of the jungle. Inside every speck of earth

there might have been a whole Hill hidden. But I hadn't had time.

Now I would have to be in my room or with people all the time, because I "can't be trusted".

I've been making a list of all the people I would like to stay in with me.

- *Mandy.*
- *Tracey Beaker.*
- *Nefertiti.*
- *La Xana (Fairy from Asturias).*
- *Lady Gaga.*
- *Marina (from Stingray).*
- *Mum.*
- *Real Dad*

I made some more lists: normal things, things for not going off with, things you can do in your head, celebrities I'd like to 'splore' with, good hiding places in movies.

I needed to make a list of my lists. But none of the little lists was finished. Anyway, how were you supposed to finish a list? Just have the top ten maybe? But that isn't Truth, is it? That's how the Ugly Truth grows! You crush it down and it sprouts. Like a centipede with ten segments and ten legs on each segment and ten toes on each leg and so on and so on. The lists on TV usually have one hundred, but that isn't true either, there are thousands of best comedies of all time, there isn't time to list all the best things of all time or the different kinds of places whose edges you can just see once. There's no reason for the lists to stop at ten, or fifty or a million. That's the Centipede. That's what Dad was now. He could explain anything with a weird story that Mum had told him or a painted stick he'd made for himself, but he just kept adding: and and and. That would be OK if it was just him, but in fact the world is much worse than parents let on to you. It is full of huge machines all the time producing lists, and maps, sending out names in groups, and none of them is ever completed, not one single journey is ever happily ended.

Downstairs I hear Mum and Dad reading from their scripts.

"I'm not going to let your friends loose on a child!"

"I'm sorry, but a child in that distress needs more help than you can give her..."

"Don't tell me what a child needs..."

"Well... frankly you're the last person to start pronouncing on what anyone, let alone a child, needs..."

A Child was in the woods. A Child was huge and babyish, wise and incredibly tired. A Child did nothing. It knew it should be stomping its big fat legs, shaking the ground, but because it did nothing it felt so tired. A Child felt worse doing nothing. So it began to make a list: Ten Best Ways To Escape When You Are In Distress And Your Parents Are Watching All The Doors.

I don't even remember which item was the one that I used.

I started realising what I'd done only half way down Prison Lane. I was running out of time. It was downhill, but it behaved like an escalator running the other way. If I stopped I would go back to the top. Maybe all the way home. Up and down the lane I went, back and forward. I didn't know what to do until the sound of a train's rattle made me remember bones holding up a ceiling. That's where I was going. I couldn't get out of the lane until I'd remembered why I'd had to run away.

I slipped back into quick time and I was surfing the escalator down to the bottom.

There were no ticket people at the back way to the station. Dad had showed us this sneaky way in so we could avoid the ghosts of people in olden days watching the hangings. I didn't have any money, but I knew the guards on the train wouldn't mind. They would just suck their long teeth. They're part of Dad's organisation. My Dad is in charge of millions of people. He knows all these places.

I was strong now. If the first train didn't stop I could get on the track and stop it. Didn't need to, though, it was already in the station, trembling. Coincidences are less rare than you think. I started to run for the first coach, and then there were other people running. These were the patterns. You began to run and others began to run. You had to get in the real pattern and the real time. The doors were closing and I jumped on board just in time. The engine made an angry sound and we set off very slowly. People on the platform were shouting and waving. I grabbed a seat at a table and started looking out of the window. I love the bits by railway tracks. When the world has fallen to pieces, these are the places where no one goes, where we'll be safe. On the platform there were people I recognised. They were pointing into a window further back down the train and then at me. Like there was something back there that wanted me.

The Thing? The Ugly Truth? Or the birds, maybe?

The people on the platform were dropping back as the train picked up speed, scuffling with a man with a white ping pong bat. All part of the pattern.

As the trains leave our station they curl around a bend. Then they straighten out again. I forced myself to look back up the train. Patterns. Rows and rows. The usual same passengers as everywhere; no explorers this time. No monsters, either. No A Child, no Stories, no Caretaker. Autons, every one. I could see into each coach as it came off the bend and straightened up, slipping back into line, I could see new rows of passengers, the usual same passengers. No monsters, no A Child. Autons, every one. Second coach, third, fourth... What if they just kept clicking into place, forever, and the train never ended and I was stuck here, with row after row of robot-people rolling off the machine, frozen here forever, for being scared. Fifth coach of autons, sixth – Dad. I sat back into my seat. I sat perfectly still. I held my breath. I was exactly IN PLACE. Precisely part of the pattern.

But my Dad is a superhero and he saw me with his X-ray eyes.

Chapter Twenty-Seven ~ Swamp

...let us remember that this modern movement is only the latest stage in the slow revolution... which began 150 years ago, when Englishmen 'long in city pent' first began to feel a strong urge to escape.

(*Shanks's Pony*, Morris Marples)

After the train, things changed. Nobody said anything, but there was always someone around. Ben not so much now, but Mum, Dad, Nanna and Gramps. And doors – there was something wrong with the doors. I could never get anywhere!! Things had closed in a lot since the train. The patterns had tightened up, there wasn't as much to explore as there had been. In fact outside of me there was no space at all now. There was a sort of corridor that Mum, Dad, Nanna and Gramps were using to move around, but nothing else.

Ben must have misbehaved once too often. This must be to do with him.

I wasn't going to disappear though. Just because everywhere else had begun to. Even my name on my Literacy Book. First the A went and left LICE. Then I was ICE. Next CE went. CE means Christian Era. Which is something to do with History. But 'I' stayed. I watched the 'I' for ages. Trying to keep it there. Kind of hoping it would fade, actually. Just to see. 'I' didn't though. 'I' stayed all night, while other things went. Things that 'I' knew I knew, and 'I' knew I knew they were there too, but 'I' couldn't see them any more. Other people's faces. Colours. Anything to do with lights.

Reflections were the last to go. I had to get around in a mist now.

I could only travel if I followed special rules. On the stairs I must take three steps up and two steps back while counting to a thousand. I could only go on to the next three up and two down if I ended the last three up and two down on an even number. If it was odd I had to start again at the first step. Most nights, Dad would carry me.

Dad was wearing something new every night. He was interviewing for jobs. After he brought all the paper and crayons and pencils home, he found he couldn't pick them up. Or "couldn't pick it up". I heard him shouting at Mum that he didn't care what he did, he only wanted to make money for me and Ben. I didn't believe him.

Each day Dad would come in to see me in the morning in a new costume: his wedding suit, the shoes that make him limp, then a white suit with three overcoats, and a baggy thing that made him look six years old. One day it was something like a clown. At night he'd be angry because they'd turned him down again. The more interviews he did the more he changed into the people that nobody wanted him to be.

He'd had to carry me out of Drama Workshop in a new red suit and a yellow tie. Even though I couldn't move anything else, my eyes still worked. We'd been doing drama games when I got stuck. I knew I was only putting it on. I was doing what Mum had taught me for Scrooge. The routine I had to stick to. It was nothing to do with anyone else. I didn't listen to our Drama leaders. I just fixed on doing the right thing.

Mum said I was trapped in a nursery rhyme. But I wasn't, I was just 'behaving', like I'd been supposed to. It was all on purpose. I didn't need to go on a journey to solve our problems, I had to stay still. I had to finish the story in my head and then we could all begin again, in real life again.

And I was right, because after a while something happened in the world that had disappeared. It didn't all come back, but it became clearer. Less misty. It looked like icing on a cake now, like on one of Dad's old black and white videos. In the mist I'd been on my own, in a dirty cotton wool cloud, comfy in a way and sweaty and warm. But there were other things in the new grey sugary world. Little crowds of Stories who chattered to birdlike things. In the shadow of the scuzzy trees was The Ugly Truth, clumsy and hairy, a giant that dribbled and spat. The birds would twitter and the Truth would blub. They both said the same thing: that the other didn't exist.

Then, one day The Ugly Truth started to fade. I was so happy I danced through the grey trees until I couldn't make my legs work any longer. When I looked down my feet had gone. The remains of my legs were fading too. Below my pockets I was icing. I tried to hold a story above my head, in case it sank into the goo. Then, like water suddenly sucked down a plughole, wooosh, the rest of me had rushed away. I tried to feel what it was that was now seeing the dirty trees, because I *could* still see them, even though all of me had gone. What was left was the last thing I'd been looking at. The tv was playing the same image of a tv over and over and over.

Mum came. She pulled all the icing sugar leaves straight and she smoothed all the wrinkles out of the grey dirt under the trees. I told her that I had to tell her a story, but she said I needed to rest. I told her that I couldn't stop thinking about disappearing and that I was frightened. Mum was really calm. As if she dealt with disappearing people every day. But afterwards I could hear her crying outside the huge door. I realised, like Dad must have, that disappearing people have a kind of crappy power. Power to make things more crappy. And I wanted to use it even though I knew it was wrong.

Dad came to "tuck me in". He was wearing an old fashioned jacket that he must have borrowed from our Great Remains. He didn't say anything about getting the job so I didn't ask. He was looking less like Dad now. He seemed older. All the lines that made him Dad were falling out of his face. Soon all that would be left would be a huge hungry nought.

That night Crappy Power came to me. He was dressed in a cowboy suit and a musketeer cloak and when he spoke his teeth stank. He whispered all night. Plots and plans. I couldn't quite hear what they were, but I told him I'd be ready. When I sat up to get my ear nearer to his smelly mouth I noticed that the icing had gone. There were no trees, no scummy leaves, nothing. Just Crappy Power bending over me. I still couldn't hear what he was saying. When I lay back the light came on, Crappy Power ran away, and the icy sugar forest ran back in, full for the rest of the night with Stories who kept yattering together about something or other and running around in the crunchy leaves, like my bed being eaten by a monster with silver foil teeth.

Towards morning it grew quieter and I was scared again. Stories were meeting under the trees, discussing. After a while they came over in a gang. They said there was going to be a war with Crappy Power in Panicky Woods and only the part of me in the letter 'I' would be allowed to fight.

In a place in my brain I'd been making up a list of rules for the club of 'splorers of ordinary places, but before I could finish it the battle began. It went on for days. The sun would appear and then disappear like a very slow turning on and off of my bedroom light. I couldn't speak. I'd go to wipe my mouth and it'd *be there!!* But before I could get any words out it'd go again. I couldn't tell my story. It sat at the bottom of the bed, ignored. All I could do was sweat at things. Whenever any part of me reappeared for long enough I would use it to pull the sheets round me and make myself hotter. Mum and Dad were taking turns to sit by the bed, sometimes they would switch back and forward quite a few times in a second. They sat like commentators on sports TV, but they didn't say much except how much they loved me. Never that they loved each other. They seemed to be watching my eyes. I wondered if I could do Morse Code blinking. I tried, but my eyes disappeared. I couldn't see if they saw that. Everything I tried to do went wrong. I stopped trying. Instead, I watched the battle of Crappy Power and 'I'. It was quickly over.

In the grey mist I felt my way towards the new grave; the Story-Crows were jumping on it – three steps forward, two steps back, 149, 150, 151... aaah! Again and again having to go back to the cemetery gates, coloured like play clay. I found the only way I could get closer was thinking about rivers, rain cycles, and estuaries, and jumping fish, reaching my fingers out like streams. I felt my way across the green lichen. It took days to get to the first letter. A centipede counting out the numbers. The gravestone had all the same flowers as the alleyway. But always, all the time, in one little unnecessary room in my head, with just a chair and some magazines and a broken sewing machine, I kept trying to reach out. What was it? Please... my dirty fingers and chipped nails feeling into the dents "IT'S THE... IT'S THE SORT

OF..." No, please! "...OF ROAD..." I could feel that everything would come down now. Everything would fall. "IT'S THE SORT OF ROAD THAT CROPS UP EVERYWHERE..." Lies! Everything and everywhere was lies. Dad said the list only referred to *kinds* of places in books and movies, nowhere real, but I had remembered now. On the way to The Hill, in the story, Dad had said he was on a road, and he called it "...THE SORT OF ROAD THAT CROPS UP EVERYWHERE..."

Those places that we found *were* real.

And now I was going to walk that road, thank you very much.

Chapter Twenty-Eight ~ The Dream

> ...it (mythogeography) is also a geography of the body. It means to carry a second head or an appendix organism, in other words to see the world from multiple viewpoints at any one time, to always walk with one's own hybrid as a companion.
>
> (*Mythogeography*, various and anon)

Running off hadn't worked. Plots and plans. That's what were needed.

I lay very still so no one could see me thinking. I daren't use paper, I had to make the plans in my head. Draw maps inside. Assemble the kit without getting off the bed. And it worked perfectly. It was all so very much better in your head; on paper the ideas stayed in order. In your head they were changing around all the time. Of course, you can do that in IT class too, but in your mind they move quicker than your fingers do.

The journey was much clearer.

I couldn't take Ben and Mandy, of course. Mandy had never been that interested, anyway, I took her the first time because I was scared to go on my own with Ben. Once you're honest about one thing, you can be honest about other things.

And, anyway... anyway, Ben isn't allowed out of his room, for cheeking. It would just be me and Dad. I was in the kitchen now. Mum said she agreed. "What's more important than feelings? But I hope you thought about asking me along too?" She knew I hadn't. Mum only travelled in brains and I had to get out of mine.

We would all pack the rucksacks together, she said. Even Ben would be allowed out of his room to help. I could hear him playing my cds. And as long as me and Dad got back in time for Christmas to see Nanna and Gramps, it was our holiday to do what we liked with.

Mum was sitting on my bed, but I couldn't hear her now. She was looking at me. Her mouth wasn't moving. It was getting late.

We should have been packing things for my journey. Maybe we were having a break? I couldn't see anything packed and I knew I shouldn't be in bed yet. I needed to be ready! Anyway, I told her what Mandy had said at the very beginning of our adventure. That Dad had never seen what was under The Hill, that he only knew what his 'imaginary friend' Wally had told him.

"Mandy guessed it from the start, didn't she?" said Mum. "It was Wally who did all the subterranean exploring for Dad. Do you know why Dad didn't see the underground city in his story?"

I shook my head. I had no idea.

"Me. My fault. I got in the way. Dad's story that you found in the attic - I read it after. And that's what it's about: love getting in the way. I'm afraid that's what most people's lives are about – trading love for ambitions, and ambitions for love. So Dad invented an 'imaginary friend' to do all those things I stopped him doing. Except grown ups don't call them 'imaginary friends' – they call them novels or poems or nagging or work. And when art and fighting fires didn't work any longer, who should appear again? Wally."

I didn't like art or work.

Mum said I should go to sleep now, to rest my mind.

I don't know how she thinks my bags are going to pack themselves. But I was tired and I knew something would happen to make things right. We were in an organisation, of millions of people: Japanese, insects, bearded examiners of angels. They would all help.

I released the tanks of air and allowed the metal craft to sink.

Next morning Mum made us all a special cooked breakfast with our favourite: bubble and squeak. When we'd finished everything on our plates, Mum cleared the table. She said: "Leave the washing up. You go now. I'm going to look for The Hill in my own way," and she gave me a wink. She knew the code? Not to look in order to find?

"Aren't we going in the car?"

"No, young lady, you need to go on a proper journey."

And I saw her give Dad a funny look. But he missed it.

After I finished my hot chocolate, we put on our rucksacks. Dad was bringing along a door knob made of stuff that old radios were once made from. He said it might help open doors. He said he'd found it under The Hill.

Mandy was at her window when we left. She was much older now and I was embarrassed to look at her. Mandy's Mum was clearing ice off the windscreen of her car. I hadn't realised how cold it would be. I hadn't been out of my room for weeks.

We didn't wait at the alley, but went straight in and down the steps to the path. Our feet left marks in the snow. Where had that suddenly come from? We walked through the trees. The leaves broke like glass. The insect sculptures didn't look so good. The one Ben had knocked over had been put up again, but it was more like a bus shelter now. I showed Dad where we met Mister Binns, but there was no moon to make a head and no night for a coat.

We didn't wait for a bus, we went straight to the '**hub**', although I didn't actually feel us walking – no *one foot in front of the other* for us; we slid. Dad nodded and pointed out where someone had thrown an egg at the Spiritualist Church. "Eggtoplasm," he said. We stood in the almost tall grass, but nothing new happened. In the High Street I showed Dad where we'd swallowed our reflections. Dad said it must happen to shoppers all the time. They were copies of copies of copies of copies of copies of copies of copies...

As we walked by the building voted the most ugly, I said they should knock down the Ziggurat Centre, like Mum said, but Dad said that every time they try to knock down buildings, people try to stop them because they are kept up by dreams.

"Are dreams really *made*?" I asked him.

He said. "There have to be dreams. Even if they're only handbags. That's why I wrote about The Hill."

I showed Dad the empty space where we'd fed the ghosts and he laughed. This was much better. Now Mum and Dad said things they were really thinking. And they did what I hoped they would.

Further away, up on the High Street, the crowds were churning around and around. Out of all the jumbling, *the boy in the puffa jacket* emerged on a long curve, leaning his body over his skateboard as it slid across paving slabs, throwing himself this way and that, always *about* to smash his head on one of the lampposts. Dad was watching and gasped, but at the last moment the boy threw out his arms and caught the post in both hands, spiralling down it until he landed, kicking his board into the air with one foot and taking off with the other, disappearing into the crowds.

I thought of the boy's backwards hand and that he'd been pointing us in the right direction. "Everything in the universe has to move in one way or the other," said Dad, twisting his wrists.

In the Cathedral Square, Dad sneaked me into a pub. Two grumpy men looked at us over their beers; they were insect people in disguise, part of our organisation. We ducked through a tiny door and down some dark spongy stairs. The carpet ran out and we were on uneven stone tiles.

"This is the heart of all my exploring," said Dad. The air was damp. The walls were made of crumbly rock, but one side had a long window in it that didn't look out on to anything but more crumbly rock. Dad pushed me closer. Behind the glass, just below the ledge, a skeleton was laid out. I wasn't scared this time. Because there hadn't been a curtain or a door. No plots nor plans. Over the bones was a sign: *Birth is the first step unto death.*

Outside, the sun seemed to be shining brighter. We passed the hospital where Ben and me had been born, turned down a side road that said "cul-de-sac", and followed an alleyway to the Weightie Tree where the old tribes had once met. At the bottom of the path was a big hospital building made of glass, where washed sheets, picked up by robot arms, were shaken and folded, a procession of linen ghosts. On the estate unhappy boys were shouting the F word and Dad nearly said something to them.

I knew that now was the time to end the walk and go home. The robot bed sheets had summed it up, and I knew we should catch the bus back. We could go and have some Turkish salad, Dad have a coffee. Talk over what we'd seen. Get kissed. Maybe Dad could go back to being a fireman again. He wasn't out of breath yet...

Things jerked, something in the clean sheet machine had

slipped. We were in the countryside now - I could do that, jump forward if I didn't like what was happening – but I didn't know how to wind back.

We climbed over a stile, picked our way round a rusty bed frame, and up a green hill. In the grass, someone had left a village of tiny wooden toy houses.

"Is this *your* Hill, Dad?"

"No, Al, long way to go yet."

We followed a muddy path down through an old, disused quarry that changed to being not old or disused and we got told off for being there. The man told us all about the stone and how it had all once been an ancient desert and how they could tell from the rock which way the wind blew three hundred million years ago.

"An accidental museum of wind, Al!"

As we left, Dad winked at the man. We were in an organisation of millions.

We followed a busy road. 'The Sort Of Road That Crops Up Everywhere.' We met an artist pushing a stuffed goose on a tiny cart – he said the welfare people wouldn't let him use real ones.

Dad's mobile rang but he couldn't work out how to answer it. A 'V' of geese clanked over the valley below. We had come to huge gates.

"Ah," said Dad, as if he knew where we were.

"Do you know this, Dad?"

Because I knew. It was the way to The Big House with the skeleton. I could hear in my head the shrieky voice of Dom from *Dick and Dom In Da Bungalow*: "This week's spooky bogey-man moment sees Alice and her Dad brave the terrors of... The Big House!!"

At first the drive was so long that I didn't worry about what would happen if we ever got to the castle. But it speeded up like the Prison Lane escalator. The deer grazing changed into a line of men in uniforms, carefully examining ground marked out by fluttering plastic tape. A policeman leaned into our path.

"Excuse me, sir, miss, you're on private property."

"I'm sorry", said Dad, exchanging passwords. I didn't want anyone to see my face in case they accused me of killing the lambs.

"Is the house open today?" asked Dad.

"No, it's never open to the public."

"O."

Dad's "O" hung, in the air, hungrily. The policeman looked at it, irritated.

"There's been an accidental shooting."

I pulled at Dad's arm to leave and we both fell over in the road. I tried to get up, but Dad wasn't helping. I knew who it would be. The lady in the purple and silver dress. The policeman's hand pointed backwards like an arrow.

> *"We've been together now for forty years,*
> *An' it don't seem a day too much.*
> *There ain't a lady livin' in the land*
> *As I'd swop for me dear old Dutch."*

"Hadn't you heard, sir?"

"I've been away," said Dad, "Only just getting back to normal now."

"That would explain it, sir. Lovely lady. Do you have an interest in the case?"

"I have an interest in everything, as a member of the human race."

I couldn't think of the words to get us out of this. The story had got stuck. We were lying in the gravel. My legs and arms felt very fat and full of air. Dad was heavy, like in his chair. The policeman and Dad were talking round and round in circles like Mum and him would every night.

I jumped everything forward.

The policeman had gone now. We were walking away, but I could see over my shoulder that in a room hung with old paintings of ladies dressed like Mum, firing arrows, there were people, old and similar to each other, like a family, and they were leaning over something, anxiously, as if someone was dying in bed. But it wasn't, it was a model city, a toy version of our city. And in the middle of it were hundreds of Ziggurats.

I asked Dad if he thought the beautiful lady had been murdered. He blew air out of his mouth.

"Maybe it doesn't mind, Alice. Who knows what pots and pans there might have been..."

I thought for a moment he said "pots and pans" instead of "plots and plans".

"It doesn't *matter*..." I corrected Dad. If it was Dad.

"No, I mean *mind* – The Big House doesn't *mind*."

The tapestries swung open. The skeleton was there. It was sitting in a chair. For a moment the ghosts of the Ziggurats were all around, circling, about to pick the last pieces from its bones. Then the mists danced one last turn and whirled away. The floor was cluttered with pots and pans, but they faded too, memories of plastic play-kitchen toys. Someone else was in here with me.

The skeleton began to talk.

"Alice? Can you hear me?"

It began to push itself up from the chair. It was unsteady, as if it hadn't got used to doing without flesh.

"Nancy? Nancy!" hissed the skeleton.

And Mum appeared in a huge cloud of light. She stood by the skeleton and they glowed. Like the lovely lady.

"Did she wake?"

"I wouldn't call you without good reason, dear."

The skeleton inched nearer. The light hung around its bones like old clothes. Mum leaned closer.

"Alice, try to sleep, lovely..."

"Mum..."

"Shush, now..."

"But, Mum..."

"Do as your mother says," said the skeleton.

"All right, Beryl. I'll do this."

The skeleton harrumphed and sat down. I could see a face at the door, polished and shiny, and the shape of a man dressed in overalls.

"Alice, you have been very poorly, and you're so tired, lovely. Try and rest as much as you can..."

"But why am I here? I'm supposed to be on a journey..."

"You're not going on any journeys, lovely..."

"But you said I could!"

"No, I wouldn't ever have said that..."

More lies.

"You did, you idiot!"

"Dear o dear!" tutted the skeleton.

I had to get back to the dream. They were making me so tired here! I turned over so I couldn't see Mum and the bones in the chair. I closed my eyes as tight as I could against the light. I could hear someone "there, there-ing" and I felt a hand on my back, that might have been bones. I hugged myself as tightly as I could, forcing myself back into the story. We had been coming away from The Big House. Dad would still be there. He'd be lost if I didn't help him find The Hill again and see the city inside. We had to beat this stupid, traded Love!

But it's hard to get back into a dream once you've come out of it. I climbed into the tiny submarine, and lay down, and began to think.

List of new dreams:

1) *Ben makes cakes from mud and serves them on plates in a smart restaurant. The manager is a tiny man with a look as wide as a country, he wears a black coat that is beginning to swallow up the restaurant, the white towel on his arm is a slope, down which knives and forks ski...*

2) *Mum and Dad are dancing together in a green field, the clouds in the blue sky are shaped like mountains. In the woods there's a hidden band, dressed in smart orange uniforms. They play old fashioned music with saws, hammers and huge sheets of paper. The conductor keeps complaining about flies...*

3) *I am doing my homework at my school desk when I shouldn't be. I can also see from a bird above that there is no one else in the school. The bird flies higher and I can see there is no one left in the city. Then, right at the edge, tiny because the bird is so very, very high, something begins to move into a street. I can't see what it is properly... I try to turn over, but it's in the corner of my eye. It's a huge shape...*

4) *There's a submarine stranded in our street. All the*
students are leaning on it. And it topples over, rolling
down the road, smashing into the prison wall. Behind the
bricks is a curtain which opens in the middle and
thousands of tiny human skeletons the size of dogs come
running out. They disappear into all the houses on the
road, but none of the students seem to notice. I try to get
them to stay in the road, to run away with me, but they
say that they are all in Love and Love stops you doing
what you want...

5) *A cloud of breath finishes its own fugue across the sun.*
Warm light like gassy butter wanders about in the
wintry lane and I decide that the 'museleum' and the
painting of the lightning lady from olden times would not
be playing any further part in our dreams. I say so to
Dad, but when I turn to see what he would reply, he is
thin, like the buttery light. Like human net curtains.

There was some snow, deep in the brambles by the roadside.
Stories floated around our heads, heading off in a 'V' down the
valley, clanking.

We turned off and followed the line of electricity pylons.
Dad's ghost said "pylon" is the name for the doors between the
different rooms in the Ancient Egyptian afterlife.

Chapter Twenty-Nine ~ Binns and Hill Ltd

> ...organisms have the power to bestow 'form' on inorganic matter or on dead meat. It is this mysterious force called life that is responsible for 'thoroughly transforming' the 'edible object... into the eater.'
>
> (*Vibrant Matter*, Jane Bennett)

As we walked under the cackling lines I talked to the ghost about movies I wanted to live in. 'Spirited Away', but without the giant radish. Faded Dad said he wasn't sure if I would know any of the films he wanted to be in, and said a word, but because I didn't know the name in real life I couldn't hear it in the dream. It came out as "Blah Blah".

We passed ponds and dens, waded through scratchy ferns and into tall trees. We might end up walking round in circles forever if me and Dad both had the same shorter leg.

Somewhere off in the trees, a creaky-cranky music started up. Like when Mandy and Ben and me met Mister Binns the first time. We stopped in a little clearing, three piles of branches lay in the open space. The pipe music was coming from somewhere on the other side. Dad stopped unfolding the crinkly chocolate bar in his see-through fingers.

Suddenly the whole forest began to shake and wave and I knew what was coming. The huge shape had left the city. Bushes and ferns bashed and danced. All the different pretend characters of the forest – the fairies, the pixies, the goblins, the elves, all that crappy nonsense and stupid stuff that grown ups tell you and that actually really scares you – were churning around in the dirty yellow leaves, forming into one big swallowing shape.

I couldn't help shouting: "It's the scary man!"

Dad grabbed me before I could run. His fingers on my puffa jacket sleeve were wriggling like glass shrimps. The face of the forest shuddered and tripped forward.

Shooosh!

A scummy curtain parted and out crashed Robin Hood and his Merry Men: a man in a green Santa costume twelve feet tall and a gang of blokes dressed mostly in the same colour, with a woman in a bright red coat, pulling by the hand the most miserable man in the world, even if you included our Great Remains. This man had even given up on remaining.

"Look oo it uuurz!!!" shouted the huge, snotty Santa. Behind his shovel of a fake white beard it was the wild man, the scary man of the forest, for real. We were in the story! The green gang looked doubtful and nasty, but the wild man said: "It's all right, we know 'em." He came over to punch Dad in the shoulder and we fell over. I felt proud. Our Dad is friends with the scary man of the forest, with Green Santa, with Mister Binns himself, with Mister Everything!

"No point in goin' that way," says Mister Binns. "Us just tried again this marnin'. Day after you'm been 'ere they'm already gat the fences up! Barbed wire, the lot. The real thing – concrete posts, 'lectrified wire, and the notices, now 'ere's the clever bit: they'm *look* old!"

He shook his head and his giant's beard snaked.

"Tunnel's full o' rocks. Cam'ras on trees. We gat find another way in."

Dad said that Mum was doing research on maps and documents that might show where old mines and tunnels once were.

Was she?

He reached in his pocket, but Dad doesn't have a mobile.

The woman in red pointed her thumb. We all looked as hard as we could into the yellow.

Dad whispered that we had been followed. There'd been geese.

"And a periscope," I said.

A giant above the trees carefully placed a cup of water on the toy trunk and settled into the skeleton's chair.

Red Riding Hood said we might be being watched. The fairy roads had been ruined by railway tracks - why wouldn't they steal the steam engines and hide them under a hill? We could see them if we didn't focus our eyes.

You don't find anything if you look for it.

In the yellow-grey, I could see another, brighter, fizzier yellow, like one of those glowing vests that workmen wear. It was flapping on the body of a little man in brown overalls.

"That's Wally Eager," whispered Dad. I'd seen him somewhere before.

The wild man raised a hand for no one to speak. Dad waved and we followed. No one seemed surprised that they could see the trees through Dad's hands.

We tracked Wally Eager through the forest to where the ground began to rise. The Hill looked how I'd imagined it. Wally was crouched almost halfway up; we could just about see him lift a metal cover and lower himself in.

Once the lid had closed, Mister Binns led us up the grassy slope and we gathered round it. First he put his ear to the cover, then carefully lifted it. Beneath was a darkness into which the rungs of a metal ladder faded.

"There be light down there," Binns whispered.

The merry men went down first, then Dad, Mister Binns at a squeeze, me, the old man and his daughter. At the bottom of the ladder we found a long, cold corridor, lit a greenish blue the colour of mints that Nanna likes. The passage ran off in two directions: the bent over wild man and his gang took one, they had plots and plans. Dad led the rest of us down the other.

I had to start planning this dream. I had to face up to Mister Binns. It wasn't enough just to let it happen. I needed plots and plans of my own. But I'd realised that you could let two or more Stories run at once.

Our corridor began to drop through The Hill, just like the tricks I played on myself to get to sleep. Things were cancelling each other out. Way ahead Wally was leant over a box in the washy green wall into which he was working a long piece of wire. There was something angry about the way he was. Patting the last of the flex in place, he swung the lid of the box closed, snapped shut his tool case and disappeared through a door, letting a mild clang run down the corridor.

The door was thicker than I expected. Dad levered it opened, and the Red Sister wedged a coin in the hinges so we wouldn't get shut in. On the other side was another corridor, the same sad green, but in this one there were signs. And doors. And, far off, in the dim distance, there were people. Not wild gang people, but creepingupthecorridortowardsus people.

I had that fat feeling in my legs again. I whispered to Dad: "Did we find all the places on the list?"

"We're here." He shrugged. The list didn't mean anything.

It was easier to see the approaching faces now. They weren't the faces of piskies though, they were human. But not the usual sort. Firstly, they were all very, very old. In ordinary light they would probably have looked very, very white, like beluga whales, but under the watery blue bulbs they seemed transparent, like aquarium tanks. Their clothes were smart but very old-fashioned. Ancient. Most of them were in uniforms; some green, some blue.

When, at last, one of the old people noticed us, she seemed pleased.

"Hello," she said. "How are we feeling today?"

And all the other pale, watery faces turned to see who she was talking to.

"Is there anything you want?" one of the others asked.

I thought I heard one of the old soldiers whisper something about "disturbed", but a shush of wind blew it away.

This was the strangest place in the entire world. We moved through hundreds of elderly people, aged desk clerks, old tea boys and wrinkly typists, soldiers and officers; there were multiple copies of each one. I recognised the different models from my school book on the Blitz; but they had grown much older recently.

No one told us off, no one asked us what we were doing or explained themselves. We wandered through the corridors at the same pace as the elderly army. The men beamed at tatty maps on large wooden tables; old ladies very, very slowly typed from crumbly notes onto crisp, yellowing paper.

"Will you let us help you?" One of the typists smiled.

She had stood up and was walking unsteadily towards us. I held out a hand because that seemed the right thing to do. She didn't lean on it; instead she held and stroked it. I thought I could see another person, behind her, moving her arms.

"Hello, there, how are *you* doing today!" said a slow, hoarse voice. A thin man, holding a peaked cap against his side, was supporting himself against the jamb of the door. "Nothing to worry about, no reason to fuss," he said.

Dad had gone. The Red Sister and her dad had disappeared too. They were only ever characters to get us here. It wasn't real Dad, it was the sort of Dad that had come back from the 'fugue'. The giant Binns and the worker Wally were what was real down here. I had to finish the story with *them*.

I ran out of the room, almost knocking over the old man with the cap. There were hundreds of doors at each of which was an aged soldier who would begin to salute as I went through; each room led to more and more rooms, all of them the same – stained tables, kind old people, more old guards on the doors.

Finally, I found a door that didn't lead to a room, but to a new corridor. I tried to find a stone or something in my pockets to put in the hinge. There was some silver paper from a chocolate bar that I didn't remember eating, but the door crushed that to nothing. I went through, anyway. The lettering on the signs was odder, thicker:

EMERGENCY PLANNING

How would you plan an emergency?

Beyond the door, more rooms, inside the rooms were again the same tables, chairs, guards, posters about the end of the world. But there were also huge rooms now, their signs said: 'Cinema', 'Library', 'Reading Room', 'Canteen' and 'Quarters'. All of these were empty and in darkness. Their lights worked, once I'd felt around for the switches, which fell with a loud hunk and ching. In these rooms the posters had gone but you could see their shadows. I went from room to room, wondering if I really wanted to go into the final one: "'Mortuary'.

Its light switch fell with the same damp clunk, and there was a moment, before the bulb fizzed, when I thought I heard dead bodies stir themselves inside greaseproof paper bags and flesh scrape on table tops. But the room was no different from 'Cinema' or 'Library': neatly swept and completely empty.

Jump forward.

Jump back.

I felt fat arms again. I pushed myself along, like the hospital machine pushed the sheets. At the door I could see old ladies carrying away piles of videos.

"Hey!" I wanted to shout – but I choked on invisible smoke. "Those are D...d...!!!"

I felt the hug of their big, red, watery eyes and I could hear them arguing among themselves about "experts" and "letting the doctors do their job".

The only door I hadn't tried didn't have a sign and was so warped and twisted around itself that it was bigger at the bottom than at the top. I pushed gently. The light was already on and in the middle of the room, seated at a large desk was the oldest man I had ever seen. He was one big white wrinkle, his eyes and nose and mouth almost swallowed up in crumples of skin.

"Hello", said The Wrinkle. "Will you let us help you?"

"If I can", I said, as Dad would want me to.

"What's wrong, my darling?"

I told him about the Frogs.

"I see", said The Wrinkle and he stroked the badge on his cap. "Leave it to me." He tried to stand, but couldn't and fell back in his seat. He looked around him. He had the same posters on his walls as I had on mine.The eyes and the teeth that had emerged like crabs from shells retreated into their crumpled machines.

"Do my best..." he mumbled.

Outside, a chattering, yelling wave of pent up energy came rattling through the corridors. Wally Eager, gripping the edges of the 'Ops' room door, was shouting instructions and waving his electricity repair clipboard. The wild man and his Mummers came running through the rooms. I saw Wally step away from them. The huge wild man's beard flopped on his massive chest, hanging by a single piece of elastic. The merry men dragged heavy sacks. They pulled one of the telephones from the wall and ran off. What were they? I saw Dad wander past the door. Our journey was churning around and around underground. People began to pack things away. This was the end for The Hill. It had realised that I had realised.

"Hey!"

A very old Ben was walking across the room, his freckly arms held out in front of him in a strange clutching shape.

"Is that you?" he said to a shape of nothingness in the shadows that now turned its mustardy head, black soot rising from its matted hair, smoke drifting from its mouth. Things were getting mixed up. There were too many Stories loose. I hadn't got time now to tie all the ends together as well as sorting out everything else! I'd got to cut out some of these things, before Wally the Caretaker swept me up with his broom of knives. I sort of wished and Mum came rushing in, wearing the Sister's bright red coat, filling up the space with "happy" and "wonderful", and "miracle" and "family", as the room was cleared of phones and maps and boards.

"You can't stay down here," Mum was saying.

An emptier man was making a big speech about what a disgrace modern life was. He said we should burrow further down.

"You're not well," Mum said to me.

I couldn't think of anything that had happened since I walked into the unnecessary room at our Great Remaining Relatives. I should have heard sirens and hooters, but all I could hear was the tinny 'beep beep' from the smoke detector in our downstairs hall.

I wanted to slip away, back into the minty light of the corridors. But Wally Eager was there, shouting: "I can keep it all going!" He tried to usher the army back to their desks, but they slipped very slowly past him. The care-taker of souls was in dead trouble. And that meant he was dangerous. I had to keep his eyes away from me.

I peered around the door. Why had I been so happy among these old people? I looked at the dark shapes where the posters had been – "Pink was there," I said to myself, "the dolphins there, the Wallace Collection there..." Everything was a horrible version of something else. I let the Stories hover around me for a while, like swarms of helicopters, with no need to push the button, only to Remain. I just "needed to rest", then I'd get better. But the care-taker was here, and the whole thing was turning into pretend. How was I supposed to "rest"?

In the corridor the old people still had things to clear away, but they'd started chatting and laughing. They began to lean against the walls and tell stories. I knew where this was and I knew what this was. This was the crescent with the monkey puzzle tree, the snow and the Christmas crackers. These were my Great Relatives in the olden days, when Mum was my age, and the fire was glowing and we were sinking back into the soft armchairs and eating mince pies. The tape was running backwards. First Ben had been old, but now the Great Relatives were young again, and I was Mum when she was a little girl, when there was no Dad.

Behind the glass of the viewing gallery a large man, his grey moustache flaring upwards, his eyebrows like ashes, was holding out his arms, palms upwards. Beneath the gallery, I saw a movement in what I'd thought was an empty space. Two old ladies, one in a green uniform, the other in a pinny like Nanna's, were moving a section of the floor back into place. Before the gap closed I saw something like the edge of a grass sports field or a huge green carpet. As the section clicked into place, they turned to check they hadn't been watched, but saw me looking. I expected them to exchange looks, but they didn't need to. The old lady in the pinny smiled and the one in the green uniform winked, both put their right hands over their right eyes and disappeared behind a curtain I'd not noticed before. It was the insect people, the Japanese hunters, the seekers of angels. Even down here we were organised, even here I was part of something, part of the organising of space.

I took a careful step into the corridor and, without warning, Wally swung round the corner explaining something to Dad, who now popped up at his side. Wally saw me and winked.

"Ah, Alice, I was wondering where I'd find you – look! It's Wally Eager, just the same Wally as before!"

"But Dad, you said..."

"I know, but I was mad then. Wally's been telling me the most amazing things... Alice, this isn't the real bunker, this is just the top layer... it goes down and down and down... and on each layer they think they're the real thing, they don't realise that there's a deeper organisation under theirs - it's just like you said!!"

But that wasn't what I'd said.

"Dad, I'm scared. I don't like him. We saw him in town. He's not a 'splorer, Dad. He's a caretaker. He collects things. He's trying to keep you underground."

"It's all a misunderstanding, Paul. She's young, she's smart. She's put two and two together and made seventy seven. That's... how many levels I've found."

Dad turned to Wally and showed him his doubt.

"Well, not 'found' exactly. Deduced. I need you to help me with my researches. I've talked to some of the folk here and they talk about a completely modern layer, about five down..."

"Really? That's amazing..."

Don't be taken in, Dad, don't let him take you down there.

"... but what are they for, Wally? Exactly? Your researches?"

Wally moved between Dad and me. Over Wally's shoulder I fixed onto Dad's uncertain eyes and I cut the air with my flattened hand.

"Dad..." I knew I had to break the rules of The Hill. "I know that you... lied to me because you needed to. Or there would have been nothing." It was a big risk. "It's the same with him."

Dad turned to his old friend, and I saw something rising. He was coming back!

Wally half-raised his right arm and with a flattened hand he cut the air. He didn't even bother to turn round to score the point, but at the third cut the hand began to direct stragglers in the corridor back to their desks.

"Please, Dad... it's ghosts he's interested in. Do you see how everything is so *nothing* here? These are places for collecting things that aren't going to cause trouble anymore. And you'll be part of his collection if you don't stop him!"

I didn't see Dad's reaction, because Mum woke me up. It was daylight outside, although the curtains were closed and the landscape patterns in the material glowed like film locations.

Mum brought me up my medicine. She tried to rush me taking it, in case Dad caught us.

"I have to go to sleep, Mum..."

"Just take the big tablet..."

"No, it's a really important bit. I have to save Dad."

"You can't save Daddy, lovely. You need all your energy to save you – go on, take the tablet and remember - it's all about you..."

I took the tablet and as I was passing it from my hand into my mouth I saw that it was grey and shaped like a tiny submarine. I didn't need to swallow it. It swam down my throat, 'sploring inside.

Wally shouted his orders again. To stay at our posts and carry on. A few of the old people tapped at the phones but the lines were dead as before. There was nothing to carry on *with*. It was time to get out of Dad's stupid Hill. It was a secret for the sake of one.

"Fire the missiles!"

As Wally screamed his order he thumped on the tables, pushed an old lady here, an old man there, shouting into their faces. Even though I'm only nine I felt really angry with him. But I knew that it would only add to all the bad under The Hill if I tried to shout, if I tried to hit and kick. A cloud as rough and big as a duvet was stuck in my mouth. I squeezed my hands into fists to force the dream to DO SOMETHING!

Dad came rushing into the room. He was wearing his fireman's uniform and carrying his axe. He chopped Wally down like a tree. Wally shook for a moment and keeled over. The old people grumbled, but they weren't Remaining now. The last untidy things of ours were picked up from beside the skirting board. Wally, lying flat on the floor, was shouting at Dad about handing him over to the army for "professional treatment". Dad was saying that I would get better, quicker on my own. "A change and a rest."

It was a trick!! Wally Eager wasn't my Mum or anyone else. Dad had invented him so he could beat him. This was my dream, but these were Dad's tricks. He'd got inside my head and set me all these missions so I'd end up believing what he told me! His uniform began to peel off. I could see right through him! Dad had taught me too well! I could hear myself shouting these thoughts, but no one else was taking any notice, there were so many other voices in the room, all telling the others to shut up, and that I needed to hear just one voice, and that I needed quiet and calm, and just to "do nothing", and then it would start all over again with them arguing about "something that needed to be done" and who was to be the one, quiet, calm voice that I needed to hear. In the middle of all this Wally Eager and Dad were pulling and pushing each other around the map table.

How had I got on the map table?

Dad knelt beside me. "Don't worry, lovely, I won't let them catch you." He pushed me off the table and lay down in my place.

The ancient yellowing man pushed Wally away and stuck his thumb on the middle of the map. With his nail he ripped its surface.

"They're going to spoil everything," I said to Dad.

Dad was breathless. He sat up and choked, smoke crept from his lips. I wondered if it was OK for someone who once swallowed a cloud to be down here. I looked over the edge of the tabletop and the mist had climbed halfway up its legs.

"We need you out of here."

The old man in the stitched and patched green uniform and the peaked cap jumped to his feet, clicking his heels together as he rose from the swirling smog.

"Prepare to evacuate the facility!" he announced and gave a huge, slow wink.

Behind the glass screen, the man with the big grey moustache shook his arms as if paddling words. The old people jerked in a choreographic shudder. I felt a wave shift frequency and I began to move with it. In the corner of my eye I saw Wally Eager heading down a set of stairs that had appeared at the far end of the room. A draught of air seemed to blow open door after door down and down through the layers of The Hill. I glimpsed for a moment many different rooms, with the same lighting as the stadium for the Ladies International: filled with massive versions of the unnecessary room – but instead of the mist of tired breath in the cold night air, there was the smoke of a factory, churning out lies about everything and everywhere. And following the caretaker into this machine was a slow stream of glassy-eyed and uniformed elderly.

"Wally Eager was what I was before I met Mum," said Dad. "But I know what's different from then - I have responsibilities. Not to disappear."

The elderly army was now streaming through the room, and, shakily, down the stairs to the layers beneath, an ants' nest on the march, old arms carrying things that were far too big for them, attic after attic stripped by trembling hands. As we tried to weave – where to? – through the army, the gentle flow from the different rooms held us back, and we gave up and allowed ourselves to be moved by the aged current.

We checked each layer as we passed down through it. Dad said to try to keep in our heads a picture of what was once there and how things had once been. But the picture I kept getting was the diagram of moles' burrows from my Learning magazine.

"It's no trouble coming out to help in a time of need."

It was the lady typist who had held my hand.

"And how are you doing at school? What's your favourite subject? And do they still teach you manners? And have you got a big family? And what are you hoping to get for Christmas?"

Dad gave me a 'don't let me down' stare.

"It's OK, thanks. History. Yes, but it is called something else now. No, only me and Mum and Ben, but he's naughty now so he's not part of our family, o, and Great Great Auntie Beryl and Great Great Uncle Tony, and Nanna and Gramps, of course. Bratz and a painting set."

I saw the old lady's fingers close more tightly on Dad's arm. She looked far ahead, as if she could see great things and far off lands. The stairs ran into a corridor. As the crowd surged politely onto it, a huge cavern unfolded in front of us, its ceiling way above us, its floor far below, and in the depths, in a carpet of greenish steam, like kids lined up for school assembly, were uneven rows of smoking, hissing, shining, sparkling STEAM ENGINES.

I'd forgotten about them.

It wasn't just the engines. The whole cavernous hall was magical. I had put my head into a massive brilliant spar box. Precious gems sparkled in the walls. And by the sides of the huge engines were piles of jewels; even in the dimness they dazzled. The jewels were being crushed down into powder by old men using the backs of their shovels, and then fed, as dust, into the furnaces of the engines. Out of the trains' chimneys was pouring the mist, the green, minty mist. I knew where this was – the Cloud Factory, the universe underground, this was the place where our problems had begun and our dreams been woven. Where they'd used things they shouldn't have and smashed them into the stuff that Dad had swallowed, the mist that stops you seeing what's really on the other side of yourself. The Thing that keeps you in unnecessary rooms.

Down below I could see the old man pulling a trolley of Dad's things from my bedroom, making ripples in the green vapour. Like luggage at an airport. The man stopped and began to load the things through a door into one of the carriages. He looked up and blinked. Dad had got it all wrong when he'd said that the trains were dead. They were shiny and ready and fired up! A few old people were already in the carriages, while knee deep in mist others were polishing the name plates and shovelling crystal dust. Old men in overalls clustered around the engines, crouched like Wally Eager over his box of wires. Everywhere there was the hiss of steam, the hunk and ching of metal on metal, and the raw screech of flames. Through it all the sleepy old army wandered, mostly ignoring the carriages and disappearing down exit stairs to the next layer.

"We're leaving now," the old lady typist whispered. And she began to lead me by the hand away from the army. Our train was the first on the line. Behind ours were three or four other trains, stretching into the shadows, and then more and more on track after track, all pointing to one single set of rails out of The Hill. "Very good idea," said Dad, and he began to help the old lady and me up the steps. It wasn't like the carriages on modern trains. There were benches around the walls.

"Not exactly Pullman, is it, dearie?"

Dad said: "They're really for supplies, Alice."

"O – "Alice"! What a lovely name! What do you think of our Wonderland?"

And I said that I thought it was the best Wonderland that

there had ever been, even counting EuroDisney. Dad looked disapprovingly, but the old lady backed me up: "O, I know what EuroDisney is, darling!"

A yellow flap of shiny vest shot through the steam outside. Dad leapt straight out of the carriage. Wally Eager was screaming at our driver and at another man and he began to pull them from the engine. The two elderly men did their best to fight back, but before Dad could reach them one came bumping down the metal rungs of the ladder and fell into the mist.

Dad leapt straight up the rungs, holding his hand out to the driver and placing himself between him and the ranting Wally. The driver fell back against the controls of the train. There was a huge flare of flames and sparks and cinders. Billows of emerald, sapphire and ruby smoke erupted round the cab, swallowing Dad, Wally and the old driver, swelling bigger than the train itself. Throbbing on its surface, the cloud winked as it began to mushroom above the engine; wriggling across its swelling surface were what looked like thousands of fireflies or maybe burning helicopters. I remembered, from Dad's story, the cigarette light in the shadows. Wally had been behind that too.

For a while, time didn't work properly. Dad, who had once swallowed a cloud, had now been swallowed by one. He had disappeared again. A flare of orange lit up the smoke and went out. The cloud became still and began to thin, floating in strands towards the cavern roof, releasing the fireflies with strange popping sounds.

At last Dad reappeared, covered in brownish ash, a rag from somewhere held over his mouth and nose. In his arms was the old man who had fallen, his eyes closed, his mouth shut tight, the ash on his face like a mask. Dad carried him down from the engine and up to our carriage, lifting him on board. The old man let out a big "phew" of relief, farted and lay still.

"I'm the fireman now!" Dad was shouting, holding up a shovel full of black crystals. Making fire, not putting it out. The lady typist and me shouted and cheered. At last we could go home! Dad began shovelling and the bruised and dusty driver began to turn wheels and pull levers.

At the end of the cavern, next to the mouth of the only tunnel

out, stood the huge-moustachioed commander, down from his
glass booth. There, beside him, wrapped in a soldier's green
cloak, and prodding the commander with a twig-like forefinger,
was The Wrinkle. The commander nodded, his moustache
nodded, he raised his speckled hand, but before it could fall, he
and The Wrinkle were showered with burning helicopters and
they began to singe. All around old people were bursting into
flames. The piles of crystals were going off like fireworks
squirting multi-coloured sparks, carriages were beginning to
glow and melt. The mist on the floor of the cave was turning
brown and rising. And wading through this chaos, as if they were
on a shopping trip, were Robin Hood and His Merry Men, Mister
Monster Binns and his Magic Mummers, Spike and the Big Boys
Gang, escorting a wheelbarrow full of jewels towards the mouth
of the tunnel.

"Why do you have to take the bits that keep this all going?" I
shouted. I got down from the carriage, because Dad wasn't there
to stop me. I didn't want to half come back like Dad.

"Why do you have to take treasures that will spoil everything
everywhere else?"

"You'm weren't gonna use 'em, you'm only complain now *us*
'ave 'em – now you'm gone all artistic!"

"I'm nine!" I said.

And it seemed to echo round the cave, above the shouts and
the roar of flame coming up like orange curtains hauled by a
clean-sheet machine. I took a step closer to the Monster,
standing straight like I was in the choir. He straightened too and
winked like stars. All around us carriages were burning.

"We need to move!" I said. "You have to come with us! And
and and!!! If we leave anyone behind, then we will never..."

I knew that there was SOMETHING that we would "never".
There was definitely SOMETHING. It had to do with the
machine, the bits of the engine, that if one screw came loose,
then everything flopped around, flapping like an injured bird.
And with a person it was the same. It was why Dad hadn't really
come home yet and why Monster Mister Binns had to come with
us now. He was our guarantee of everything. I pulled at the
bottom of his fake white beard. It snagged and I thought for a

moment it was real. It came away and it was Dad's face underneath. Dad – a massive Dad who had never *wanted* to come home.

"Now you'm done it, young lady!"

Behind Big Mister Binns the Merry Men were burning like candles. The Monster snatched his beard and hastily snapped the elastic back around his ears. But there was a firefly in it now, and Santa was red at last. Binns was right: I'd done it. Huge flames were lifting everywhere like the red velvet curtains at the panto.

The show was about to begin!

"Let's get out of here!!" And with a big harrumph our engine jerked forward, a clatter running through the train from front to back. I could feel all the connections. "And and and!" shouted the couplings. I looked back and all the carriages were on fire, flames were licking at cargo from the Cinema, Library, Emergency Planning, Operations and Mortuary.

At the window the typist was waving, shakily but wildly. The great engine at the head gave another huge shrug and shook its carriages forward. All the trains were now attached to ours. All aflame. The smoke had reached my neck. I had to decide.

Running through the mist, I had no idea what it was I was running on.

The steps to the carriage got higher and higher as the train began to pick up speed. Why didn't Dad slow down? And then I remembered – he never slowed down, he always had things to do, at home, at work, even when I was tired out and had the stitch he always walked ahead, shouting at me to catch up. Telling me to "walk it off". I was running as fast as I could. I was alongside the steps now, but they were too high. I was going to miss the only train out. One stumble now and ... I felt my toe catch on something small, something that slid under my tread, I was pitching forward, my mouth nearly in the brown smoke, I flung out my arms for balance, the trip seemed to speed me up and I was rising, I was careering upwards, I saw my knees and then my ankles appearing from the smoke, the bottom rung of the train steps was lower than my waist now, and, as my trainers finally reappeared I saw beneath them a flash of purple, then yellow, red and green.

I was running on jewels, running up a mound of gems.

I jumped.

Inside the carriage the old lady typist was clinging half to her seat and half to the old, still, expressionless driver.

HARRUMPH, HUMPH, HUMPH, HARRUMPH, HAAAAARUMPH, HAAAAAAAARUMPH!

With great, shuddering jerks we seemed to pull ourselves free of the flames. I could see them shaken back along the trackside, re-gathering. Up ahead, old men in blue overalls, flares leaping from their hair, were pulling down on a long lever, lines of metal were moving to allow us onto the main track. Thin and freckly hands clutched a little tighter and a great burp of green crystal smoke shot up to the ceiling of the cavern as we began to pick up serious speed.

The old lady slammed the window shut so we didn't suffocate in the tunnel. By its mouth, the commander and The Wrinkle were mostly mist now. Mister Binns, inhaling everything, his huge face, white beard and all, rising out of the smoke, a pillar of circle and square. Suddenly, the light of the cavern disappeared behind us and we were in darkness. The volume control on the crunching and panting was turned right up. I thought I could hear the high, thin voice of the old lady somewhere. I felt her hand on my arm, cold and scared. I reached out and found her other hand and we squeezed.

It wouldn't be long now. Not at this speed. But the darkness just went on and on and on.

Then I remembered something – something that was holding everything up. Something that meant that there was no way to carry on the story AND get out of the Hill... because, in Dad's story, when they're following the old steel railway track through the trees and into the tunnel, they reach up, they reach up and they touch the ceiling of the tunnel, they can feel the tiles! Dad had dreamed the tunnel too small!

There was a clang, and a vicious shaking, first one way and then the other, a sound like grit under a door, the train shuddered hard and, and, and burst from darkness into light with a terrible grinding yowl! White tiles, in savage splinters, spat and cut the green till it bled red soil streams.

The old people in the carriages screamed. Partly delight, mostly fear. They covered their eyes. In chattering voices they told each other, above the screaming metal, how they could not believe how bright the light was. I wondered if the sun had got hotter while we'd been underground.

Around us the fields were vivid green, bright like food colouring. We were slicing wildly through the surface of the huge cake. The tracks were buried here, grown over by grass, but the steel wheels of our steam engine were feeling them out. And where the soil was ploughed by our wheels, it came up the same red as moulding clay, looked as good as Easter Egg chocolate.

Ganesha was the god of this place, god of all that is sweet and escapes from bad things.

I looked ahead, and we were turning over the field like a farmer would, putting a red slash through the whole countryside, aiming an arrow towards the city. No one would laugh at Dad when we ploughed up the truth and showed them the hidden tracks all the way up the High Street!

A tiny tremor, inside the continuing metal howl, nudged the train a little. Points, maybe. Then another tremor. A sheep perhaps?

Then we hit a mountain.

We all leapt into the air. I hit my head on the window frame. The old lady typist seemed about to fly, but caught the edge of the window and swung like a skinny monkey. Then a horrible sound, like a million of Dad's beer cans being scrunched up. For a moment we seemed to go even faster. As if we'd come off the axles and were sliding along like a massive metal toboggan! I heard the deep, unnatural squeals of cows panicking. The sun shook and leapt from one side of the carriage to the other. I was in the air again, but flying backwards this time. I hit the back of the carriage, next to the old dead driver, and all the air burst out of me in a big 'hunk!'

This wasn't like Spike Binns' crash – this time there was going to be clunking and hissing and clouds of steam.

The world stopped suddenly, jerking us forward, but fixing *everything else*. We were all flung down to the front of the carriage. Outside, the fields were fields again. Cows were cows. The sun was stuck, right way up. My nose was bent against the wood and when I tried to sit up a warm throb of pain ran up my back like an electric toy. On the window were little blobs that when touched made pink streaks over the green outside.

My head began to ache.

The roof had stopped caving in and the old lady typist was still hanging on to part of it, the toes of her old fashioned shoes just touching the floor of the carriage.

I tried to say "jump", but it hurt to think in words.

The old man was stretched out in the middle of the carriage as if he'd been carefully laid there. Big sheets of steam waved past the window and turned into nothing above the fields.

I knew the train was ruined. One of the outside doors had come off its hinges. I wanted to be in the green field, picking its icing-sugar blades. It took a long time for my head to let me. And then I had to hold it, like a Celtic water goddess, to stop it falling off. I wondered if anything would grow from the smear of blood.

I didn't get as far as the door before I was in the field. The grass had come into the carriage. The broken doorway had gouged up a great chunk of it and I walked on its softness out into the sunlight.

A cold wind hit me so hard I almost fell.

There were other people in the field by now. I saw Dad. He was laid out in the grass, carefully, like the old driver. I couldn't speak, but I could wave and I pointed to the train. I didn't want Dad to go away. Ever again.

The front of the train was buried in the earth, only the top of its chimney exposed, gasping smoke as if *it* had now swallowed the cloud.

I looked the other way and I could see the hole we'd ripped out of side of The Hill. We were nowhere near the city. It would start to get dark soon and the kids from the big school would be in the High Street. They'd be waiting for us, picking on someone else for practice.

The Hill stood there – stupid, no help at all. As if it was all suddenly going to get better on its own. Just like that.

"Come on, Alice," said the old lady. "It's time to come back to us."

Chapter Thirty ~ The End

Each new short cut you discover redraws your map of the
city, connecting the places that before were separate,
making the city more porous and more yours.
(*Sweep and Veer: Short Cuts & Intimate Routes Around
Norwich*, Townley & Bradby)

"You can't just tell her like that!" Mum was saying.

The weird thing about getting better is that it seems to
happen in a completely different way to getting ill. Getting ill
happens really quickly and dramatically and everyone gets very
excited and they tell you what they think is wrong with you, and
then while you're sick it's like a battle against time with winning
and losing, but then when you're getting better it's like no one's
trying any more and they're just letting things happen on their
own. No one seems to mind how long you take doing things, you
can waste as much time as you want. And no one can remember
anything, either. No one wants you to talk about why you got ill,
or how you got better, they just want you to do it, magically, in a
weird bedroom space where no one cares about timetables.

So, without time, getting better is all about coming back to
space.

At first I could make out its shape. There was a big rectangle
of light. And blobs that moved. Certain fixed things. A chair.
Then two chairs. Books on my shelves so tightly packed that they
didn't look like they were there for reading. I tried to work out
what the pattern was. Why did J. K. Rowling come before
Michael Morpurgo? It wasn't alphabetical order, but there was
something.

"I told you she wouldn't like it," a voice was saying.

In my dream I remembered not being able to remember
anything after visiting the unnecessary room at the Great
Remains. Maybe I'd broken down there, got stuck there, and
everything after that was the dream? Why else would Great

Auntie Beryl and Great Uncle Tony be bending over me now like crinkly velociraptors, stalking me from both sides?

And where was Dad? Hadn't he carried me out of Drama Club? Or had I imagined that and dressed him in all those costumes?

I realised about the books. They'd been arranged according to colours. The blues flooding down from the top left until around the middle where they became purple and then red, bloodiest at the bottom right.

"Can you hear us, dear?"

Is this what a ghost at a séance feels like? I considered tapping on the wall with a hand under the duvet, but I saw a whole new story growing; a feathery thing on huge legs that would run off among crackling trees and never be caught.

"Hello, Great Great Beryl."

That wasn't quite right, but she smiled. Not quite the old vulture smile she usually had, but something she'd been saving up for a rainy day and was spending now.

"What are you doing here?"

The dolphin was arching out of the blue, blue water. Pink was still posing. It was my bedroom.

"Mummy's at work, Alice. Uncle Tony and I are looking after you today. We all take turns, dear."

I was a camp they were guarding.

Great Uncle Tony coughed, as if he couldn't think of any better noise to make. Great Auntie Beryl shot him a look like a harpoon, but when she looked back it had fallen away and the smile had returned.

"We've been with you a long time, dear."

"I've been away," I said.

"Yes, but you're back now, thank God." And she really was thanking God.

"Would she like anything?" suggested Great Uncle Tony. He couldn't quite bring himself to speak to me except through an interpreter.

"Go and make yourself useful, then – what do you want, dear? Squash? Fizzy?"

"Tea, please?"

"O, very grown up. We've been giving you the wrong thing obviously. Tony?" And her face sharpened again. "Sweet!!" she shouted at his back as he sloped off. "Take no notice of him, Alice, he's too shy to show you how much he's enjoyed looking after you. He's always been up, trying to find out what you'd like, fetching you water, asking you questions."

I thought of The Wrinkle and the old people on guard.

"Where's Dad?"

"O, he's... Mummy will explain."

I looked out of the window - the curtains were drawn right back – at a clear blue sky. I wondered if Dad was 'flying a desk' now. There was no cloud in the whole frame. In the distance I could hear the angry buzz of the police helicopter. But no desks.

The light fell around the room, stretching it out. It seemed far bigger than before. There was so much in it and everything so detailed, so sharp. It had to be as big as a football stadium to get it all in. The door seemed a mile away. No wonder Great Uncle Tony was taking so long with the tea.

"We've been here ever such a long time, you know, dear."

"Thank you," I said, detecting that that was what was asked for.

I suppose I'd hoped for a Wizard of Oz ending with all the family gathered round the bed and me recognising them from my dream. "And you were the commander and you were the typist and you were one of the merry men..." I wasn't even sure about Great Uncle Tony and The Wrinkle, now. The more I listened to Great Auntie Beryl and looked around the room the further and further away the dream was slipping. It wanted to be off, to be doing something other somewhere else, it didn't want to hang around here drinking sweet tea and having to behave for the Great Relatives. I let it go.

Later that day, as I was sitting up in bed eating macaroni cheese with strong cheddar on the top – Great Auntie Beryl's recipe, I'm sure there's sugar in it, she's like an ancient McDonalds – Mum and Dad repeated their appearance at 'A Christmas Carol'. Mum waving Dad in. Dad wearing a suit with tiny lines running down it, as if it were made from giant feathers.

"Hello, big lovely!"

He gave me a huge hug and I felt along his back to make sure he was real.

"Is Ben still not part of the family, Mum?"

"What on earth do you mean, darling?"

"He did bad things and he had to leave the family..."

"No, darling, Ben is still part of our family. I think our family's got bigger not smaller... and closer as well..."

Dad ever so slightly flinched.

"Where is he then?"

"He's at Woodcraft Folk, lovely."

O, right. So, the dream wasn't any more true than anything else.

Dad had sat on the bed and it was creaking.

"Careful with the bed, Tony... Ben... er...." Great Auntie Beryl had done that thing that adults do when they run through loads of names before they get the right one. Like they show you that they don't actually think about *you* until they have to fit the name. I thought Dad would get really angry and say something, but he seemed to actually enjoy being annoyed and he swapped a quick smile with Mum. They never did that before. It was too good to be true.

"Are Great Auntie Beryl and Great Uncle Tony living with us, now?" I asked Mum.

"No, no, darling, they've just been very, very lovely to you, looking after you when I've been at work."

I looked at Dad. The hero. He was doing something else now.

He shrugged. Great Uncle Tony raised his eyes, Great Auntie Beryl tightened her smile.

Dad was fine. Old Dad, same Dad. He wouldn't change.

I remembered now....

Mum had taken us to say goodbye to Dad. She'd meant hello.

It was at an another art gallery. The entrance was like where you wait for planes for going on holiday, but they didn't want to see our passports. You just went to a desk and they told you where the person was and in what war. Dad was in Drake's War, the lady said.

Inside were the galleries; they were long and thin and the paintings and the special photographs and the labels were on the walls. Just like the not-so-private view, everyone was ignoring them.

They'd brought Dad here from the fire in the place inside with all the smoke. Where Dad had breathed in the whole place, Mum said. Mum said they'd found him lying outside, very poorly, very still. And that we were something something something something something. Blah Blah.

Dad was in a room, but there was no guard on the door. No old ladies. No veiny soldiers. He wasn't in his costume. And they had taken his boots. Mum said he was so clean because they had washed him, but in the cloud place he had been very sooty.

There was more art on the walls, but no one else but me seemed interested. So I didn't even mention it. Not even the print of the dead huntress, with the angles and the bow, the plan and the plot, the men around the laptop, laughing by the cars.

We said hello to Dad. But he couldn't reply yet because of the cloud inside. He had to stay very, very still, keeping his mouth open so it could all come out slowly.

I thought maybe he wasn't talking because he was sulking – Mum had said he didn't like the gallery system.

The system made him look like a place. Like a big empty airfield on the top of the hills.

I told the young lady that I thought Dad would like to have his fireman costume on again. She said: "yes". And she wasn't just saying that because later in the High Street we saw Dad in it.

Mandy had held my hand in the car. She said she had known what we had been doing. Our Mum had told her Mum. And all the time she'd been imagining where we were.

As we drove away, The Hill began to drop behind the trees.

"We were under that hill," I pointed. "Dad was under That Hill. He was a fireman bringing out all the people who were trapped in there."

And I wondered if, even though I hadn't really described it properly, that that's what Dad's mission had been all along – to save a world?

"Poor ghosts," said Mandy, as the last bit of Hill disappeared. "They'll be getting hungry soon."

Mandy's Dad dropped us off at the Art Gallery. Mum had rung on her mobile and she'd said that she had something to show us and that she'd meet us.

Afterwards we walked back through the town. By the Riddle Spike.

As we walked, I went through the list. **Dreamscape** – was that the broken bedstead we'd passed on the hill where we saw the spire framed? **McCurdey**, something that isn't what it seems, like the funfair dummy that turned out to be the body of an actual cowboy? **Geometrical Space** – the big store at the end of the High Street. **New Menhir** - the Riddle Spike! **Revolutionary playgrounds** – hmmmm...

The train hadn't reached the High Street. It had stopped where no one would see it and now 'they' would cover it with sheets and keep people off with tape, and after a while it would disappear. Maybe that was because we hadn't completed the list.

"But Wally Eager was real, wasn't he, Mum? That bit was true!"

Mum shook her head. I hadn't expected that. I'd only asked her so she could say "yes".

Now I looked about for the frogs.

"I said before, darling. Wally was a fictional character. Your father made him up more than 20 years ago. There are thousands of Wally Eager's – people tend to think that coincidences are more unusual than they really are..."

"Where's your plank then, missus?"

It was the frogs, on cue.

"Actually", I said, "we did discover something, actually – a very large hole, actually..."

The frogs were hopping again.

"No, honestly, it was virtually a city, but under the ground... and back to front..."

The frogs reached new heights.

"Yes, yes - there were tanks. And fire engines! Hundreds of fire engines, waiting for... a crisis."

One of the frogs put his finger in his mouth and made a 'plop' noise, sending his companions into a jig.

I hadn't seen tanks or fire engines, so why did I say it? I suppose they must have had some, if it was a real Reserve for an actual crisis. I just hadn't thought about them at the time.

"Where was this?" one of the frogs asked.

"Come along", said Mum.

"The Early Learning Centre!" another answered.

"Your Dad's a loony! He's found a hole... with tanks! In his hole!!"

The frogs had collected quite a crowd.

"Mum, please, let's get out."

I was trying to pull Mum away. But she was trying to pull me. We were stuck.

"I'm going to explain..."

The crowd edged a little closer. The frogs stepped back. They knew they could rely on Mum to make a fool of herself even without their help. This was how it all worked. There were frogs everywhere. Green, sad, lonely and stupid things that could only think in a pack, could only smile when someone else was suddenly hurt as bad as they felt, could only feel real when they were showing off the lies they made us live.

People in the crowd were already chuckling. But others looked angry, glancing from Mum to us, as if *we'd* done something wrong to make this happen to us.

Mum had just reached "shock... coming to terms... some respect, please... I know your head teacher personally..." when a line of red, like a crossing out on a spelling test, filled the far end of the High Street.

"RINGARINGARINGARINGA!"

A lonely town crier come to announce our humiliation to the High Street.

RINGARINGARINGARINGARINGA!
RINGARINGARINGARINGARINGA!
RINGARINGARINGARINGARINGA!
RINGARINGARINGARINGARINGA!
RINGARINGARINGARINGARINGA!
RINGARINGARINGARINGARINGA!

RINGARINGARINGARINGARINGA!
RINGARINGARINGARINGARINGA!

A thousand town criers!! All in their bright robes!!

The crowd turned towards the cacophony of bells, fanning out as they were hit by the waves of sound. Between the dispersing shoppers I saw not town criers nor red robes, but three abreast, row after row after row, fire engine after fire engine. Ringing their old bells. The old drivers in the old uniforms. The people of the underground city in the heart of the clone city, for everyone to see.

I thought the whole world might suddenly flip, like Dad had said the whole planet would someday soon, and the North would be South, and the South would be North, and the sky above would be the roots underground.

"He said that!! He said that there would be fire engines, Mum!! Look at them, they must be a hundred years old!! He said that!!"

The frogs shrivelled on hot stones.

"Look at those old drivers!!"

The crowd gasped in ripples as they saw the salt white faces, marbled with excited pink and violet veins. In the cab of the nearest engine, the commander with the giant moustache was saluting us! The Wrinkle sat by his side prodding in our direction! And next to them was a very old Dad, in his costume now, in his boots.

"They've come from under the ground!! Our Dad was there!"

Dad had turned the whole High Street into a huge **Z World**! In front of the last minute Christmas shoppers was a whole universe uncovered! And we'd almost completed the list!

Stories ran up and down the High Street, a wild Chinese Whispers, accurate enough for a thousand or more shoppers to stop and stare into the pavement, willing their eyes to be X-ray beams, stumbling, and re-adjusting, at the thought of what might have always been beneath them.

"Whatever next!!" said a lady with a big, old-fashioned shopping bag, which cannoned into Ben.

As if in answer, a tank in the centre of the fire engines, a gun metal Sea Slater escaped from its tunnel, began to slew to one side, sweeping one engine backwards and heading towards the edge of the gathering crowds, who turned and fled as quickly as they had surged forward. The elderly man, whose head and shoulders poked from the tank, was yelling down the hole he was standing in, and the tank wound left and then right, but rather than slowing it began to gather speed, sending the crowds leaping and diving again. Just missing a travel agents, the tank hiccupped over a kerb and onto the little square, pushing aside a statue that seemed to wave it on its way. The old head had disappeared from above the tank now, the opening was sealed. The tank speeded up across the flat surface of the square, bent right, ploughing the pavements, and then left again, turning up more slabs, and headed for the glassy front of the new shops.

We could all see the people behind the glass. We could see them notice. We could see their faces. Their eyes were swimming, panicked fish watching a cat swooping towards their glass bowl. They were disappearing deep into the building, a shoal of horror-filled tails, as the tank clipped the Riddle Spike, turning it on its side, a silver ice cream cone dropped by a giant robot, then smashed into the glass front, bringing it down like falling water, splashing and leaping on the pavement, sweeping across the square in waves of sparkling splinters.

From the far pavement, we saw the tank burrow deeper inside The Ziggurat. A piece of green and yellow camouflage in the shining city, a piece of the countryside burying itself into the new foundations. The tank seemed to slow, turning in a circle, bringing down more walls and screens. A clothes shop on the first floor abruptly collapsed into the main entrance hall, an explosion of falling reds and blues. Coats and jeans. The tank ploughed into an electrical goods shop and set off a display of metallic blue sparks, showering upwards and setting fire to the floors above.

"The gods are showing themselves!" mouthed Dad inside the cab, as the front part of the building folded open like a plan, toppled forward, detaching itself from the main part, then leaned, wondering for a moment, before flopping with a sigh and a crash onto the square.

It now looked just like one of the diagrams in my Learning

comic. Or the poster of cuts of meat in the old-fashioned butcher's Mum makes Dad take us to. The tank was showing us 'how things work'. Inside the diagram were the last of the crowds. Scared security guards still doing their jobs, assistants ushering the last shoppers down the emergency exits. A man erupted from the toilets, holding his trousers up with his hands. Beneath him the floor exploded in a great shower of water and poo. The tank was opening up all the secret places. On the top floor the counter with all the supermarket cash tills tipped forward. Everyone in the High Street held their breath. There was a tiny shower of sparks and all the tills opened together, a sprinkle of coins fell through the ruins, followed by a shower of paper, soiled in mid-flight, each stained note turning over and over on itself, spreading from the shuddering building towards the gaping crowds.

On the exposed second floor, the film on the widescreen TVs and plasma screens was frozen at the same moment, as if transfixed by the flying wee and poo and money, multiple Mikes and Sulleys gobsmacked inside their tiny prisons. Then they too fell and smashed into bits on the floor of the entrance hall, joining a growing pile of things and cleverness.

Above and behind us, the people who worked in the High Street shops were pressed against the windows. "Like at a hanging," Dad mouthed. Like the magical mathematician watched the murderers swinging round and round on their ropes, jerking and kicking; him in his twisted turret.

A huge beast was dying in front of us. And we just couldn't stop watching. The green light dying in the eye of the stegosaurus, when I'd first realised that everything would end. Fantasia. Nothing is the same.

All around us people were jumping up and down, getting ready for the money. The cloud of pooey notes approached in an orderly descent. Fingers reached in anticipation. Feet away from us now, the cloud of cash seemed to slow.

I saw Dad look up and down the High Street. He raised his hand, cutting the air slowly. I knew what he was thinking. Because he'd talked to us about the High Street. About how it had been a road for a very long time. Ancient Egyptian coins had been dug up under it. It had been the route for flint weapons, carried into the forests around The Hill. And tin. And clotted cream from Phoenicia. And Mum's Mum and Dad had always got caught up in a big traffic jam here on the way to their holidays, before they built the by-pass and the motorway.

I knew Dad was thinking all that travelling was about to pick up all this money and whisk it out of the reach of our fingers.

And that's exactly how it happened. For about two seconds. The wind rose, from the direction that the travellers had always come: Romans, tourists, elders, worshippers of Mercury, souls of the pharaohs, funerals of the cholera dead, promotion winners. The orderly procession of cash stumbled, and with a leap it shot about in a swirling mass of swapping and bargaining and arguing, like everything that went on inside the shops every day was acting itself out, but just out of reach of the crowd. Like something that just happened. Because a tourist fanned herself with a guidebook on the other side of the world.

The remains of the big shop were very slowly collapsing now, and from the dust that rose from the fall of its parts a new shape was forming. Not a shape that meant anything, not that looked like anything. It was kind of square, and kind of circular. And it rose up like a pillar. And at its top, billowing up towards the white and blue sky, it was shaped like around the top of the hotel with the white tunnel. I couldn't tell how many sides the pillar had, but I knew it would be eight.

"Wow," said Ben. "Please can we go home now, Mum, and watch the rest of this on the telly?"

Later on, Ben came home from Woodcraft Folk. He'd cut his finger with someone's pen knife and he was very proud peeling back the plaster to show me just how deep the cut was and how he could pull the two pieces of skin apart.

"We'll put some antiseptic on that," and Mum escorted him out.

"Do you think they should allow them to take knives?"

Mum was shouting down the stairs to someone. It was much harder to know who was in the house than before.

I knew that Mum and Dad's getting on better was only

pretend. Not for my sake, but because pretending was part of getting on. I knew Dad wouldn't ever leave us for good because he needed somewhere normal to come back to from the Disappeared World that he would carry on going to. To be with the jewels for a while to stop him from getting sick. And Mum was happy because everything – so she thought – was going according to her theories. It was perfect – she had pretend patients and she could pretend that home was the same as work. And we could all share the same common enemy now that Great Auntie Beryl and Great Uncle Tony came to visit us almost every day. I overheard Mum saying to Mans's Mum that she never thought this would happen without one of them dying.

I used to think our family was a bit sad. Some of the other kids' Mums and Dads were much more lovey-dovey in the playground. But then those were the ones that 'had affairs' or said they'd stopped loving each other and it would get nasty and the kids would have to leave the school because they were going to live somewhere else. It was far better to have pretending parents than real ones.

I was surprised how happy I was. I shook very slightly with happiness all the time. Like tea in a cup that someone has disturbed.

I'd heard that in the dream? Yeh. There were old soldiers. But I couldn't remember the details now. The Stories had left long ago and there was only a sense of the trees and a hill and some places in the town.

Chapter Thirty-One ~ Better

Whether this archive exists outside the framing of an image by Escher, or whether it is constant only in the inconstancy of dreams, this is the archive that contains all others.
('Archive of the Impossible', Jason Hirons, in *Tremblestone* #Four)

As soon as I was well enough to get up I started looking for moments when I could escape to the Disappeared World. It was harder now, because the Great Remains were on guard almost every day. Even Nanna and Gramps, who never came to call, had taken to "popping in, just for a moment, love". And it was true about Ben, he hadn't been thrown out at all. While I'd been away he'd started reading. He could already do words and things, and when I was having my bath each night I had heard him grinding them out with Dad, and Dad getting annoyed and then I knew Dad would close his eyes, or stare at the bookshelves. Just the same as he had with me. But now Ben wasn't just doing words, he was doing whole books on his own. He'd dive in and wouldn't come out until he'd finished the lot. He could swallow a world in one go.

But there were gaps: when Mum got home and started on the tea, when Dad was supposed to be getting us to bed and must have forgotten or when the Great Remains argued. Then I could escape for a few seconds, a few minutes, an hour sometimes in the Disappeared World.

It was different there from before. It had been a kind of dead playground, like the edge of town where all the burned down garages and dumps are. It had felt always still, fixed, some bits divided into squares. But it was far more alive now. Although I never saw him I always felt the caretaker was about, with his broom of knives. And the toys – A Child, the Ugly Truth, the Crow Stories – they were more commercial now, more like merchandise, flogging themselves round the concrete ruins.

Perhaps our visits had spoiled it. I remembered that going there
had been like skating down smooth slopes that you couldn't ever
fall over on. But now on some days hard things would come in
waves. And Dad was there.

Things in our world were different too. It wasn't just our
suddenly crowded house; outside had moved on too. Nanna took
me for a walk down the alley and along the valley path. Mum
drove us past the **Hub** on the way to Kids Club at the arty
cinema. We walked into town to buy Ben some new books from
Waterstones and we passed by the dump for ghosts. But none of
them fitted on the list anymore.

And there were three new Ziggurats, almost ready to open.
Mum said that there'd been an explosion; a lady in a long dress
from another religion had been trained on her computer by
people who 'they' never caught, but not very well because her
bomb went off too quickly and it was only her it hurt. This was in
the toilets, and even though you couldn't see much damage 'they'
had to rebuild, and so 'they' had taken the chance to make it
much bigger this time. But I knew that wasn't true, and that the
lady who'd died was a huntress; because the men in the car park
needed a sacrifice so 'they' could put the plan on their laptop
into our High Street.

There'd been weird hot weather after Christmas and the
nettles and ferns in the valley had sprung up early and were
already hiding the insect sculptures. The wasteland on the **Hub**
had been cleared and benches installed. The ghost dump was
piled high with wood, cement and huge cubes of grey bricks on
wooden pallets for a new mini-supermarket.

But I don't mind.

Before the dream, *that* Alice would have been scared, or
would have got angry at things changing. Like I did with Dad. I
wanted him to be the same, always, but now he's different I
know that it *is* him there, on the edges of Disappeared World.

And it was the same with me. Mum says I'm "a zealot" which
is a person who believes something so much it makes them crazy
and hard to live with. How can you believe too much in the
truth? But you can. Before I realised, I told Mum "we have to live,
all the time, exactly how we believe and never, ever pretend or lie

– that way I'll never go mad!"

"I'm sure that's true," said Mum, "but you'll send everyone else around you completely round the bend!"

I put a new toy in the Disappeared World – The Zealot. It's selling really well.

Lately I've noticed that I don't really mind Mum telling me off. In fact, quite a lot of things that would have bothered me once don't anymore.

Things carried on in school, at Brownies, painting and choir. I still need extra help in maths. But nothing bothers me about that now. I don't mind if one of my school friends wants to break friends with me, I don't mind if Mum sends me to Brownie camp with the wrong things, I don't mind if maths is hard, I just get on and struggle with it. I don't even mind if someone knows I'm trying to help them. I don't mind if people know I've been ill. I don't mind, but I do matter.

Chapter Thirty-Two ~ Late Santa

> In the twentieth century, those adhering to Utopian
> principles have worked between 'art', 'politics',
> 'architecture', 'urbanism' and all the other specialisms that
> arise from separation. Utopians aim to 'create' a 'new' world
> where these specialisations will no longer exist.
> *(The Assault On Culture*, Stewart Home)

We all decided it was very funny.

The idea of going on a Santa Special in the middle of a heatwave.

Great Uncle Tony had suggested it. Great Auntie Beryl had tried to shut him up, but he'd found a leaflet while tidying up the downstairs cupboard.

Great Uncle Tony had been tidying every day, working his way through the house. It was his new hobby. Suddenly there were gaps opening up and things that had been lost for years were reappearing:

A spongey dinosaur that Ben had grown from an egg and was now shrivelled and starting to fossilise.

A letter to me from my cousin that had never been opened. (Not very interesting.)

A green - possibly cheese - sandwich that looked like a tiny, hairy sofa.

Great Uncle Tony was very proud of his finds and wouldn't be shut up about the leaflet. The moment he said "steam" Great Auntie Beryl was on to him, but he just kept ploughing through the storm.

"We've missed the Santa Specials, but they're doing some Winter Wonderland Runs and we could pretend? You like steam trains don't you, Ben? Alice? Wasn't Paul's father a bit of a trainspotter?"

Mum got the giggles and had to go out of the room. Ben laughed because everyone else did, trying to top Mum's hysterics with screams and squeals. Great Auntie Beryl gave Great Uncle

Tony a "now you've done it" look, but there was some kind of weird affection there.

I didn't really mind that he'd mentioned steam engines. Everyone knew that Dad and me had gone mad. It wasn't a secret, and just because we'd both had "delusions" (Mum calls them) about steam engines, how was Great Uncle Tony supposed to remember everything? Dad had forgotten every important thing I ever told him.

So, we had to go. Otherwise it would have been like we were scared. Nanna and Gramps had to be invited, because they were now part of the extra family. They probably didn't want to come – even though Gramps *is* train-mad – but they obviously thought they'd better or it would look like there was something wrong with steam engines, that steam engines really might set off on their own across fields, that steam engines really might plough up the centre of town, that steam engines might really be the top layer of a conspiracy that went down, floor by floor, to the very centre of the earth.

That's how we all came to be packed into an old carriage, waiting for the whistle and the wave of the flag.

It was sort of horrible, but in my new skin I didn't really mind. It was a sort of horrible because I knew everyone would be watching me and having to pretend not to. They'd be checking that I wasn't looking out for Wally Eager or Mister Binns, or for the enthusiasts who dug up the tracks, for the melted spectacles and the ruined cardboard from 1947, the third track, or for the mouth of the tiled tunnel into The Hill.

Mum wore a red coat!! I saw the moment when she realised what she'd done. I knew why she'd done it. Because Great Uncle Tony was going to dress as Santa and she wanted to fit in with the fun, show him some support. Instead, she'd made herself part of the cast of our 'delusion'. Ha ha ha! Wait till I tell Mum's friends from work!

Of course, there was no Hill, no Mister Binns, no Wally Eager.

There were lots of hills. And any one of them – or even all of them – might have had a secret city inside. The steam train *was* run by enthusiasts. It wasn't like usual trains, though. No one was paid, Mum said. Which is weird. There was no Santa (Great Uncle Tony's effort consisted of a red bobble hat with a piece of torn printer paper sellotaped to his chin), although they did have Wee Willie Winkie and Doctor Foster and the Ticket Collector was a huge man with a wide face, and his evil puncher might have been useful for labelling the ghosts he'd stored in the mail van. But he wasn't Mister Binns, though he just *might* have been Wally Eager.

We were in the Refreshments Coach, Dad and me. Sent to fetch crisps for Ben and squash for Mum. If we did OK maybe Mum would let Dad and me go off on one of those walks where we didn't know where it was to. Dad had found they served local beer, so he was having that and I had real ginger beer.

Dad didn't wear the green Santa outfit in the end. He said he'd thought about it, but it was "too much" for Mum. When he said that, his fingers drummed on the formica bar top. All superheroes have to pay some sort of price for their powers – Dad's was that although he didn't know truth from lies, his hands did.

"You're not supposed to drink beer. It's bad for you."

He used to get angry when I bossed him about. He'd look away, at bookshelves or hills or gutters. Now he looked me right in the face.

I'd told Mum the story of my dream. I'd told her that it had felt like I'd really been away. I told her that I knew – even in The Hill – that I'd known I hadn't really been there. Mum gave me the old "it's you talking to you about you" and I liked that, because that meant somewhere inside me I had The Hill and hundreds of steam trains and rows of fire engines and Mister Binns and, wow, he was Everything. But I hadn't told Dad – although I knew Mum would tell him one day, perhaps.

"Mum says that when you pulled Mister Binns's beard off, it was me underneath? Is that true?"

"Mum wasn't supposed to tell you." (But I didn't mind.)

"O well, people do lots of things they're not supposed to."

"Don't you think you were there?"

"Under Spike's beard? You think it was me all along? The wild man – that that's what I was searching for – in all those places?"

"In your dream he was you."

"Not dream . Story... maybe..."

"Mum says they're.... de... lusions." (I still wasn't sure about 'delusions', they didn't sound any better than 'lies'.) "But that means they're not true. They were, weren't they?"

"I don't believe they were lies."

"So, was he you in your story?"

Dad thought for a long time. Outside a river snaked beside the curving train.

"That's your Mum's theory: 'you talking to you about you'."

"You didn't answer my question."

I didn't mean to be nasty to Dad, but I wanted him to answer.

"I suppose Mister Binns is what I'd like to be and Wally Eager is who I'm frightened of becoming. I didn't mean to make it as blunt as that, but – was it as obvious as that? OK, that's sort of what's underneath the story."

"Mister Binns is everything."

"What?"

"He's everything."

"Well, he's sinister, isn't he? He's mysterious... he can't be literally everything, he'd be even more lonely..."

That's sort of what Mandy said, about something else. And she was wrong too.

"He's a super hero. He doesn't have to stick to the rules."

"A pretty weird kind of a one ...."

"Who are you, Dad?"

"What?"

"You know."

Outside, the river was churning over large rocks. Dad looked away and out of the other window. Here the ground rose up steeply from the train track. Someone had stuck hundreds of garden gnomes and fairies with fishing rods and tennis rackets into the green bank. A sign said: 'PIXIES HALT'. Magic stops here. But I couldn't stop now.

"You were our super hero, Dad, before you swallowed the cloud. Then you hid behind your books and we didn't know where you were. And then you disappeared completely. I didn't think anybody was looking for you... and I didn't think you *wanted* to be found."

"Mum was..."

"Yes, but how can you tell if that is any different from her just being angry? She says that's why she gets angry, but how can you tell? That's why we went to find you, Dad – because you and Mum were just playing at wanting you to be found."

Dad jerked, just like he had by the Riddle Spike.

"... did you go off to be with other people?"

Dad wiped a hand across his face as if he were taking off a fake white beard, slowly. Slowly, so he could put on another piece of disguise.

"You weren't *really* mad, were you?"

"I don't know, Alice, I really don't know."

"I do, because I thought I was pretending too, and I couldn't stop it and that's what the thing people call "mad" is."

"Not "mad", lovely..."

"Why don't you ever answer me?"

"I'm trying... that's the truth..."

The huge, hairy ticket collector was ordering a beer at the counter.

"I *really* don't know. I needed to get away. And now I have. But whether I really chose to or not... that's what I don't know. I always half knew and half didn't. Half wanted to get away and half wanted to come back. I really didn't know my name or who I was, but I knew if I wanted to know that I probably could. But I also knew that I was putting it on, that it was *all* an act, and one I couldn't stop. So, yes is the answer. I was... "mad". Stark, staring, raving bonkers, actually. Off with the fairies. The first citizen of La La Land."

The hairy ticket collector shot a glance at us over his shoulder, but turned quickly back to his beer when he saw that I was watching him.

"Is there a place you go to that isn't really the same as the real world?"

"My writing?"

Was that all it was?

"Dad, when you were on your journey, you said you met other

people, groups…"

"Did I?"

"Well did you?"

"I must have done. Other travellers. People in parks, in hotels."

"No, different to that. Do you think there's an organisation of people like us, who are always half-travelling?"

He looked around the train – as if I'd meant passengers on Winter Wonderland Specials.

"People on 'fugues' you mean? What sort of organisation? A charity, do you mean?"

He was pretending.

"You know what I mean. People who recognise people like us."

The train was slowing and a metal whisper passed between engine and and and carriage. People were beginning to shuffle along bristly seats, dragging bags and rucksacks down from the racks. There wasn't much time.

"O?"

And now he did seem to really try to think back to something. He screwed up his face as if he were forcing up the cover and squeezing down the metal ladder into the tiny submarine.

We were passing sidings. Old wooden trucks with freshly painted signs for gravel and lime companies, a little steam engine that was so fat and squat it seemed to have been sliced off a real one. An engine that was rusting orange out of black paint, a dome like a soldier's hat in the middle of its tube. And a long line of faded green carriages. In among all this were five or six people, winding through the wrecks, one making notes, another prodding the ground with a red and white stick; a third – in black clothes, her hair in tight black curls – looked straight up at us and put her right, black-gloved hand over her right eye, palm down.

When I looked back to Dad he was doing the wiping thing again to one side of his face.

"You want to know where I really went?"

The wanderers were hidden by the green carriages. Their

insides stripped bare, bits of upholstery peeling down.

I looked at Dad very hard. Or at the space that Dad was pretending to be in. To force him to be real for once. We had less than a minute.

"OK," he said.

Just like the dream, but backwards, the train was straightening as we drew into the toy station, and I could see one carriage after another as they cleared the bend and showed themselves. Three carriages back, Mum was pulling our things from the overhead rack, Gramps helping Nanna sweep something from the table, Great Auntie Beryl ticking off Great Uncle Tony, who was smiling out of the window. Ben was pulling at Mum's top. He'd be complaining about the non-arrival of the crisps that were still lying on the table between me and Dad, shaped like The Hill.

"OK. Where I really went? Where I really wanted to go? Away. That's all, that's where. Not very nice, is it? But neither was what I was feeling. A real hero – rather than one who'd learned how to play the part in a uniform... a real hero would have stuck it, Alice, stuck it... but I've always been selfish, I've always wanted to be something special. When I got the chance to be a fireman, and it was just luck... it was my big opportunity to do the magic thing, to put together things that don't usually ever mix: what I wanted to do plus other people..."

Ambitions and love.

The world outside had stopped moving. The ticket collector was opening the carriage door. Wee Willie Winkie was already on the platform, white like a ghost, his candle held out in front of him.

"The smoke took that away from me. I couldn't bear it. I wanted to do what I wanted to do. I stopped caring about anyone else. I knew that was wrong, terribly wrong, because deep down I did care – I did love you, and Mum and Ben and it was only this stupid wanting thing that wouldn't let me show it... this thing I had to get into a... a space that was so close to people and yet never quite there... just a few inches to the side... it let me... let me be... and I went back in..."

"Where's my crisps!"

My little brother was two carriages away now, worming around the families who were pulling on huge coats and woollen hats, four young people from somewhere far away threading their arms into strange, box-like rucksacks, and an older man with white hair caught in the middle of a story told to a thin man with a stringy black beard, grabbing things from the air as they packed up maps and sticks. Any other day and Dad would have taken this chance to break off, to float back to Disappeared World, to draw down the blinds – but on the steam line we were already partly in his funny so-close-but-not-quite-there space.

"You're right, lovely. It is "mad"... better get back... erm... Most people never get the chance I did. I hope you do. That's why Mum goes to work, always checks everything to do with your school, you know... because we want you to get the best chance. But you have to get your head down and do the right thing. That's what I'd like to do, but I can't get out of that space anymore. So, if I sound a little cranky, that's because bits of me are made up from other people, so you'll know why, eh? OK? OK, it's no excuse, but it's life."

I only had one more question.

In my head, like a racing train I ran through the places:
Dreamscape, McCurdey, Geometrical Space...

Mum's wrong, the dreams were not just me talking to me about me and Dad's story is not just him talking to him about him. That's a Wally Eager kind of thinking. Mister Binns's way sets the dreams free!

"Dad..."

But he was gone. Disappeared into the invisible world.

"Next time you go for a walk, I'm going too."

"Uh?"

On the way to the steam railway after our pretend Christmas lunch (with real presents), we'd driven past a hill shaped exactly like the rounded pyramid of crisps that Ben was fighting his way to under rucksacks and through families. Around the bottom of this hill the trees had been cleared and there was a big sign up:

"Underground Paintball Arena: The Battle For The Tunnels".

At home, under my bed, rolled up like a tube, is a big square of paper, and every night, before I go to sleep, I don't think of sinking into the ocean anymore, but of taking a walk along its lines. It's the map of Dad's journey that Mum made. Though she says she doesn't remember one, so I had to make a copy from memory – but I know she has the real one in her grey box up on the living room shelves.

I've been back at school for two weeks now. I'm fine.

When I finally told Mum The Whole Story – which is a castle that looks like a bird perched on the grave of an Ugly Truth – about seeing Dad with the Insect People, about the Sawing Hand, the Second Journey, the Frogs and Everything, I knew by then that the steam train was a fevery dream. Mum said I'd probably remembered seeing Dad talking to tourists when he did The Thing. Maybe they *were* tourists. I knew there were people who you could see, even though they were partly in the Disappeared World too, explorers of the things everyone else ignored, people who you might meet one night in some panicky woods. I'd see Dad with them again, I knew that, no matter what he said.

Mum had explained about how I'd got poorly. It was just the same as getting tonsillitis, she said. I got Stories. Because, she said, when things make so little sense that your brain begins to shut down, silly Stories can help to keep it going until it can start up again properly. Stories invented themselves – stuff like Dad being part of a secret organisation, or that a little kid might find out something about hidden army places, or that all things were connected. Mum said that these Stories were the wires you can use to start a car if you lose the key, you plug them into someone else's battery for a while, but that doesn't mean you and them have to drive round together for the rest of your lives. That only happens with love (which is a kind of madness, she said). The Stories made up connections of their own, so it could start me up again. But now it was time to disconnect, she said. We all lived in the same world and she and Ben looked just as closely at that world as Dad and me ever had, and that our family were the important connections to always hold onto and that she would

213

never disconnect from them.

I didn't want to carry on being poorly, so I didn't have any problem believing that the steam train was a dream and that the Stories were just theory-godmothers.

Mum said she had a treat, because Christmas had been such a mess – it was a huge book bigger than I could hold, literally, called 'Amazing Places' with giant photos of the Taj Mahal and the Eiffel Tower and the Grand Canyon and places like that. Which was very clever. Because there was nowhere in it that was *anything* like that **superfluous place** where Wally Eager would still be bullying a gaggle of hungry ghosts. Or like a **Z World**... or any of the others.

Even if it was all a dream, some things are true.

There really is a tower with an eye, and empty places where ghosts are things you can feed, and putting one foot in front of the other is really *not* what walking is all about.

Mum beat Ben through the crowd. She'd cheated by stepping off the train and walking round by the platform. Now she poked her head through the Refreshments Carriage door.

"Isn't it nice to have our little girl back?" she said, opening wide her arms.

I whispered, so Mum couldn't hear.

"Will you finish your story?"

The End

I must take care not to give too much information to just anybody.
(*Comments on the Society of the Spectacle*, Guy Debord, trans. Malcolm Imrie)

About the Author

Dr Phil Smith is a prolific writer, performer, urban mis-guide, dramaturg [for TNT Munich], counter-tourist, drifter, artist-researcher and academic. He has written or co-written over one hundred professionally produced works for a wide range of British and international theatres and touring companies, and has created and performed in numerous site-specific theatre projects, often with Exeter-based Wrights & Sites, of which he is a core member [**www.mis-guide.com**].

He is Associate Professor (Reader) in the School of Humanities and Performing Arts at Plymouth University.

Phil has published papers in *Studies In Theatre and Performance Research, Cultural Geographies, Performance* and *New Theatre Quarterly,* co-authored a range of Mis-Guides with the other members of Wrights & Sites and written or co-written a number of other books including: *On Walking; Enchanted Things; Mythogeography: A Guide to Walking Sideways; Counter-Tourism: The Handbook; A Sardine Street Book of Tricks* (all published by Triarchy Press) and *Walking, Writing & Performance* (ed. Roberta Mock, Intellect).

www.triarchypress.net/smithereens

About the Publisher

Triarchy Press is an independent publisher of alternative thinking (altThink) about government, finance, organisations, society and the creative life of human beings.

It also publishes an occasional series of altThink fiction by serious people of impeccable standing. The main criterion for inclusion is that they should be very good indeed.

www.triarchypress.net/fiction

Lightning Source UK Ltd.
Milton Keynes UK
UKOW06f2114180615

253759UK00001B/2/P